Bad Timing

Bad Timing

A NOVEL

Betsy Berne

Villard New York

Copyright © 2001 by Betsy Berne

All rights reserved under International and Pan-American Copyright Conventions. Published in the United States by Villard Books, a division of Random House, Inc., New York, and simultaneously in Canada by Random House of Canada Limited, Toronto.

VILLARD BOOKS is a registered trademark of Random House, Inc. Colophon is a trademark of Random House, Inc.

Library of Congress Cataloging-in-Publication Data
Berne, Betsy.
Bad timing / Betsy Berne.
p. cm.
ISBN 0-679-46318-6 (acid-free paper)
1. Manhattan (New York, N.Y.)—Fiction. 2. Pregnant women—Fiction.
3. Jazz musicians—Fiction. 4. Single women—Fiction. 5. Adultery—Fiction. I. Title.
PS3552.E7295 B3 2001
813'.6—dc21   00-040833

Villard Books website address: www.villard.com

Printed in the United States of America on acid-free paper

24689753

First Edition

Book design by Meryl Levavi

To my parents, my sister and brothers,
and to Hilton Als

"Remember, you can't sweep
the funk under the rug."

—Bootsy Collins

ACKNOWLEDGMENTS

My thanks to Jennifer Rudolph Walsh, Bruce Tracy,
Deborah Treisman, and Barbara Jones for their insight
and encouragement. My thanks also to the MacDowell Colony,
Kevin Thompson and David Kuhn, and Pearson Marx
for their hospitality.

Bad
Timing

CHAPTER

I

I REALIZED I WAS CRACKING ONE SATURDAY MORNING IN JULY WHEN I found a mouse in the half-full—well, half-empty—water glass by my bed.

The room was close and sweaty, suffocatingly so. It had been a hot and surly summer in Manhattan, and summer in the city is more than anything a psychological season, a season dictated by income bracket. (The lower your bracket, the longer and hotter and smellier summer is.) Summer in New York can make a loser feel more like a loser and a winner more like a winner. The winners usually beat the summer by leaving, and by now most of them had long since gone. My neighborhood was inhabited mostly by winners, so the streets were pretty deserted. I could see all the way to the Hudson River from the windows lining my loft, and the view was sullied only by a stray loser or two. My own summer strategies varied with my fluctuating income bracket. This year's income said long summer.

I'd gone to bed very late the night before, though I knew that I'd have to be up early. I'd been invited to Long Island, and it's easier to be a guest when you're a little foggy. I hit the alarm without looking at it and made my way slowly toward the kitchen. When I went back into the bedroom I saw the mouse in the glass on my crowded night table, less than six inches from where my head had rested moments before. It wasn't even dead. It was very much alive and struggling to get out.

I ran to the living room and called my brother, who was in no mood to help. He told me to go back in there and throw it out the window. I informed him that I was unable to go back in there. "Just go back in one more time, cover the damn glass, leave, and when you come home it'll be dead," he said. I told him that I couldn't get that close to it, nor could I face a mouse corpse later. He said, "Jesus, I don't know—call Mom," and hung up. My mother had been a renowned rodent killer in our youth. I called her.

She said, "Go back in there, honey, bring the phone, I'll go, too. What is wrong with you? Damn it to hell, just throw it out the window, honey, and don't call yourself a feminist if you can't even throw a mouse out the goddamn window." I wasn't sure that last comment made sense, but I let it go. Finally I called the feminist who lived upstairs, and she marched down and disposed of the mouse without incident.

It was time to take a look at the big picture.

•

My slow but steady demise had begun with an unlikely encounter one night a couple of months before.

We had met on an early spring night that was damp and raw, after a particularly grueling winter from which no one had quite recovered. My neighbor, who generally made appearances at every party in town, had told me about a party—a trashy magazine party at a trashy new bar—a hot trashy new bar, which made it even trashier and even less appealing. This wasn't exactly an invitation; my magnanimous neighbor said he would see to it that I'd get in, but not in his company. My neighbor is a slippery sort who prefers to move about town unencumbered so that he can adopt the appropriate persona for each occasion, and I am the kind of person who might inadvertently blow his cover. He also happens to be black, which means that his persona is a far more urgent matter, in some cases a matter of survival. Luckily, he is a master of disguise, and people of all colors are generally smitten with him. I am white, a white Jew to be precise, and smitten; he is an original, and he has no choice, really, but to be slippery. (My neighbor lives only a few blocks away, and he and I often pass the time by making enormous crass ethnic generalizations and congratulating ourselves on our brilliance.)

I felt it was my duty to go to the party in order to continue an ongoing, albeit desultory, mate search. I can simulate a suitably sociable façade as well as the next person, but an escort would make things easier. So I called Victor, who serves as my human oasis. He is something of a dandy who dresses in Victoriana and S&M jackets with exotic jewelry. On a summer day he is often decked out in a billowing skirt, or linen bloomers paired with a light cotton vest. His head is hairless except for several tiny, well-placed patches and some strategic twirly strands, and he sometimes sports Hasidic earlocks. But by now I no longer notice his appearance, nor do I question the purpose of his cane, even though he has no limp. Victor is not even remotely concerned with the mate search. He has his own ideas about the human condition. But he does love a party. And like me, he is an artist who is slowly losing the ability to do the fawning necessary to revive a faltering career. But neither of us had thrown in the towel yet, and there is really no place more conducive to fawning or searching than a party.

Outside the trashy new bar there was a groveling and expectant crowd. My neighbor had kept his word, and I breezed right through, and Victor—well, no conscientious doorman could refuse entrance to Victor. Inside it was cavelike. You couldn't see out and you couldn't see in. The walls were tinted the pale hazy ochre that is designed to flatter those who are getting on in years. It was almost embarrassing to be there when most people in our age group were home guarding their sleeping progeny, yawning and struggling through the last hour before they could respectably turn in, too.

I've never spotted an interesting stranger from across the room at occasions such as these—everyone tends to dissolve into a blur—and by now anyone who looked interesting turned out, on closer inspection, to be not a stranger but someone from my past whom I'd either forgotten or hoped had forgotten me. But tonight—perhaps thanks to the full trays of vodka being spirited past by insectlike waitresses, or the pot a wobbly art dealer had coaxed me into trying at the door—I wasn't bored. Victor and I stood in a corner and watched my neighbor hold various people in thrall. My neighbor looked a little weary. Holding crowds of people in thrall can be exhausting. He motioned us over, so we settled into the unsightly stuffed furniture that crowds new bars for those getting on in years. My neighbor and Victor are allies. When they enter a social gathering together, people look up. They communicate with each other by a flash of the eyes or a discreet nod, and they make an impenetrable and arresting pair. They launched into their own convoluted discourse, and I took the opportunity to gaze around.

Then this guy came along. I didn't know he was still around; I'd heard he'd slipped out of town—a New York "timely" disappearance. He was one of those big-wheel-behind-the-scenes guys you always heard vague rumors about. I still remembered hearing about him when he'd just moved to town from Paris years ago and was causing some commotion. He was a kind of a renaissance man, a jazz whiz kid—a bass player—one day, then an impresario who owned a jazz club the next. He'd been something of an enfant terrible in jazz circles, and no one knew why he'd stopped playing. But mystery was always welcome in these circles, and he was mysterious with class.

I used to tag along with my brother to his club, before it became infested with tourists and businessmen, before it became what my brother, a jazz musician himself, referred to as a "soft-dick jazz club." This guy could play and he had a real presence—he looked like he'd been zipped too tight into his human suit. I was surprised to see him at a very stuffy exclusive art event a few years later. He looked trapped and I liked that. The friend I was with introduced us, and this guy looked right past me to the door. Later I asked my brother what his story was. He said this guy had been the real thing, a musician's musician, and then he passed on a few of the rumors—one or possibly two ex-wives, an uncertain number of kids, a very fashionable society-type current wife—and some "extracurricular activity" on the side. So I had some background.

He sat down with us and began riffing with my neighbor about an uptown multicultural arts festival they'd suffered through together. The guy referred to the festival as a "coon fest" and commented on some of the standard notables. "Oh, yeah, they rounded up every creative Negro in town," my neighbor said, and they both smirked. I smirked, too, but I couldn't really participate. They continued riffing on this one and that one, my neighbor graciously playing the straight man.

Eventually I couldn't resist; I whispered to my neighbor, "Come on, there must have been at least a Jew or two."

The guy heard me and said, "Oh yeah, more than a few—this was a first-class coon fest—and you know a black man's really made it when he owns a Jew." I laughed outright and he tried not to. Soon he was ordering rounds of drinks for everyone—except himself. He nursed a glass of red wine forever, using it primarily as a prop.

Others joined us, among them an artist I'd known when he first landed in New York, Minnesota-sweet and earnest. Now he was semifamous with a fake English accent—and insufferable. We made room for the artist and somehow the guy ended up sitting across from me. I was wedged in next to Victor. He turned to me casually and asked, "What do you do?"

I told him I was a painter and that I'd started writing recently to make money. He didn't blink at the ludicrous nature of that statement—most people did—and he moved in closer. He insisted I have another drink, but I demurred and sipped water cautiously.

"You don't drink?"

I told him that Jews were more likely to be drug addicts than drinkers.

"Not the ones I know—they're both," he said. Then I confessed I never drank too much because I was sure I'd end up in a heap in some forsaken corner. I'd never said that out loud before.

He asked about my work. "My ex-wife's a dealer," he explained. "I do some collecting." We discovered he knew a dealer I'd shown with recently, and he said curtly, "She's a crook. But she's a crook with an eye. You must be talented to show there."

I told him that my father used to ask me if my musician brother was "talented." Would he be "successful"? It had driven me nuts to have to explain over and over that, yes, he was talented, but talent had little to do with success.

"You're right," he said. "Forget I said that."

"Okay. Anyway, he never asked me again after the *Times* decided that my brother was talented."

"Who's your brother?" I told him and he said, "He's your brother? I know him. Yeah, I saw him play in Paris. He's good." My brother did not play soft-dick jazz, so I was surprised. "I used to play the bass. Well, sometimes I still do—"

I interrupted. "I know that. I've heard you play. I used to go to your club—oh, a long time ago, before it was, before it was . . ."

"Before it was jive? Is that what you're trying not to say?"

"Well, kind of."

His insidious charm was making me loose-lipped, and I was almost relieved when the creepy artist leaned in. He'd been watching us closely; he must have known this guy was a collector. "So you've gotten hitched," he said, addressing me but giving the guy a just-between-us-guys look. "How brilliant. I suppose you've moved to elegant uptown quarters."

"Oh, no, no, we just . . ." I began, but the guy took over.

"I live in the East Village—I wouldn't call that terribly elegant."

The artist had stopped listening; someone really famous appeared, and I said to the guy, "You liar, you don't live in the East Village."

"Was it that obvious?"

"To me it was. But you're not as bad as him; that guy was asking for it. I mean, his whole life is a lie."

"You're sure I'm not as bad as him?" He was trying not to laugh again. Then the artist turned back to us and went on and on until the guy got up abruptly and walked away. When he returned, he apologized to me.

"I'm not much of a group person. I have no tolerance, and I've got the kind of face where it shows—unfortunately." I assured him that I shared a similar affliction, but he refused to believe me. "Oh, no, you've got a pleasant face." He moved in even closer and gestured with the glass of wine. "Are you sure you don't want a drink?"

My neighbor, who'd been watching us with his third eye, reached behind Victor, nudged me, and hissed, "Be careful."

I laughed him off. "Don't worry. I'm not stupid." I rarely lived in the present, much less enjoyed living in the present, and I was determined not to let anything spoil it.

The guy and I started talking bad TV, one of my favorite topics and a safe one. "Oh, yeah," he said, "bad TV is great."

"So do you let your kids watch?"

"I only have one . . . here . . . I mean, yeah, most of the time." He pressed his lips together. I snickered. I wasn't stupid.

His eyes were deep and dark and steady. They were eyes that listened hard—and judged hard. But I had grown up surrounded by eyes that judged hard; it was familiar. I approved of his eyes' judgments—and he understood my shorthand. The eyes and the gentle voice made me confide recklessly things I sheltered closely in my battle to seem normal. My neighbor hissed and nudged more frequently, and I just laughed. This guy, he brought out the laughter in me. I was doing entirely too much of it. I laughed when I told him about my heart problem, a valve that was misbehaving, and the inevitable surgery—a topic there was no need to broach and one I always assiduously avoided broaching with anyone, even myself. I laughed when I mentioned the numerous dead friends I'd accumulated in the past five years. I laughed when I told him that maybe the art career for which I'd forsaken all chance of normalcy wasn't going according to plan. He watched me and listened closely. When I laughed, he didn't flinch. He hailed from the dark side, too, so he got the joke.

A resurgence of small talk seemed unlikely after the maudlin detour, but we managed. I regaled him with stories of my crazy family and my crazy brothers.

"So I gather you're not a big fan of men," he said.

"I don't think they're any worse than women, do you?"

He nearly smiled, and then he said he didn't have any experience with brothers or sisters; he was an only child—well, actually, an only child with an anonymous father, possibly still at large. "It wasn't what you think," he added. "I wasn't just another statistic. My parents got married too young. He left when I was barely conceived, and then, well, by the looks of things, my father may have been a white boy. Wouldn't you agree?" He laughed without smiling—a forced cackle.

"I don't know. I guess it could go either way." I caught his eye deliberately. "What kind of statistic were you referring to?"

He studied me and continued. "My mother was a professor. We did okay." With another cackle his eyes became deeper and darker but less steady.

I changed the subject to the anxiety of getting old. I could tell he had it bad. "But you're not old!" he insisted. (The pale hazy ochre was doing its job.) I told him that I was—that girl years were like dog years, so I was much much older than he was—and he nodded. "You just might have something there."

I added that I didn't care, since I didn't particularly cotton to the young people; I cared because I wanted a kid, not because everyone had them these days but because I'd always wanted one, and besides, I was sick of just taking care of me; I wanted to take care of someone else. And then I clammed up. He'd been close to me, but he sat back in his chair then with his hands on his knees; his eyes became muddy. "It'll happen, don't worry." And he smiled a tender smile. He wasn't the kind who wasted smiles, so when he did smile, it was momentous. He continued to insist that I wasn't old. I think he had decided I was young and that was the way it was going to be. It made a far more suitable scenario.

He was unbridled and bold in the brains department, and well-versed in obscurities. The list we had in common was long. For a while we shared opinions—more often harsh opinions—on the sticky webs of music and art people we both knew. Then he stopped suddenly and asked, "Hey, is there dancing upstairs?"

"Aren't you too old to dance?"

Not quite yet, he said, but he hadn't been dancing in so long, certainly not since he'd been back in New York.

"I dance," I told him, giggling, "but mostly in private, when I paint."

He asked what I listened to, and I said I had an extremely narrow musical range—mostly funk and old soul—and I told him I'd seen one particular group led by my hero at least twenty-five times, with loyal Victor by my side. That made him smile the momentous smile. He tried to one-up me by reciting some funk mythology, but I knew more than he did and I won. He liked that I won, and I appreciated that. He did it again, the smile, and I confided my secret fear that I would still be screaming along to the Walkman and dancing wildly while painting when I was wizened and sixty-five. He laughed. I knew I sounded like a nut, but I could tell he got it.

He was handsome enough in a hollow, bony, sharp-edged way, but handsome had never done much for me. It didn't explain why a terrible and inexplicable urge came over me to grab one of his limbs—any limb, I wasn't particular. I couldn't recall ever having had an urge to grab a stranger's limb in a public place before. I had to grip the arms of the stuffed chair to circumvent an unseemly grab. Just about when I got the limb-grabbing urge, my neighbor and Victor stood up to leave. My neighbor eyed me suspiciously, but he didn't know the half of it.

Once they were gone, the guy moved in for the kill, not that it was much of a contest. He was getting impatient. He'd finished his glass of wine, and when he let his hand graze my knee, it felt like silk. Forgoing my chaste water, I drank clear vodka, moving closer to the Scarlet Letter.

"Let's go dancing," he said. Fine, but I hadn't a clue where to go anymore and neither did he, and the only two people I knew who would know had just left. "Well, let's go upstairs," he said, exasperated. "I bet there's dancing up there." I knew full well that there was not going to be any dancing in the tiny hellhole of a lounge upstairs, but I agreed. I welcomed any opportunity to change position.

I stumbled up the winding staircase, and it was just as I thought, crammed and claustrophobic. All the leftover, desperate people were jammed wall to wall. I must have lost my balance because he put his hand on the small of my back. "I won't let you fall down," he said gruffly. That made me slump into the only available chair and resume gripping. We had reached the state where there weren't any words left to keep us in line, and silence wasn't helping matters much either. He perched on the arm of my chair, no doubt to prevent my gripping, but that was no good. So he crouched down in front of me and I could no longer avoid the steady gaze; he was awfully near and I couldn't help it and neither could he, so we kissed.

I had always demonstrated a modicum of decorum, even in my youth, yet here I was in a public place—a trashy trendy bar, no less—flagrantly welcoming the advances of a relative stranger, a married relative stranger. I could only assume that I'd been bewitched. It was ridiculous, not to mention somewhat indiscreet as far as marital mores go, although why I was worrying and he wasn't is perhaps more interesting.

"We should go," I whispered, unable to break away.

"Where?" he murmured into my hair.

"I don't know," I croaked, and I wasn't being coy.

"What about your place? You live around here, don't you?" Lines didn't sound like lines when he said them.

It was a kaleidoscope outside the club, with a ragged line of double-parked cabs blinking in the rain. We lurched into one of them and continued the teenage groping session. The cab delivered us to the door of my building, and then we faced the awkward long march up another set of stairs to my loft. When we reached my shabby pink couch, I mumbled, "I guess we shouldn't go to my bedroom." What he could possibly have imagined I meant is beyond me. How could he have known that, true to my heritage, I was preparing for the end of something that hadn't quite begun? I wanted to avoid the presence of his ghost in the room that provided my only sanctuary.

"We'll see what happens," he said steadily.

He made me forget everything. No one had made me forget everything in such a long time, and a relative stranger, never ever. There was only his bold, urgent self released from under its smooth surface, and his words, the tender sweet talk and the not-so-tender sweet talk, and my replies, and I was no longer anywhere near the shabby couch.

•

We ended up on opposite ends of the couch, me hunched in a corner and him sprawled. I was frozen, frozen in fear, and the voices in my head had returned. He fixed an unswerving stare on me, daring me not to look away. I shut my eyes and played dead.

"I want to see you again," he said, in a cadence that made the cliché sound original. And then cryptically: "I told you something I've told very few people. That's not my . . . I mean it's not like me."

I figured out the something, and I knew that this wasn't a lie because there had been such an instinctive trust between us at first—before sex had made us cagey. On the other hand, under the circumstances, I had no choice but to view him as a liar, and a seasoned liar at that. I didn't hold it against him. He struck me as the kind of liar who genuinely believes the lies that roll off his tongue, who believes in the act of lying in the same way others believe in religion—it's ingrained, not malicious. He was the kind of liar—a flawed liar—who hadn't started out as one but who'd acquired the habit so as not to expose a scathing candor that was far more threatening and could have got him into worse trouble. I'm sure he assumed I was lying to him, too.

I nodded. He asked if I'd be around the next day. I looked blank and shrugged. He was intense and unrelenting, as seasoned liars tend to be. When he said, in the dark, lullaby voice, "I'll keep trying until I get you," I answered glibly and scornfully, "Oh yeah, yeah, right."

This only fired him up. "Not oh yeah, yeah, right—I want to see you again," he said, acting insulted, which made me act more scornful in my vain attempts not to believe him. "I'll call you between ten and twelve tomorrow," he finished with a flourish. I had to get even with my own tough-girl act, up a couple notches from anything he'd seen yet. It was an automatic reflex, a feckless attempt to deflect the all-too-foreseeable future.

We'd skipped blithely over the part where you launch into the melodramatic married discussion. I'd smiled glazed smiles over amusing anecdotes about the kid early on, but even early on, the alienating phrases *wife* and *married* had never crossed his lips or mine. He knew I knew. I knew things, already I knew way too many things about him. At least, I thought I did.

"Don't you have to go home?" I asked abruptly. I wanted to get him out of there before he realized he'd made me forget everything. He started to button his shirt, and I saw his face turn impassive as I continued: "Do you have everything?" thrusting the jacket at him. I watched him disappear back under the smooth surface, and I detected hurt in his eyes, but I couldn't stop. "Did you forget your belt?"

"No," he replied, still staring.

"Oh, right, you wouldn't be the type who'd bother with a belt."

He looked at me then like I was a child and if he didn't take the bait, if he waited long enough, I'd get over it. I teased him some more. Just to make sure he was aware that I knew his type, that I wasn't stupid. My teasing was like his lying—ingrained but not malicious. I had learned all there is to know about the fine art of teasing from my brothers, until I grew thick skin and could tease like a man. My teasing might have felt unwarranted to a stranger, but this guy didn't feel like a stranger to me—that was the problem—and I couldn't allow him to see that he'd made dents in my thick skin.

2

AFTER HE LEFT, I CLEANED. CLEANING WAS A GENETIC TRAIT IN MY FAMILY, on the female side, particularly in times of stress. At four A.M. I was vacuuming in a fervent quest to atone for my sins. I woke up a few hours later, another genetic trait. My people got up at dawn, even if it meant suffering through the day too tired to do anything. I wasn't sure that I was coherent, but I had to report in to someone. My neighbor wouldn't be up for at least three hours— he had genes that allowed sleep. My musician brother might not be awake yet either. My brother's behavior was no longer predictable. He had a girlfriend now, or as my mother often despairingly referred to my brothers' girlfriends, a concubine, an overseas concubine, but enough of a concubine to make him act smug and mature. He might just be smugly repudiating his genes by sleeping.

As I staggered around cleaning I looked for confirmation of the night before. I browsed around the shabby couch area and found a souvenir—a thin sliver of a credit card. My proud plan of action had been not to call under any circumstances, but the card put a clear crimp in the plan. The card was a circumstance. I decided to call my brother. Better to wake one of your own.

He wasn't asleep. I described the situation carefully because there was no telling whether he was going to act smug or go in for some vicarious thrills. My brother, who's always on the road, is no stranger to off-the-beaten-track behavior between the sexes. As I told my tale, he was skeptical, understandably so, but not smug. Still, by the time I got to the line "What about your place?" he couldn't hold back.

"This guy has balls—he was playing you like a Stradivarius," he said, amused. I began to bristle audibly but he kept going. "And by the way, this guy really could play. I never could figure out why he quit. Like I never could figure out why his club sucks so much now. That place had potential."

"What about the credit card?"

"You know I hate to say it, but he's supposed to be pretty cool; he helped out a lot of guys when he first had his place. I mean I really hate to say it, but he took chances on guys who were really out, guys nobody would hire—and he actually paid. Like that guy, remember that cellist, I just played with him, you know—"

"What about the credit card?"

"That's easy." My brother sneered. "Go shopping."

"Well, shouldn't I call and tell him?"

"Yeah, right—call him, maybe you can get me a gig. That place really does suck now even though nobody'll admit it 'cause no one wants to dis him. I must say though, he does pay."

"No, really."

"What are you, nuts? Under no circumstances do you call." As an act of mercy, he left out "You really think he's going to call?" Men trust men much less than women trust men.

The next obvious step would be to consult a girlfriend. Unfortunately I was in the process of giving the silent treatment to my closest girlfriend, and the married girlfriends with children—the majority, by now—might not take to the situation. And to tell you the truth, the girlfriends in general were a diminishing group. I no longer had the first and second string I'd sustained in my youth. Some—not all—had taken the husband-and-children deal to extremes and it had become an insurmountable barrier. The Grim Reaper aspect to my life—that is, the steady death toll (let's just say it was a bad run of luck) encompassing not just AIDS but suicides, heart attacks, brain tumors, you name it—had also weeded out some. Then there were those who couldn't handle being around all that death—not that I blamed them—and that weeded out a few more. Anyway, friendships in the city are fickle, cyclical; there's always someone newer and more glamorous fading in, and sometimes old friends fade out for a while. One of my dead friends used to rotate the speed-dialing patches on his phone routinely in accordance with the rapid ebb and flow of glamorous and not-so-glamorous friendships.

I decided to risk waking my neighbor. He has a way with listening, my neighbor does, with his solemn eyes and graceful hands moving in perpetual consternation. One time, after the final-straw death, the one that broke me, he took me to a movie where I laughed so hard—and it wasn't even very funny—that I began crying, and later at the coffee shop the crying turned into a jag, and my neighbor never wavered. This was one of many public breakdowns that occurred that year without any warning. I referred to these untimely and unprecedented displays as publics. My neighbor is a homosexual, which makes him that much more attractive to female crackpots of all ages. They flock to huddle under his kind wings, and there are times when he can't take it. I used to have the crackpots-huddled-under-the-wings syndrome until I lost one to suicide, and while my predilection for crackpots had not abated, I learned excessive huddling under wings is no solution for either party. I try not to abuse the privilege of my neighbor's kind wings. There was no need to huddle under at this juncture, but we could certainly indulge in some ribald humor.

"I'll get back to you," he answered curtly. My neighbor operates like a flesh-and-blood switchboard, but I had just enough time to tantalize, and he recanted. "Hold on, I'll get rid of this call."

At first we chortled uncontrollably. There was no need to go into any sordid details. We had developed a set of infantile stock phrases to describe any action—or lack thereof—in our private lives, and there was an unspoken confidentiality agreement between us. I tossed around the stock phrases, and he bantered back. He was a little undone—and perhaps insulted that I hadn't heeded his warnings—but not terribly shocked to survey the rubble. He knew this twisted town too well, and no doubt he had a backlog of data on the perpetrator—or thought he did. Like I thought I did. It was an occupational hazard in this tiny town that posed as a gigantic metropolis.

He got into the black-and-Jewish thing immediately. My neighbor and I like to think we have debunked some myths. We have discovered that black people and Jewish people are more like than unlike, much more like than the general public would have you believe, although we are aware that they also have some genetic traits that are diametrically opposed. My neighbor happens to have a penchant for mousy, balding Jewish men, more specifically, short, spectacle-wearing, mousy, balding Jewish men, a compulsion I do not share. He is often puzzled by the genetic behavior of the mousy, balding Jewish men he likes. One mousy, balding Jewish boyfriend would open his eyes, vault straight out of bed, and rocket through the door to purchase a fresh gray copy of the *Times*, not to read leisurely but to scan hurriedly. (The Jews don't like to miss anything.) And plans, plans, plans, and the endless scheduling, what was with that? I tried to set him straight, gently, by pointing out the historical roots of such behavior. Plans and scheduling are important, I explained, because my people never know when we might be yanked out of circulation. Thus our lives take on a dire sense of urgency. He said, Well, yeah, his people knew all about being carted off, and yeah, they had the sense of urgency, too. But plans and scheduling? What you have here, I explained, is a prime example of one of the diametrically opposed genetic traits.

"Do you think he'll call?" I asked eventually, with what little was left of my pride.

"Well, there's the black thing, the time thing, you know," he said pragmatically. "But wait a second—he's got a substantial amount of white blood in there, doesn't he?"

"How should I know?"

"You'll be able to tell soon, take my word for it. Well, even if he does, the black genes always dominate in this area so I'm sure he wasn't up at dawn with the Jews. He probably doesn't get to work until noon. Those club creeps never do anyway. I know he's got this Mr. Nice Guy rep, but I don't buy it. I remember when I used to hang out at his club, before I hated jazz. He thought he was Mr. Supercool. I was just a kid then. God, it was a long time ago—before his club was such a joke; it must have been before I knew you. You don't remember?"

"No." I was growing hesitant about taking the purported facts at face value, since the perpetrator was one of his own kind. My neighbor was harder on his own kind—understandably so, since it does take one to know one, judging by my experience with my own kind. I wasn't sure I should be heeding his words.

"Believe me, it could take him at least a week to call. Why'd he come back, anyway? I heard he'd split for good." He paused. "Hey, does he still buy art? Did you talk about your work with him?" Changing the subject. He wasn't eagerly anticipating future huddling.

When I brought up the credit card, he echoed my brother's response regarding shopping. I said impatiently, "C'mon."

"Call if you want, but I say that's his problem." He changed topics again: "Were you careful?" He knew that wasn't one of my strong points, and he didn't need much of an imagination or a backlog of data to wager it wouldn't be one of the perpetrator's strong points either. He chastised me—this day and age and all— and I couldn't come up with any excuses. I couldn't very well tell him I'd been bewitched.

"Hey, maybe there'll be a love child," he suggested.

"Don't even say that out loud," I said. "Anyway, I'm too old, one night, there's no chance."

"You could get a show out of this." He was revving up. "Black-mail him—collectors rule these days. He probably still knows people. He'd have to get you a show if you threatened a love child."

"There's an idea." I was coming around. "But you know how I feel about the kid thing—I'd rather keep the love child."

My neighbor was on a roll. "Listen, get the show, worry about the love child later. You can always keep it. You can say it's mine."

I considered this. "Then we could fake a marriage and you'll make it into the will." One of my major goals was to get my neighbor into the family will, since he had no will in the offing. My aging parents were in the throes of living a miserly, will-enhancing existence, a practice common among the Jews—in this instance, to ensure that the bohemians among the mad progeny would not end up entirely penniless in the distant future. One of my father's favorite lines was "I don't buy new clothes anymore. Do you know why?"

"Why?"

"Because I'm going to die soon!"

"Got another call," my neighbor said. "Should I take it?"

I was relieved to let him go. I didn't divulge the real secret be-cause I wasn't prepared to divulge it to myself. I had fallen for this perpetrator, and that was not my style. He and I had shared a sin-gular wavelength—a dark wavelength not so easy to come by. I hadn't met anyone who actively embraced the dark side since I'd tangled with Jack—who had dropped dead soon after, one of the heart attacks, the last-straw death, the one that broke me, before we really had time to give the wavelength a chance.

It was now past the ten-to-twelve "I'll keep trying till I get you" calling period, and you know what wasn't ringing. I resumed cleaning, although there was very little left to clean. The giddiness was beginning to subside, and the gloom was moving in, heralded by soppy platitudes from the song lyrics imbedded in my brain via the headphones. I was approaching pathetic. Holding a credit card hostage was also pathetic—and juvenile—behavior. The thing to do was to avoid human contact by leaving a message. It was three o'clock. The timing was superb. The perpetrator would be languidly engaged in a late lunch, if my neighbor's genetically based assumption of a noon office arrival was correct. I could leave a cold and haughty message and then settle in to wait.

Unfortunately, I could no longer stave off some uncomfortable introspection. The adult behavior I'd witnessed in some of my peers was still eluding me. As an artist you weren't encouraged to grow up. In fact you were treated like a child, so you tended to respond with childlike behavior. I used to think that adult behavior went along with producing offspring, but that was not necessarily true. Offspring were often just props to enable parents to look adult. I'd come across many more adult kids than adult parents. So that wasn't it. This adult behavior, it was a subtle but enviable way of being.

But there wasn't time to concern myself with adult behavior now because it was crucial to act before the cutoff point for even a late person's lunch. So I dialed, and when I heard the slow, easy hello, I dispensed with a greeting and rushed headlong into a babble allowing no room for interruption. I stumbled over my name and, like quicksilver, recovered. "You know, from last night. I found your credit card."

"I wondered what happened to that" was the laconic reply.

I wondered what happened to that? Where was his ethnic sense of urgency?

"Well, how are you?" he continued.

"Tired."

"I know," he answered. "I had an appointment here at nine, and meetings all day. I haven't had a chance to hire a secretary since I've been back, so I couldn't get out today."

I silently cursed my neighbor and his genetic miscalculation—perhaps there were some pale genes in the mix. My own voice—uncommonly high-pitched—was echoing louder in my head than the perpetrator's, whose delivery proved as disarming now as it had been during the early-morning hours. I considered mentioning that I'd been up since dawn cleaning. Instead I simpered, "Well, can you go home early?"

"Not a chance. I'm supposed to drop by an opening, and then I've got a dinner tonight—business. Record people—one of the lowest forms of humanity—from Munich. It's the last thing I want to do." There was an awkward pause while I calculated which opening he was referring to and whether I should nonchalantly attend. I was about to resume simpering when he continued. "I was going to call you, but I lost your number."

I didn't bother to honor that with a reply. One of the fundamentals of jazz is improvisation, working directly from the unconscious. Improvisational lying isn't that much of a stretch.

"That was nice last night," he purred.

"Yeah, it was nice." Those damn lines, they tripped me up. The simper became higher and squeakier, which was even more disturbing. "Well, anyway," I started and became paralyzed. There was a longer, more dangerous pause.

"Are you still there?"

"Uh-huh," I replied flatly.

He chided me. "You were going to say something. What were you going to say?"

"No, I really wasn't going to say anything. I mean, I don't know what else to say."

"All right then." His voice tightened. "Listen, can I send a messenger down for the card this afternoon?" He said it hard and polite.

"Uh-huh."

"Can you put it in an envelope?" Real hard and polite.

"Uh-huh."

Can you put it in an envelope? Where did that come from? I was fully equipped to handle the complexities of the working world. I had no intention of flinging the card into the arms of a messenger. Perhaps I'd played the role of bohemian artist too well. After that sorry debacle of, I guess you'd call it a conversation, there wasn't going to be a chance to rectify the situation.

When the messenger rang the buzzer I obediently handed him the card in a manila envelope. Then I took stock of the situation. There was no earthly reason to seek involvement with a married perpetrator. I wasn't the type. Besides, I would make an unconvincing partner in crime because I was an unconvincing liar. And this attached perpetrator came with progeny. A far more serious level of crime implicating the innocent. So what if I'd come across a wavelength? There had to be more than one wavelength out there. I averaged roughly one a decade, which wasn't exactly encouraging, but look at this decade—I'd come across two. One dead and one legally attached.

3

I DIDN'T HEAR FROM HIM. BUT EVERY TIME THE PHONE SANG OUT IN THE still loft, I'd leap to my feet, break into a sprint, and get all twisted in the headphone wires. There'd been a few minor meltdowns since Jack, but this was a major defrost and I was taking some time to ice up again. I'd been rattled—no doubt disproportionately. I was especially stumped by the perpetrator's "I'll keep trying till I get you" finale. It had seemed to indicate that feelings were somewhat mutual. Why would anyone, even a seasoned liar, albeit a flawed one, go to the trouble if this weren't the case? With a no-nonsense farewell, he could have made a clean escape—that is, relatively clean.

But I had to get a grip. I had a show coming up and a magazine article to write, and gene-driven guilt was rolling in waves all over the loft and drifting into the sanctuary, where I'd been doing more than a little time. Spring wasn't helping. My neighborhood wasn't laid out in a geometric grid of gray New York blocks. It was a magical enclave with quiet, quirky charms. It was a strolling kind of neighborhood, and on spring weekends it began to fill with strolling groups of all kinds: middle-aged parents in sweats toting the standard toddler and infant, packs of tourists with their guidebooks open and faces up, intrepid elderly couples from uptown. Everyone was outside my windows saluting the new season. Those spring days, as nightfall approached—and it never came soon enough with the irksome time change—cabin fever would descend and I'd prowl around the loft like my late cat used to.

While I refrained from stalking in the world outside, I did do a little discreet research—and a fair amount of deluded stalking in my head. My recovery was long overdue. So what if my base instincts were in obdurate rebellion? There was no excuse. Except, of course, for the wavelength excuse. Except for the speed of his wicked wisdom. Except for his body's impatience, the fury seeping out from under the smooth. I had the impatience and the speed, perhaps without the wisdom, and the fury, the fury maybe not so well hidden. But the fury hadn't fazed him, and besides, his made mine look tame. His made mine feel mild, normal, wellmannered. His soothed and relieved mine. But some forms of relief are not meant to be and are destined to be fleeting.

Eventually, after three weeks, a regime of solitary confinement—broken only by one-block outings to forage for food at the local deli—served its chastening purpose. Time and will sent the episode and its star scuttling into a dank corner of my mind. There were vestiges. I was still doing a little sanctuary time, some neck craning at hip restaurants when I did get out, but nothing I couldn't brush aside. It was just a stage, a melancholy what-was-I-thinking stage.

Then there was something else. One afternoon I was trying to write the magazine article. I was writing about lipstick—about whether brown or pink lipstick was going to be the best bet in the summer to come. Brown was the spring's hot ticket, but my editor had let me know it would be in my best interest to make a case for pink. This was my latest solution—not fail-safe by any means—to the financial standstill I had reached alongside the art market's crash. I knew enough people in the writing world to forgo paying another long, loathsome set of dues, even at this late date, and breezy writing for women's magazines was miraculously contributing to my coffers. It was also contributing to an old-fashioned identity crisis—I was not exactly proud of my role as beauty expert—but dwelling on that problem would only induce more gloom.

I was particularly gloomy that afternoon, and every time my loyal companion, the phone, sounded, which was not very often—it was as blue and green a spring afternoon as you were likely to see in the city, and not many were shuttered indoors in solitary confinement—I frightened the caller off. Hoping to blame the bad mood on a culprit more physiological, I consulted the calendar and was suddenly and irrevocably jolted out of my haze. For an hour I remained seated, counting and recounting the days—and then the heartbeats. My bum heart was skipping an undue number. Sure I'd joked with my neighbor about a love child, but then, nothing was sacred between the two of us.

This was sacred, so sacred, that I buried the jolt instinctively in a corner of my mind that was even more dank and festering. I resented the jolt. The perpetrator had finally taken a ghostly seat in the dank corner, only to be suddenly whisked back to the front of the room through a presence that was ephemeral, but a presence nevertheless. It was still early. I was agitated with the show coming up. There were more than enough excuses where those two came from. My emotions were running rampant because of the defrost—or had they been running rampant because of the potential presence? This was, after all, a symptom that could swing toward either verdict. Face it, any symptom could really swing either way. My friend Perry, who was a member of my race's royal class—the southern version, a different breed altogether—once told me that at our age all hell breaks loose in the body. Because the womb is crying out for a child, she said. We laughed. She hailed from the dark side, too. Perry's womb, however, was no longer crying out for a child—she was married, due in a few weeks—and I was no longer laughing.

My mind and heart had betrayed me; now my body appeared to be following suit. It was a vile betrayal. What I really would have liked was to go into reverse, back to a time of comfortable, predictable semimalaise, not a jarring, up-and-down jagged despondency. I calculated that I still had some time before I could reach a conclusive verdict, and anyway, I wasn't sure I could handle it. Verdict or no verdict, the dank corners of my mind were overflowing and pressing in on the ostensible subject at hand—whether to wear brown or pink lipstick and where to find the best one once you'd decided. All I could focus on was pink babies—or, come to think of it, brown babies. And as for decisions, I had a potentially more crucial maybe-brown-or-maybe-pink decision on my mind.

•

When I heard the sound of my loyal companion in the distance I lunged for it on the first ring, determined not to drive away whoever it might be.

"You haven't called. Do you hate me?"

"Mom? No, no, I've just been . . . busy," I answered.

"Oh, honey, you're busy, I'm glad, thank God. I just hadn't heard from you in so long." So long was one week for daughters, two months for sons. It was part of a genetic double standard that didn't always add up to two. "I just felt like talking. Listen, we don't have to talk. If you don't feel like talking, God forbid, don't talk. You're busy."

"No, no, it's fine. What's new?" We were straying from our

regular routine. Normally I'd initiate the five P.M. call and we'd talk while she broiled my father's steak. I'd recite my latest professional accomplishments, if I could summon any up—I was never one to confide in my mother with dirt, unless, of course, it had been thoroughly scrubbed and disinfected; she'd attempt to weasel out information about the other siblings; we'd analyze the grandchildren and the quality of their upbringing—thank God two of them existed—and then we'd ramble.

On a good day, there was no one I'd rather talk to. She was, after all, the original crackpot who'd taught me—unwittingly—to befriend the countless other crackpots I'd since befriended. However, if things were not going so well, she was the last person I'd choose as confidante because she was, first and foremost, a professional mother. Her voice would become low and tense with stifled hysteria, and any commonplace temporary setback would take on overwhelming proportions for us both. She simply cared too much. It was more expedient—and kinder—to spare her.

I repeated, "Mom, what's new?"

"Oh, nothing, really. I was just making his goddamn dinner and I thought I'd check in. How are you?"

"Oh, okay."

"Okay? Okay. What exactly does *okay* mean?" She enunciated each syllable through clenched teeth like a criminal prosecutor.

"It means fine, good," I begged.

"No, you're depressed. Believe me, I can tell. You're depressed. I knew you were depressed. Goddamn it to hell. I knew it. I told him you were depressed. He said, 'Stay out of it.' He said I was imagining things. Don't be depressed, honey."

"I said I'm fine. Fine means fine." My teeth were clenched, too. "I told you I've just been busy. I've got the show coming up and this stupid article to write."

"Aw, honey, don't call it stupid. Don't put the writing down. I think you're damn good. All kidding aside. Maybe it's because

I'm your mother. I honestly don't think that's it." She paused dramatically. "Don't knock it—you're successful and you're making money. I can't remember, is it about liposuction or lipstick?"

"Lipstick." My mother was generally oblivious to beauty products and rituals, but her only spark of vanity, and I hesitate to call it that, involved lipstick: an initial seven A.M. smeary application of thick Revlon True Red from 1952, which rapidly feathered into pink and was never reapplied. "So have you decided whether to come up for the show?"

"Honey, I think so. We won't be in your way. We're not going to stay over. The hospital won't give Daddy the day off." She wouldn't let him retire—"Over my dead body; his brain will rot"— and she still called him Daddy, which I never noticed unless we were in public.

"You're going to drive all that way and then drive back the same night? Are you out of your mind? It's not worth it."

"You don't want us to come."

"No, no, I want you to come."

"You don't want us to come."

"Mom, I do, I do, but it's just a group show. But come, great, great. In fact, there's probably going to be a party afterward—you can come to that, too."

"Oh, no, honey, no party—who needs that shit? We'd only be in the way. We'll just come up for the opening. He wouldn't miss it. You know we love to drive. It's nothing—five and a half hours. Worse comes to worse that lazy son of a bitch can drive. Hey, where is Daddy? He should be home by now. Do you think he fell asleep . . . Oh, there's his car. Let me go, I have to put the asparagus on."

This call threw me off-kilter, not that I wasn't already off-kilter. Although all I had done was withhold information, it didn't sit well. I would hardly have been capable of conducting a clandestine affair. (I mustn't forget that was no longer the problem at hand. I was already regarding the original problem with fuzzy nostalgia.) Honesty was not merely a virtue, it was one of the ironclad platitudes in my platitude-ridden, faux-Ozzie-and-Harriet upbringing. The stress is on *faux* here, because there was something going on far more treacherous beneath the surface layer of platitudes. In truth, my family had a law-of-the-jungle kind of thing going on. To outsiders we presented a united front, but at home it was another story: We watched our backs, acted cool, learned to be perpetually and candidly sly, and only the strong survived. My neighbor was always perplexed after a session with my family. He said he had never witnessed a family that shared a meal as though it were a highly competitive athletic contest.

We were also gigantic. My three brothers hulked around at six feet four, and my mother was close to six feet tall, even when she was hunched over, which was most of the time. Our benefactor, my poor father, however, who had been barely six respectable feet in his prime, had shrunk down to five feet seven after half a dozen hip replacements and two back operations—"the cripple," we called him fondly. Now he had to look up to me, the baby of the family and the runt of the litter. At five feet nine, I had believed myself to be diminutive until I left home for a progressive boarding school, where I towered over the true diminutives, rich blond girls from the city.

Although all of us had long since left home, most of us—the oldest, the jazz musician, and I—were still on top of one another, all in the same city. Only my middle brother had made himself scarce, having hightailed it away from home at the first opportunity. He had escaped, in theory, across the country, but it was not a pleasant or an easy escape. It was a sixties-style escape with all the sixties accoutrements—drugs, radical politics, mental institutions. I believe he even lived off the land at one point. He still moved around a lot, never staying at one job or in one city too long. Even though he'd been destined to lose from the starting gate, it was still painful to watch—and no doubt contributed to my soft spot for others who'd been destined to lose but did whatever it took not to.

My oldest brother—whom we addressed as Your Majesty, the King, and who gleefully beat down any attempt at insurrection among his siblings—was convinced that my father had chosen my mother for her big tits, but my father denied it. They'd met young and shared a desire to get the hell away from their own families, so they built their own baroque dynasty. My mother ruled while my father loomed ominously behind the scenes. My mother referred to his menacing presence as "he," as in "Honey, you know he's always right," or "You'll be screwed when he finds out." But by the time his ominous presence materialized, most of the physical and psychological repairs had been hastily attended to by her. Needless to say, on a journey when the family had to spill over into two cars, he sat stony and alone in his until I went and sat beside him.

Having two parents who still craved each other's company after half a century, whose version of a less savory world entailed making crude jokes to each other like "Who would want you and your flat ass anyway?" or maintaining harsh judgments on the few friends who had stepped out of line decades ago, was really more of a curse than a blessing. It fostered unrealistic expectations. My expectations had lowered over the years, but they weren't nearly low enough. My father always had a good platitude on deck if questions of love or marriage came up—not that he and I ever really mentioned either topic anymore, since discussion of personal life was inherently protected by the familial policy of silent communication—and it was generally something about just being reasonably comfortable. It had sounded plausible when I was younger, but it had grown stale and it certainly didn't apply to his own situation, which was much more than comfortable, much more than reason dictates. Nor did it apply to mine now.

•

The call left me hollow. I headed directly to the sanctuary and took to my bed. My mother's crusty veneer and shantytown tongue veiled untold compassion driven by extremely sensitive radar. You usually couldn't tell, but she hurt easily. I knew because I was my mother's daughter. I was also his daughter, complete with the scathing judgments based on impossible standards. It would have been a difficult combination to navigate with anywhere, but it was especially hard in this small town, this relentless town that seldom forgot or forgave.

My mother's radar had tracked a crisis in the making, and I wouldn't have known how to begin to confirm it. The term *married man* would not have worked. And I doubted that "single mother" would go over too well either. I sprawled out on the bed, staring at the high pink leak-stained ceiling.

I was one of the very limited number of women who remained pink freaks after the age of five. The sanctuary was pale pink and was filled with cheap street furniture that I'd accumulated over the years and painted white. It looked like the kind of quaint little room you'd find in a shack by the beach. In the sanctuary I could pretend I was at the beach—on a rainy day, that is, since the windows faced an airshaft and there were never more than a few weak rays of light streaming through at odd times of the day. There was a big metal bed my friend Sam had made for me. It was two inches too short, so the mattress tipped a little over the edge, and it was so heavy that I'd never be able to move it. There were photographs on the walls—several of my dead friends had been photographers, and I had a whole wall by my bed consisting of nothing but pictures by dead friends and pictures of dead friends. There were pictures by living photographer friends on the other walls.

One of my older paintings hung on the wall opposite the

bed. It was pink, too, a morbid dirty pink with a lot of scratchy tentacles surrounding a murky object in the center. Some said it resembled a heart with one or two aortas too many. Others found it disturbing in a grisly, visceral, or sexual way. Grisly sexual art was trendy these days, but not my kind: it had to be more obvious or ironic—so obvious that you'd look at it and think, I can't be right, that's too obvious, it must be over my head, but it would turn out that your first throwaway thought was usually right. I guess that's where the irony came in. Anyway, whenever my neighbor ambled by the sanctuary, he'd cover his eyes and crack, "This room must make men just shrivel right up. You might want to consider some redecorating." But I didn't see it.

I began to mull over my situation and then did everything in my power not to. My favorite form of avoidance was a nap, but I was not a successful napper. All the men I knew could go down at the drop of a hat, particularly the ethnics. Every time I saw a movie with Victor he'd be dead to the world at some point, and my neighbor could even drop off during an arduous dinner party. As for my musician brother, his day was one long nap, interrupted by spurts of work and phone calls. I, on the other hand, usually had to sedate myself with several over-the-counter sleep potions in order to attain a measly hour of escape.

I swallowed and waited. I put the pillow over my head to simulate darkness, but I could still hear the Wall Street broker who had moved in upstairs. It sounded like she had purchased a new pair of boots, perhaps riding boots. I pulled the pillow around to cushion my ears and had difficulty breathing. I lay facedown for a similar, less suffocating effect. Then I curled into the fetal position. The fetal position made me sit back up. It was all wrong, both in concept and execution.

I got up and settled into another prone position in the only other avoidance area in the loft: the shabby couch perched close to its jaunty mate, the TV. Another neighborly problem presented itself: The band downstairs had begun a rehearsal. At least they weren't jazz musicians—just a group of failed generic musicians playing failed generic music. I started to drift—that is, until I remembered. This was no longer a plain shabby pink couch; it was the scene of the crime, a possibly more odious crime than I'd even suspected.

In the end I gave in to ritual. Busy people had appointments, errands, nine-to-five lives, or a steady succession of drinks, dinners, and lunches to keep them distracted. We nonbusy people were a vanishing breed. I'd toyed with the busy life, but it had never really suited me. My mind was my business. The busy people imagined that I was lolling around the premises all day. They didn't realize that the creative process involved working at all hours—because you never knew when you might hit your stride. There was no question that too many plans—even just making the plans—would disturb the process. Merely leaving the premises for a carton of half-and-half could disturb the process. Downtime was essential, but the downtime had to be filled, too; it was littered with bad magazines, half-finished books, and, most important, a few TV programs, preferably reruns, playing at salient times in the day. My favorite rerun was on at six, that hazardous time zone when day shifts into evening and the busy people shift into second gear, or third, or fourth.

Between 6:09 and 6:18, depending on the first commercial's appeal, the phone would usually ring. Today it was 6:13 and I was staring at the TV without registering.

"Wow. Brandon should never wear shorts. He looks awful," my brother said. "Do you think he and Kelly are going to break up?"

I took a quick glance. "I've seen this one, and I know they're going to," I replied brusquely. "You know who she's going to end up with, don't you?"

My brother feigned surprise. "Not Dylan!"

"Yup." I was smug. "Come on, you've seen this one." My brother always pretended to be one of the busy people. I knew better.

"Yeah, I've seen it—a hell of an episode. A fine acting ensemble."

"How about Dylan's goatee?"

"He looks like every asshole in this town—Donna's looking good though, isn't she? Are those tits for real?"

I had to focus. My mind was pretty cluttered, what with the pink and brown lipstick, the pink and brown babies, and now Donna (who was wearing red lipstick and, I can tell you, it was all wrong) and her breasts. "I think I just read somewhere that they are. You know what? I think I also read she's going out with the guy who's not blond—"

"Well, I just turned it on for a minute," he broke in, and without a good-bye he started to hang up. Under everyday circumstances this would be acceptable; the call would have served its purpose—a brief exchange to reassure both of us that there was another one of us out there. But not today.

"Wait, do you have to go?"

"I have to practice. I've got that gig next week."

"Okay then."

"You sound weird," he said. The family was not accustomed to choked whispers, and certainly not to audible tears. If you shed a few by accident in the old days, the brothers would move in close to make sure the few multiplied, so it was easier to stifle the initial shedding.

"Well, I may be overreacting or crazy, but remember that guy?"

"Oh, Jesus, I thought you were cool about that. You are crazy. I told you, just get over it—it was one fucking night, he's never going to call, and it's a dead end anyway. On the other hand, I could use a gig that pays—I hear he sometimes hires guys who can actually play on Sundays."

"No, no, no, I am over it, I swear. It's just that I think I may be pregnant."

"Oh, Christ," he said. "How could you be so stupid? Oh, never mind. Are you crying? Oh, Jesus. I didn't mean it. Forget it. I'm sure you're not pregnant—there's no way. On the other hand, it's probably just your luck. I had a feeling this was going to be trouble. Though I could use a new bass player. You never found out if he's still playing, did you? Hey, look at what Donna's wearing now. Tits or no tits, she looks terrible. Unbelievable."

"What's she wearing? I turned it off."

"Oh, it's too late. She changed. So why don't you just take a test?"

"I think it's too soon." I was still teary but relieved at having finally confessed to someone.

"I hate to tell you, but it's never too soon. You can take one of those tests the next day if you want. Didn't you know that?"

"No, I didn't. Last time I had to wait. I guess that was a while ago."

"Well, go buy one and take it. Call me back and tell me what happens. What a drag. I'll tell you one thing—from now on I'm wearing leather condoms, or maybe a steel girdle. What were those things the Roman soldiers wore when they went to battle?"

•

The drugstore was just around the corner, but in order to get there I had to run the gauntlet of three brand-new, not terribly sedate outdoor drinking establishments that dwarfed the three relatively sedate veteran outdoor eating establishments. No matter how surreptitiously I tried to slink by them, some acquaintance would notice me and call my name loud enough that a few other heads would turn to greet me, too. Whoever said this was a cold, unfriendly town has never visited my corner.

Your average New York corner is entitled to be boisterous and unruly. But until now there had never been anything New York about my corner. My corner was the gateway to the enclave where wide forsaken streets were lined haphazardly with pockets of buildings and divided by haunted alleys. It anchored blocks of ethereal brownstones with parrot stores or Vietnamese souvenir shops on their ground floors, stern factory buildings fronting for swanky lofts inhabited by rich or famous people, misshapen factory buildings crammed with seedy lofts sheltering neighborhood relics like myself, and even a few Deco skyscrapers towering over the whole mess.

Until recently, the neighborhood had held its own against repeated commercial assaults because it was guarded by a band of the uppity rich people who'd snatched it away from the relics like me. I wasn't so crazy about these vigilantes, and I crowed silently when they lost a righteous battle. However, they had been a little easier to ignore than the hordes of louder and even more uppity young people who frequented the new drinking establishments.

The owner of the new establishments was a stolid, goatlike hippie who stood on twenty-four-hour watch, like a crotchety farmer protecting his land, grinning and gloating in an attempt to ingratiate himself with the neighborhood relics. Some of the relics had caved. One painter I knew—a gray and grizzled potbellied art-world casualty—had laid claim to a stool at the far end of the bar at one of the establishments. The superintendent of my building was usually right next to him, leering. He bore an uncanny resemblance to the scurrilous super, Leroy, who inspired Rhoda Penmark to include him in her trio of Bad Seed murders. The bar was all windows, and my eyes locked with theirs every time I snuck around the corner.

I stopped and looked both ways when I got downstairs. I saw the leering super and the grizzled potbellied painter planted on their stools. The goatlike hippie was crouched beside them further ingratiating himself, although it was hardly necessary. I took off, zigzagging through the riffraff, eyes straight ahead. I'd almost made it when I heard my name. It was my neighbor calling, his grand elegant self concealed, as usual, by a baggy, crumpled button-down oxford shirt that hung listlessly over baggy crumpled khakis. He was crossing the concrete eyesore in the middle of the street they called a park. Granted, it had a few benches and one or two trees, but mostly it was littered with trash and local bums looking to cash in on the riffraff en route to the establishments. My neighbor was moving swiftly. The neighborhood presented a larger obstacle for him, as I wasn't the only relic who considered him a personal mainstay.

"Hey, where are you going?" he said cheerfully. Then he saw my face and his voice became less cheerful. "Uh-oh, what now?"

"Oh, never mind."

"Just tell me." He motioned me over to one of the benches in the eyesore, and I sat down beside him. I preferred the eyesore to the outdoor establishments, but my neighbor didn't. "I didn't get out of Brooklyn to drink another lemonade on another rotting bench on a filthy slab of concrete," he'd rage. My neighbor knew the direct route to my genetic guilt. So I must have looked pretty bad.

"It may be nothing. I mean I hope it's nothing," I began.

"Yeah?"

"The imaginary love child may not be so imaginary. I'm going to the drugstore to get a test."

"You're kidding!" His solemn eyes went big and bewildered, and his graceful hands began to flutter. "Why didn't you tell me? Listen, I'll go with you."

"No, no, no—I can't even think about that now. I'm not sure I could go through with it—not at this stage of the game. This may be my last chance, and—"

"Down, girl—I meant go with you to the drugstore." He had to raise his voice and grab my arm to break into my rant.

I wasn't sure if my neighbor understood the gravity of my

predicament. I'd emerged from the cult profamily, and while there was no need to replicate it, I wanted a piece of the action. At this juncture I was resigned to a small piece. I was willing to relent on the mate-and-kid package deal but not on the kid part. The path I'd chosen—or rather, the one that chose me, as I explained repeatedly to my mother—was not the path of a woman headed toward motherhood. It was an oblivious, obstinate path focused around the studio, a path I'd assumed I could control. I'd assumed the package-deal path was one that I could not control, it would just happen, sort of a luck-of-the-draw deal. But I no longer assumed anything. All I knew was that I might have had the whole thing backward. And now I knew I wanted the kid part of the package deal more than I had ever let myself know—sometimes you don't know how much you want something until it happens, even if it doesn't happen like clockwork, with all the essential ingredients. And now it was getting late. My neighbor might think I was making a last-ditch effort to run with the pack. I wasn't. I'd already veered so far off the path that the pack was a murmur in the distance.

I let my neighbor drag me to the drugstore, and I let him do the talking and make the purchase, and I let him block our way back home. The female members of the cult did not normally let. I had a feeling that if this saga continued to gain momentum, I was going to be doing a lot of letting.

When we got home, I propped my neighbor up on the shabby couch while I did the test. The stick turned blue before I even left the bathroom; I simply pretended it hadn't and kept right on going toward the couch. It was the last opportunity I'd have to exercise an avoidance tactic, and I was in shock, the kind of shock that hits you when a distant acquaintance calls at seven in the morning and tells you a dear friend has died. My neighbor's hands were fluttering again, and his eyes were distinctly alarmed. He hoisted himself up to stagger over to the other couch, a street couch swathed in white sheets like a newborn. He lay down there, and I spread out on the shabby pink crime scene, and we both assumed staring positions.

"Well," he began. "Well, what do you think?"

"I don't know." I covered my face with my hands, just in case. This predicament was a rude slap in the face, a cruel taunt: the dangling of a prize I had secretly planned to win. Now it was well within my reach and I might have to default. I had no qualms about motherhood—I'd mothered broods of childlike adults, and I was overqualified to mother the real thing. That wasn't the problem. I couldn't pretend that painting wasn't an all-consuming passion, nor could I pretend that motherhood wouldn't be an overriding passion—too much of my own mother was lodged deep inside me. "How can I keep it? I can't even support myself—I mean, maybe if I gave up painting and wrote about lipstick full-time." My voice drifted. Beauty writing might not even support a bohemian and a kid and a baby-sitter. On the other hand, I was moving rapidly out of motherhood range, not to mention the fact that pregnancy with a bum heart was a tenuous proposition and one that would get more tenuous with time. But a life without painting could provoke bitterness, and no kid deserves a bitter mother. On the other hand, if painting prevented motherhood, that could provoke bitterness, too. Bitterness could sneak up on you in this town, and you had to be alert and agile to dodge it.

That wasn't all. For me to foist a fatherless, not-so-privileged existence on an unsuspecting child seemed arrogant, presumptuous. I was not a movie star who could hire a staff of fake fathers, and I knew too many fatherless adults who were not quite right in the head or the heart—including the father of this potentially fatherless child. It would have been more modern to skim over the facilitator in these circumstances, but I was only modern on the surface. I flashed on him and his hidden fury and his package deal and the "something I've told very few people," which had more than a little bearing on this, and I winced. I said as much to my neighbor, but I won't pretend it was intelligible.

"Wait a minute, slow down. Screw him. You don't have to tell him. I promise you, I know his type—I guarantee he'd say you couldn't prove it was his and hang up. And screw the money— you'd figure it out—hey, what should we call it? Do you really want to do this?"

"I wish I didn't."

"I could go with you, I mean if you decide . . ." He was always going with me. He went with me to the last-straw funeral and to the memorial six months later, and he didn't even know Jack. Who in this town needs an extra funeral and an extra memorial? He went with me to put the cat to sleep, and believe me, he loathed and feared that damn cat. Eventually, my neighbor and I hit our stride lying on the couches. He'd suggest, I'd rail against. He'd go with the opposite tack, I'd rail more stridently. We didn't get very far.

I had to lie down again after he left. This going-against-the-grain business was debilitating. I blamed my erratic behavior on hormones. I'd always looked forward to blaming everything on pregnancy hormones. Just like everyone else. Exactly when did they kick in?

CHAPTER

4

LOOKING OUT, I COULD SEE THE RAIN COMING DOWN FROM A SKY GLAZED pale blue by the sun still shining. Tropical rains in the city always feel slightly sinister, but it was more likely that the sinister sensation I was feeling came from sitting alone in a dark deserted bar at four o'clock in the afternoon. The bar was tucked in a far corner of the neighborhood just north of mine. It used to be a frumpy art neighborhood. Now it was a gaudy shopping district and there wasn't a frump in the vicinity. Only a few holdout galleries were left, galleries that had transformed themselves into boutiques in order to survive, and the neighborhood was beginning to look like a slightly more upscale version of Bleecker Street. The dark deserted bar was one of the original courtly neighborhood bars and remained an institution—although remaining an institution was a fickle business in this town. There were years when it had to pose as a swinging bar to attract swingers from other parts of town, but it never quite lost its dignity. At four o'clock it was not swinging. No, it was four-fifteen.

The perpetrator had been due, at four o'clock, to discuss the predicament. The early genes and I were hunched in a not-so-dignified pose over a dignified corner table. I'd lost my dignity too many times this week—too many publics. It had been an abyss of too many tables in too many bars and too many restaurants with too much talk. I'd done it all—midtown lunches, downtown dinners, afternoon teas, six o'clock drinks. I was having publics all over town.

A sordid saga can get anyone's blood up, particularly during a listless city summer. Listless city dwellers love nothing more than to participate in someone else's sordid saga. But most are too buried in their own skins to slip into another, even momentarily, so the wisdom they offer is usually about their own skins. I was expecting the chorus of "Have the kid" and "Don't tell him" (and then the pause, and "Who is he, anyway?") from the squadron of bachelorettes. "It's your body," the hard-nosed feminist upstairs had decreed, just as predictably. "Why are you thinking about him? He wasn't thinking about you. Did he take responsibility?"

"I didn't either."

"Take responsibility now!" she yelled.

But when a smaller squadron of bachelors echoed these sentiments, I was astonished. After all, the perpetrator was one of their own. "But how would you feel?" I'd ask, and they'd shrug. Traitors.

My neighbor just repeated, "Fuck him. He'll never know."

Even the young marrieds said it. In their eyes he'd done me dirty; they assigned me the role of maiden in distress, and the perpetrator had won the part of the mad killer/rapist. Perry was unsparing: "He's obviously not from the South. One of our gentlemen would never have shirked his duties. He would have called the next day at the very least. He would have sent roses. Or a telegram. At the very least he would come to your aid now. Through telepathy, if need be. It is his duty. You gave him your prize possession. And you gave him his credit card back! And what did you get? This lover boy—he did you wrong! He should be locked up!" In her eyes I was entitled to revenge. I didn't agree. I'd been a wildly consenting maiden. Perry just needed to get out more.

I sought out a married elder a decade and a half away from the pack I wasn't running with—an elder with grown kids and an estranged mate. I anticipated sobering words of wisdom. When I heard yet another "Have the kid" and "Don't tell him" . . . "You'll figure it out," I sagged in my seat and choked on my mint tea.

Only stalwart Victor, cool and comfortable in his wrap trousers and gauze blouse (I was haggard in a limp and soggy sundress) addressed my practical concerns over drinks at a steamy garden bar on the Lower East Side. Sipping rum to the beat of his loyal walking stick tapping against the gravel, he offered his services as au pair, at a bargain rate. I trusted Victor because he was the kind of fatherless son who sought vindication through fierce attachments to children, thus conveniently bypassing fierce attachments to adults. I'm certain that day was a yes day, and we staged big plans.

I seesawed doggedly through yes days and no days in sweaty pursuit of not just a decision but of someone to make the decision. I was having trouble hearing my own mind over the incessant din of my heart and body. My heart and body didn't usually speak up, much less hold any weight. My mind was trapped in the same circle of thought skipping around like a roulette wheel. The wheel slowed down at yes but never came to a complete stop. And it continued to circle repeatedly back to the perpetrator, to "I have to tell him," then back to "I know what he's going to say," and then to a cowardly "Maybe he'll help me decide."

"How would I tell her?" I mused during a six o'clock rerun session with my brother. He'd surprised me, too. It was another giddy yes day, and he was willing to go along.

"Maybe it's time you two had that little talk. Judging by the situation, you should have had it years ago."

But my brother had his own problems, and he was losing patience. The overseas concubine had recently joined a cult, the genuine article, and our cult emphatically did not sanction rival cults. When I made the obligatory circle back to "Should I tell him?" my brother answered wearily, without hesitation: "This isn't a made-for-TV movie. Christ, just tell him."

So I called the perpetrator. Not just like that. I dawdled. I rehearsed. I wasn't quite sure who I was going to get or if he'd want to be reminded of me. This was not just a tap-on-the shoulder-at-a-crowded-party kind of reminder. It was an elbow-crack-to-the-head reminder. And what if he thought I was one of the desperate bachelorettes; that I'd calculated this conception?

When he answered the phone, I didn't stumble over my name, but I did need to pause before continuing cheerfully: "Remember me?"

"Sure I do!" It was a salacious "Sure I do," and so was the "How are you? What's going on?" that had followed. An illicit thrill pricked my relief. I scolded myself silently and kept going.

"Well . . . I'm okay. But there's this problem." I clung to another pause. "I don't think I need to spell it out."

"Oh. I see." His voice had dropped down to smooth and steady, closing in on hard and polite.

"And, I'm—don't panic and don't be mean—but I'm kind of considering keeping it."

"Oh. Well, that is a problem. I'm—"

"Oh, don't worry, you wouldn't have anything to do with it."

"Is that so? I, ah, I don't think this sounds like a very good plan. I . . . I couldn't handle . . . you see, it would haunt me."

"I know, I mean I knew, I knew how you'd feel, you did mention . . . I haven't decided what I'm going to do. Everybody told me not to tell you. I didn't think it was fair."

"I appreciate that. Oh, wait a minute. Damn it, goddamn it—another call—hold on, wait, I'm expecting an important call, don't go . . . goddamn it . . . Hello, hello, are you still there?"

"Yes."

He had regained his composure. "That would make things very, um, uncomfortable for me. I couldn't live with that. I . . . ."

"You wouldn't consider it, not even as a kind gesture?" What had come over me? This was serious. Blame it on the hormones. I heard a laugh, a soft, dry sound. The wavelength was still intact. I continued in a rush. "Do you think we could get together and discuss it?" That was not in the script either.

"Yes. Listen, I have to be downtown at six for an appointment. Oh, Christ, another call, this may be . . . Christ . . . just a minute, just a minute, hold on. I apologize for the interruptions. How about four-thirty . . . ah, no, make it four. Where would you like to meet?"

"I don't know. I'm not very good with decisions."

•

The rain had become a drizzle. A couple of dripping shoppers had come in with their packages and had caused a slight stir among the few regulars in the bar. I sucked down a soda to steady myself. I was dealing with a pro. I had to remember it was up to me, as the hard-nosed feminist upstairs had repeatedly pointed out. I had the upper hand. And I mustn't forget to brace myself against the insidious charm.

He was standing there when I turned from the window, slightly damp in a loose linen suit, carrying—not a briefcase, not him—but a crumpled tabloid. He smiled a warm, rueful smile involuntarily. I tried to disguise my own. He was slight, maybe even shorter than me. He'd loomed giant in my mind because I was accustomed to giants, I preferred giants. He looked older, too, closing in on the fifth decade rather than the fourth. I'd forgotten his worn face with the jagged planes not quite connecting, but I hadn't forgotten his stance, the belligerent, chin-jutting stance of a little boy that did me in. I hadn't forgotten his eyes either, dark and steady. They no longer looked so steady; they looked wary.

"Sorry I'm late. The rain." He said, still standing.

"Oh, don't worry. I could tell you were the late type." I laughed, more to myself. "I'm the early type, you know, my people. Your people are usually the late types. It's a genetic thing. Even if you have mixed genes, late genes dominate. And I know some other things about you. I could tell you'd be late—"

"Wait a minute. The rain, midtown—I couldn't get a cab. I mean it's true there was a time when I could get away with— rather I used to be . . . and that's why I'm never—"

"It doesn't matter. I just got here anyway." I laughed again. Nervous laughter—one of the family traits I may have neglected to mention.

He sat down in the hard chair at the end of the table and ordered wine for both of us. I was still hunched over on the red leather banquette, and I straightened up to make moving away from him seem less obvious. He looked at me quizzically.

"Why are you laughing?" he said finally.

"Aren't you glad I'm not crying?"

"I can handle a woman crying." He reprimanded me with the long gaze I couldn't forget. I didn't say anything. I wasn't nervous anymore. I was just woozy. "I was going to call you," he continued. "I've been away for three weeks, back in Paris, you know, doing some business. I'm talking to some people about starting a record company, so I'm back and forth a lot. Have you been trying to call me? There were quite a few hang-ups on—"

"It must've been some other girl." He did the gaze again, and I blushed. "No, I wasn't sure I was ever going to call. I thought you'd be mean. I thought you'd blame me. Everybody told me not to tell you." It was happening all over again, the loose-lipped phenomenon.

"It's hardly a question of blame. We're not exactly teenagers. But what led you to believe I was going to be mean? What's that about? And who is everybody?"

"I don't know why. And everybody, I don't mean everybody—just a couple of people." I took a long guzzle of wine, and something came over me. "Your reputation precedes you."

"Would you care to be specific? Who exactly are these people? And my reputation, that's bullshit." The soft dry laugh. "Christ, you're talking when I was a kid, mid-thirties, for God's sake, right off the boat from Paris, in the middle of a divorce and arrogant as hell. Well, sure I played around." He studied me with the eyes that had become more darkly inscrutable, and his mouth tightened.

"I just told some friends. I had to. They wouldn't even know who you are anymore—you've been gone a long time by New York standards—don't flatter yourself." I giggled nervously. "I wasn't trying to . . . I wasn't thinking about it like that. You can trust me." The words kept coming, but they were as much of a surprise to me as they probably were to him.

"I do trust you. I trusted you instinctively when we met." He murmured it in the lullaby voice.

My control snapped. I watched helplessly as my body sidled closer to his braced in the hard chair. "You know, you should be careful. You must have an extraordinarily high sperm count, and there are a lot of women my age out there on a sperm hunt." I went on. I told him that my neighbor had warned me about him, how we'd laughed so many laughs over that night, about the imaginary plan we'd hatched, the blackmail plan when the love child was an imaginary love child. I thought he'd appreciate a blackmail plan, but I may have been mistaken. He managed the soft dry laugh, but it was turning sour and it didn't last long.

When he spoke, it was in a taut voice I didn't recognize, and he looked past me to the door: "I think I told you. I never found out who my father was. When my parents split, he became a nonsubject—persona non grata. My mother's family, they didn't approve of him, he wasn't 'a professional'—they were an old bourgeois family entrenched in academia. Stultifying. They cut her off when I was born. We never talked about it." I could only see his profile. He'd raised his chin higher. "You seem to think you know all about me, but you don't. Marriage was not on the agenda, I can assure you . . . it wasn't . . . well, for one thing, it didn't make sense as a musician, especially back when I was on the road. But when children became involved, it became something else. My second marriage—both of my marriages—were results of preg-nancies—errors. I can live with that. I couldn't live with the idea that there was a child of mine out there I couldn't . . . couldn't pro-tect."

"Come on. What you're most interested in protecting is your marriage. But I don't think anyone would necessarily have to find out who—"

"Don't be absurd. You know how people talk in this town. And you may be right. It might . . . create problems in my mar-riage. But I'm not just talking about myself. Or my family. Or you. What about the child? Are you prepared to impose this on a child? Are you aware of the consequences? Oh, never mind. It would ruin me. For many other reasons. Personal reasons, reasons you also don't know about, reasons you couldn't possibly know about." He'd forgotten, or he was counting on me to forget? I was one of the few people who did know the story. About the original other woman, the singer in Paris. The one with the kid he never knew he had until he didn't exist anymore.

My own face was blank, but the bottle of olive oil I was gripping under the table had been stripped of its tissue-thin iden-tity. I relented. "I haven't decided anything. I can't really afford it. But this may be my last chance—my heart and everything. Then there's painting. I don't know. I still don't know what I'm going to do." An abbreviated version of the two-week-old morass shifting back and forth in my head followed.

"Why don't you adopt? Why don't you adopt a Chinese baby?"

"I don't want to adopt a Chinese baby, and I don't have the stupid twenty thousand dollars anyway." I couldn't focus with the racket in my head, and the wine wasn't helping. "You already have everything you want. I don't yet." I looked at him half accusingly and half pleading.

"That's not true. I don't have nearly enough dough. Not with a kid in New York, an ex-wife, and another kid in Paris. You can never have enough money, can you? Your people know about that, don't they?" He laughed sardonically. "You're not stupid. You've been around. You think I enjoy running a club that's jive, hiring charlatan musicians?"

For a moment he let me look into his eyes, and I detected damage—and hurt—no matter how impenetrable they seemed. They made me docile. Our eyes made a silent pact right then. Silently, we stowed away the same layers of subterfuge that had vanished instantly that first night—when we'd glimpsed something of ourselves in each other. We didn't stop talking. No, we gained momentum and we danced back and forth in our natural rhythm. I floated and forgot, and he joined me gracefully. It was too easy. We became masters at self-deception, masters at denying what drew us to the courtly bar at four o'clock on a rainy afternoon in May. We rolled out our common obscurities, and we judged our judgments. We went back to the old days: He talked about his glory years when he was based in Paris; I told him about following my fledgling brother like a lapdog to the concerts in the ramshackle lofts and the shoddy clubs that weren't yet crammed with sleek people and cash registers louder than the music. I confessed that I never could go the distance at those clubs—even in my twenties I had to be rudely awakened at four A.M. when the music finally petered out—and he confessed that he'd never felt so right as he had in those early years in Paris, when the music was starting to really happen and he was never in one place for long.

"One night in the early eighties, it was one of the last gigs we played," he was saying. "My band closed down this club in Paris—it wasn't the trio, it was the five of us, cello, sax, trumpet, drums—we were just hanging afterward, and Prince before he wasn't Prince came in with his boys, they started playing, and we fucked around."

Why didn't you just keep playing? I knew better than to ask. Instead I supplied enthusiastic "Really?"s at the appropriate pauses until he stopped short and looked at me. Cocking his head sideways, he said flippantly, "Today, did you remember what I looked like?"

I froze. "No. Sort of. A little. Oh, I don't know. Not really." Of course I remembered him, maybe not so much the jagged angles of his face, but I remembered his eyes and I remembered his every word and I remembered how he made me feel.

"Did you?" I said. "Remember what I looked like?"

"Oh, yes, I remembered what you looked like. I haven't spent a night like that in a long, long time. Have you?" His eyes were on my fidgeting hands.

"Kind of, but it was different, I didn't even like the guy, I was just . . . oh, I don't know, it was different." Trying not to believe that the night had meant something to him, I only half listened, overcome by hopelessness and fear.

"You bite your fingernails." He took my hand. "I didn't notice. You bite them so evenly."

"So?" He shouldn't have touched me. My hopelessness became petulance. "Don't you?"

"No. How come they're so even?"

"Practice, hours of practice. In the hierarchy of habits, I

wouldn't call it a particularly harmful one, would you? Don't you have habits?"

"Yes," he answered softly. "Maybe one or two. Not too many left anymore." He looked at his watch, then abruptly signaled for the check. "I have to get going; it's close to six." Then he softened again. "Well, we managed to have fun, didn't we?" He was still unable to look at me.

"Yeah. A lot of good that'll do me." And I lapsed into a bitter, reverberating silence.

He was restless in his seat, and his hands were all over the place. He was used to winning with words, and I'd unwittingly beaten him with silence. "What is it?"

I was unable to shake the silent attack. I was the one who was going to be haunted. It was bleak. And on top of it I'd been bewitched again. Through no fault of my own, of course. The run of bad luck was getting me down. It wasn't just the hormones. I raised my head, and the reliable high squeaky voice was pried loose, lubricated by a huge transparent smile. "You don't want to be late," I said. "And I'm tired. Let's go."

"Oh, you're tired." He seemed somewhat relieved but still unnerved. He tended to repeat my words when he was unnerved.

"Yeah, I am tired." I plastered another smile across my face. "I'm pregnant. Remember?"

He winced but recovered cunningly. "Oh, yes, I do, I do remember. We've managed to avoid that particular phrase up until now, haven't we?" He held the credit-card receipt tightly with one hand and tore it too slowly and too meticulously into tiny scraps with the other.

"You're right. We did. We've managed to avoid more than that, wouldn't you say? Can we go?"

The rain had stopped. It was glaringly bright, bleary-eyed hot outside, so I had an excuse to blink away anything that shouldn't have been in the eye area. We walked together for a block, not saying much, until he hailed a cab. Before he got in he turned and took me by the shoulders and kissed me hard, a kiss that belied our mutual deceit. It felt like he wanted to infuse me with something more, but he knew he wouldn't be able to.

"Shall we talk on Monday?"

"I guess so," I mumbled and started to walk away.

He shouted after me furiously, exasperated, "Do you want to, or don't you?"

I looked back surprised. Couldn't he read my mind? "Yes, yes, I do," I shouted back.

He got in the cab, and I dodged and weaved my way through the shoppers. I ran until I was wet and steamy, and when I reached Canal Street, I floated, an ominous float, the rest of the way home.

•

There were messages when I got home, from those eager for the latest news, even though the meeting at the dark bar had been a carefully concealed development. I ignored them, including one from the silent-treatment recipient, Rachel. Not that she'd noticed she was getting the silent treatment.

A perky nonethnic, she'd grown up pedigreed in the city, where she now ran a small classy company that published art and photography books. She had become one of the busy people who move in fast crowds made faster by rich foreigners and prissy art fags. Our friendship, a long boarding-school-based friendship, had begun to flounder recently. Rachel was always getting swept away by a fresh fast crowd, and even when she tried to include me, it never took. After all, who needs a human black cloud hovering over a fast and sunny crowd?

I didn't call her back. I turned on the TV. Back-to-back episodes of a very reliable program were on. I couldn't really ask for more than a couple of back-to-backs—reruns no less—my most treasured part of summer in town. It was a poignant little program. Two parents had disappeared in a tragic plane crash and left a good-looking brood of orphans behind. The oldest orphan, earnest, brawny, in his twenties, had been left in charge of his siblings: a winsome toddler, a gurgling infant, and two woebegone but adorable younger teens. There was enough hugging and door slamming to satisfy any viewer who wasn't feeling 100 percent, and tonight's episodes were priceless. The female teen, Julia, had finally begun sleeping with her adorable boyfriend (after much advertiser-placating angst), and guess what happened? It was uncanny. Julia and her boyfriend were sparring—she was undecided about keeping the baby, and the boyfriend wanted her to keep it and get married and move in with his parents. I didn't know who to root for, and by the time she had the miscarriage, my eyes were gathering moisture.

I was wavering. My decision wasn't quite taking. Just as Julia was on the way home from the clinic, weeping in a four-wheel-drive vehicle, and I was in the process of reversing my decision and trying not to weep, Rachel called again.

"How are you?" I mustered up as much chirpiness as I could.

"Really upset. I don't want to talk about it." Uh-oh, testy and bitter. I preferred Rachel's misty, undiscerning side, which provided me with a glimmer of how the other half lived. Better to remain silent to avoid more antagonism. She continued: "I've been out every night and sobbing all day, and I'm exhausted—*je ne sais pas.* I can't do anything. *C'est très très mal.*" Rachel had taken to peppering her litanies with French phrases, a practice that made me twitch. "Things with Jean aren't going so well, but I was hoping I might be pregnant. I just found out I'm not."

Rachel was one of the modern desperados who eschewed birth control without bothering to inform the man they had chosen to be the father of their child. This was one of our many chronic disagreements but one with a rare dynamic: I took the old-fashioned stance, while she went modern.

"Oh." The irony—a word I found distasteful—that was infiltrating my life (instead of my paintings, where it could have been at least fashionable and lucrative) wasn't amusing. She kept talking but I stopped listening. Because of the silent treatment, Rachel knew only a few hazy facts about the perpetrator and nothing about the predicament. "I just found out I am," I began.

"You just found out you are what?"

"Well, pregnant."

That disrupted her "I don't want to talk about it" monologue. "Who . . . oh, you mean that night? That guy? You never told me who he was. Was he handsome? I don't remember. Was he smart? He was, wasn't he? That's fantastic. You're so lucky. If only I were pregnant. That would solve everything."

"No, well, actually, it hasn't solved a thing. Actually, it's created—"

"That would be the answer to all my problems," she continued. "Oh, if only I was pregnant. You know, I really thought I was this time."

"Wait a minute. I don't think I can keep it."

"Why not? You'd be a great mother. Of course you'll keep it." I was frosty when I delivered my speech, and she didn't listen long.

"There's my buzzer—I have to run. It sounds like you've made up your mind," she snapped.

"I thought I did, but I don't know if I have anymore. I just don't—"

"I'll call you later. The reason I called was because I wanted to talk more about the party after your opening."

I finished watching the episode. Julia and her boyfriend ended up back together, and I was pleased about that but I didn't feel so good about Rachel. Maybe she had meant well. My mother had always sided with the enemy during my battling teen years. "Aw, honey she means well" was in there rock solid with the rest of the platitudes. Rachel had managed to distract me for a few minutes. The diabolical hormones were directed toward her now instead of the situation or myself or the perpetrator. Did he mean well, too?

She had reminded me of my show, something that had slipped behind on the worry list. Before the predicament had surfaced I'd been consumed with it, wallowing alternately in daydreams of sweet revenge or abject terror. The opening was another obstacle. Art openings aren't my idea of a good time even when I'm not a guest of honor. And they're never complete without a private cele-bration afterward. I was an awkward and unaccomplished cele-brator, since my family had never indulged in such folly. The last time I'd tried to personally fake a celebration was on my twenty-fifth birthday. A disaster. Rachel had suggested a sit-down dinner for thirty—this was back when I had the first and second strings of friends—and another ten for dessert and champagne. I hate dessert and I hate champagne. But I obeyed. I timidly brought up the possibility that the B-list ten might be insulted. Rachel scoffed. Never saw the B-list ten again.

This new train of thought distracted but not nearly enough. I was en route to the sanctuary when I remembered. It was Thurs-day night: Deejay Night. Deejay Night was my neighbor's pri-vate exorcism, which he enacted at a Village bar furnished lavishly in mahogany and velvet. It was a Clark Kent–Superman kind of thing; during the day he toiled away at his art criticism, and most evenings he continued toiling at social functions to ensure that the daytime toiling would see the light. It was heartening to see him behind the turntable, periodically breaking into song, dancing blindly, pretending not to hear anyone.

But there was one little problem. The night allegedly began at eleven o'clock, which was hard enough for an early person to stay up for, but it didn't hit its stride until midnight or even later. My neighbor was the original late person (the snake hid the tendency until he had me hooked), and it had been the cause of endless al-tercations between us. When we arranged a rendezvous, I would be in place, relaxed and expectant, at the appointed hour. By the time he strolled in all cheery and leisurely, my face would have turned tight and would instantly suck all the cheer out of his. Eventually I figured out the solution: drop the tight-faced routine and learn to be late. (During one late battle he informed me curtly that it was outright rude to arrive at a dinner party less than forty-five minutes late.) Once we realized it was another case of dia-metrically opposed gene-related traits and we made a few minor adjustments, it rarely caused a problem. Except for Deejay Night. I could never be late enough. I'd get close, but there was always an endless half hour where I had to keep up a steady yawn so as not to go pained and tight-lipped. I had company. By the time my neighbor staggered in under the weight of his bulging bag of discs, there was a lineup of mousy, balding, effeminate Jewish men with tightly drawn faces waiting alongside me. How was I going to manage Deejay Night in my current condition when all I really wanted to do was end this day and start fresh and more stalwart in the morning?

I called my friend Sam. I'd taken one glance at Sam in art school and decided no, absolutely not. He was a little guy with long straggly dirty blond hair, and in those days he was covered in black leather with only one accessory: a massive Great Dane by his side. I'd just been released from the progressive boarding school and was still recuperating from the onslaught of rich kids trying to be eccentric, and I pegged him for another one. It wasn't until I moved to the city and ran into him at an opening that I got it. He informed me right off he was no longer Samuel, he was Sam; and later, if I slipped up, particularly in mixed company, he informed more stridently. His blond hair was longer and strag-glier, he wore silk (they may have been polyester) Fourteenth Street T-shirts, slinky jeans, and big black boots, and he acces-sorized with the pit bulls instead of the Great Dane. We hit it off, and soon he was picking me up a few nights a week in his shiny green '73 Lincoln. Before I met Sam I drank white-wine spritzers, but Sam said he couldn't possibly be seen with a girl who drank white-wine spritzers. He taught me to drink vodka instead—he was one of the Jews who drank. There was something comforting about Sam, and it didn't take long to figure it out. He was a miniature Long Island–flashy version of my oldest brother, the King. Sam and the King got along beautifully. The King was a criminal lawyer, and Sam had committed some crimes along the way—which were never his fault, of course. The King became his consigliore. Sam called the King Scarface, and when he'd arrive in the green Lincoln at the King's midtown law firm all jazzed up in his finery, the King would yell to his partners, "The hit man is here!" and they'd all gawk.

Now Sam had a sharp cropped blond hairdo, and he mixed the Fourteenth Street look with Maine fisherman. He still wore the silk or polyester T-shirts, but now he draped plaid flannel shirts over them, unbuttoned, and recently he'd taken to wearing club-kid polyester track pants with iridescent white stripes. Sam had also stopped painting. He used to paint naked females astride flying leopards, which sounds silly, but they weren't. They captured a yearning, a melancholy beauty, that went beyond naked females on flying leopards. He got out early because of a financial "misunderstanding" with his dealer, one of a group of wealthy divorced housewives who became art dealers. Sam wasn't humble or lucky enough to stick it out. He wanted a normal life, and he had one now, with his contracting business and a few of the nasty scrawny girls that he fancied in the wings. But it didn't make up for painting, so he was always flailing away at bitterness and malaise.

He picked me up in his truck this time, with the pit bulls in the back, and as we inched our way up Sixth Avenue toward Deejay Night, I made a halfhearted attempt to gain some wisdom. His earlier advice regarding the perpetrator had been straightforward:

"Don't you remember the Kraut? Remember I had to make her suffer for the sins of her people? It was fun at first, but take it from me. Stick to your own kind."

His current advice was also to the point: "If the Puerto Rican next door can afford six kids, you can afford one." Sam liked nothing better than to offend smarmy liberals. You can be assured he was one of the few friends of mine that my neighbor allowed to cross the sacred portals of Deejay Night.

By the time we arrived, my Thursday-night friends—the cream of my neighbor's coterie—were all in position. My neighbor was shimmying away behind the turntable, with his expression of blind ecstasy. Victor was posed in front of him, immutable. He'd dressed for Deejay Night in a shift belted loosely at the waist, maroon bloomers, and a dark striped jacket with various slits for ventilation. The rest of the crowd was a conglomeration I could only guess at, students on dates squeezed on velvet couches, saucy drag queens strolling up and down the mahogany bar.

We sat by the turntable, where there were enough nasty scrawny girls around for Sam to lick his chops over. The Thursday-night friends observed a certain protocol. No one had to interact if they didn't feel like it, and you could tell by just looking at someone's Thursday-night face if they didn't. On the other hand, if you did feel like it, these nights could develop into group therapy sessions, with the Thursday-night friends spilling a week's worth, or a life's worth, of woes, and there was no need to divulge any particulars when you only knew one another on the Thursday nights. This evening I had a look-but-don't-touch face on.

At around two o'clock Sam started making noises about leaving—one of his scrawny girls was undoubtedly on call somewhere—so I said, "Go." He was taken aback. Usually I was the one half out some door, urging him to stay on without me: "You're having fun. Let me go, you'll do fine without me." But Deejay Night had sedated me, and I was in no hurry to go home.

Eventually it was down to me, my neighbor, faithful sentinel Victor, and the waiters behind the bar, sweeping, counting the loot, and still dancing. My neighbor and Victor were astonished. They were concerned, knowing my fragile state, but still they teased me. I'd never made it to the bitter end of Deejay Night before.

I woke up the next morning the way you do when someone has just died: fresh and ready to go for a few seconds, then memory intrudes and time's up. You know you're not going anywhere.

CHAPTER

5

THERE WERE ONLY A FEW STRAYS IN THE GALLERY. PEOPLE IN THE BUSINESS don't generally start arriving at a six o'clock opening until six-thirty or seven. I would have preferred to arrive late, but I was a guest of honor. I had to greet. People always complain that there is never a chance to "have a real conversation" at a crowded opening. But it's far worse when it's not yet crowded, when you do have enough time to have a real conversation, because how can you have a real conversation in an inhuman expanse of cold white rectangles under incandescent lights where you can't even sit down?

Fortunately this gallery had an austere elegance that was not pretentiously austere. It had been around long enough to establish a certain cachet, although it certainly wasn't the kind of gallery with hired help serving champagne in fluted glasses. This gallery served respectable white wine in durable plastic cups. I had time to glance at my fellow artists' work. Two of the artists painted interpretations of work from the past. This was also considered ironic, and it was, simply because it had been going on for over twenty years and no one had exposed the real hoax. One artist did fake Warhols, and the other did fake Rembrandts. The third made feminist art that could also be categorized as sexual: installations that used garbage and dresses to symbolize female body parts. Dresses as feminist symbols were a hot commodity this year—the critics had rediscovered a relationship between fashion and art yet again.

I was wearing a dress—I guess you could call it art, performance art—a navy dress that was a touch transparent but demurely, stylishly. This was a business occasion, and the importance of appearance could not be emphasized enough. You didn't want to look tarty, but you didn't want to appear too dowdy, either. The director of the gallery, on the other hand, did not look at all stylish or tasteful. She was a daffy did-I-say-that kind of gal, decked out in a rambunctious red suit—the kind of suit newscasters wear—exposing a snakeskin décolletage, which was emphasized further by an excess of costume jewelry.

From my corner I watched while she slathered a fake Warhol promo job on a collector. Protectively, I moved closer to my group of paintings. I tried to be objective about them. They didn't strike me as too terribly grisly. The fake Warhols struck me as a more grisly lot. I had a pretty grisly week ahead of me: at least two more hours of white rooms and incandescent lights, an intimate candle-lit dinner party afterward (hosted by staunch Rachel, of course), and, in a few days, under floodlights, an abortion—or termination, as they called it in the business. I welcomed this term. It was terse and matter-of-fact, without the melodrama and angst induced by the other term. On the brighter side, I'd finished writing the lipstick article, and I had some respite before the butchering—or as magazines referred to it, the editing process.

The perpetrator had called yesterday, Monday or whatever

day it was. Just as he'd promised. When I answered he identified himself by both his first and last names: Joseph Pendleton. The formality chilled me. Seeing Joseph Pendleton had served its purpose as I'd expected. I wasn't capable of ruining any perpetrator's life, insidious charm or no insidious charm—or in the process, a child's life. It was eerie, his formality. In the same distant tone, he asked how I was. I had enough time to answer okay, but he cut me off before I had time to tell him that I was out of it, that I hadn't been able to do much lately.

"I've been thinking about this problem. I've thought about nothing else but this . . . this problem, all weekend, and I can't go along with it, not only because of—"

"Oh, don't worry," I said breezily. I was out of it but the eerie formality jarred me into action. "I'm going to do it Thursday."

"Do what Thursday?" I'd assumed he'd figured it out in the bar that rainy afternoon, but his voice had a confounded, exasperated edge. "The, um, the abortion."

"Abortion? What abortion? I thought it was too soon, I thought you were going to—"

"No, I went to the doctor Friday, and I decided. When I saw you, the whole thing and you . . . you weren't an abstraction anymore, and I knew I couldn't keep the . . . it."

There was a silence. "Oh, I see." He wasn't accustomed to being caught off guard, and his voice grew even more distant and formal. "If I can be of assistance in any way, please let me know. I insist on paying for half and—"

I cut him off again, breezily. "Oh, that's okay. I think my insurance will cover it. But thanks. If it doesn't, that would be helpful." If he was going to be eerie and formal, then I'd match him syllable for syllable.

"Would you like to get together for a drink before?"

"Oh, it's in the morning, I don't think—"

"No, no, some night this week, before Thursday."

"Oh. Okay. I guess Wednesday night."

"All right. I'll call you Wednesday afternoon."

"I'm really kind of—"

"Look, I'd like to talk more about this, but I'm already late for an important meeting. I'll call you Wednesday." And that was it.

Later I replayed this scene, dissecting pauses, interpreting phrases, and I'm surprised I missed the undercurrents. So we don't do so great on the phone, I'd told myself. So he wasn't a phone person. Some of us weren't.

•

I saw them arrive. She strode ahead of him. Purposefully. She was always rushing. His uneven, plodding gait was worse than it had been three sets of hips ago. But my mother looked beautiful in her gangly, no-vanity way. She had lovely bones, and her blond hair had gone white and luminous. He didn't look too bad either, with his dark craggy face and wise eyes peering and judging from behind the tortoiseshell glasses. He was thinner than ever. The King, who hadn't arrived yet, referred to him as a "fucking gray pretzel" because in recent years he'd become excessively peculiar about food and was consequently the first seventy-two-year-old anorexic male I'd ever some across. I introduced them to the gallery's dealer, a nice enough guy, tall, balding, and wisecracking. My mother thanked him effusively for "giving my baby a chance." My father smiled his Mona Lisa smile, proof that he wasn't listening, while their pregnant baby cringed. The dealer's eyes were roaming, understandably so, and a sign in the right direction: the business direction.

I excused the three of us and coaxed my parents into a corner. My mother continued in a raspy whisper. "Thank God you're not wearing one of your short skirts, honey—I don't have the strength to worry about your pussy being exposed to the public. The paintings look stunning, and I swear, it's not because—"

"What's this other crap?" he interrupted. "They're copies. What the hell is this? I don't get it."

"Honey, don't worry, we won't be in your way. Where are your two brothers? He's not at one of his goddamn gigs, is he? And where's His Highness—he said he'd bring the kids—I've got the fucking GameBoys for them. What time is it? Oh, there's Perry. Don't worry, we'll be out of here in no time. Perry, oh, honey, don't you look adorable." Perry was about two hundred pounds into her pregnancy in a lavender floral muumuu and looked awful and miserable. "It looks like it's due any minute. Honey, you won't know what's hit you." My mother hated all southerners but was fond of Perry because she was one of us, and because she was also unwavering in her appreciation of old people.

My father was parked with my neighbor, who had gallantly shown up before the lights began to dim. Victor had fetched a chair from the dealer's office for him and stood by, elusive and refined, tracking the feminist-dresses artist, who was wan and Eastern European–looking—his type—and listening to my father. My father was undoubtedly educating the two of them on the perils of HMOs, or something equally urgent, unless my neighbor was prevailing with his ongoing research on the Jewish male. Not too long ago my neighbor had managed to pry more information out of my father about his no-good parents—liars, cheaters, opportunists— in one forty-five-minute lunch than I had in my lifetime.

People in the business, dull and humorless in tight, dark clothing, were swarming the gallery like ants. Two women in pastels toting several shopping bags each were race-walking against the traffic, and I heard one say to the other, "Absorb what you can. We'll talk about it in the cab on the way to the theater." I wasn't sure the business was happening strictly enough. My performance here was high-stakes, and I was not going to let the problem get in the way. I tried to stick with a one-two-three system. I'd begin with a warm hello. Pause a few beats for the obligatory "Con-

gratulations—looks great." A short, modest thank-you sufficed—
there was no need to list the flaws in each painting, my natural
reflex. The modest thank-you could serve as a delicate segue into
"Excuse me, I've got to say hello to so-and-so." Then, exit with a
graceful dip and swivel, and a prayer that there was a so-and-so
nearby.

The comment "I've never seen you look so good; you're glow-
ing" by more than a few guests caused a few slipups. A reminder
of the glow that was about to be terminated didn't sit too well
with me. I moved back to my paintings to eavesdrop. One prissy,
bony dealer sniffed up close to my paintings and turned to say to
his companion, "These paintings are well painted. What does that
mean?"

That's when I saw Sam. You couldn't miss him in his red plaid
shirt unbuttoned to expose just enough turquoise silk muscle shirt.
He was cozying up to Rachel. He loved nothing better than cozying up and talking dirty to Rachel, who had difficulty containing
her repulsion. Rachel had rallied to my cause—after she and I had
finally had the denouement we should have had months ago. It
was during a "Don't tell him, keep the kid, you'll figure it out" discussion and was triggered by what had become my least favorite
cliché of them all: "support system." Every time I heard "But you
have a support system," I flashed to three months after childbirth,
by which time "But you have a support system" would have become "but you—kind of—had a support system." I told her that if
she were any indication of this support system, pardon the expression, I was in trouble, since moments after I'd informed her of
my situation, she was out the door to a cocktail party.

She'd been utterly faithful ever since and had signed up "to go
with me." My neighbor had offered again but in such a way that
I knew he'd rather move back to Brooklyn. He'd been nailed to
the cross too many times for the sins of his male brethren. Even
my brother had raised a tentative hand, but I couldn't allow it.

He wouldn't know what to do. He wasn't accustomed to wit-
nessing loose emotions, especially not mine, and it would be
heart-wrenching to watch him struggling. I needed a female, a
tough, reliable female like Rachel who would accept any unfore-
seen loose emotions with aplomb and grace.

The director of the gallery, whom I'd taken to calling Ditzgirl,
was gunning for me, dragging along what appeared to be a very
disgruntled collector. She introduced us, and the collector began
to grill me. "How does a little girl like you paint these big paintings?" He smiled, and I struggled to reciprocate. "Tell me, what's
behind the work?" he continued. "I don't believe I know your
name." He addressed Ditzgirl: "Does she have a track record?" She
shrugged girlishly. Turning back to me, he asked, "What are you
trying to say with the work?"

I was going to try the girlish shrug when Ditzgirl piped up,
"She's been influenced by Dutch still-lifes from the 1700s."

Thankfully, he ignored her. "Where do you get your ideas?"

My ideas—I was wondering where Ditzgirl got hers. I was
grateful to see the King approaching, along with my giant, exuberant sister-in-law and their giant, exuberant kids.

"What is this crap?" he barked. "Your paintings are the only
decent things here, and that's not saying much. Hey, I'm kidding,
what's wrong with you, for Christ's sake? Sell any yet? Good luck.
Hey, where's that Sam? He owes me some money," he said largely
and loudly.

Ditzgirl's limp crimson mouth sagged, and the collector turned
white as the walls. It wasn't a good idea to commence with
introductions. I tried to steer the family to an area where their
loudness and largeness might blend in. But there weren't many
large and loud people in the gallery. It was more of a slender, low-
murmuring crowd. Then I saw my mother coming toward us at a
high-speed gallop with my father swaying in the rear. My other
brother appeared, registered the King's presence, and took off in

the opposite direction. My sister-in-law had the kind of face that could go from exuberant to tense in an instant, and it did so as she watched her son almost knock my father over in his haste to get to my mother and the GameBoys.

"Where's my GameBoy, Grandma, where's my GameBoy?" I could hear my nephew from the corner where I'd fled in order to act like I didn't know them. My other brother was already there acting like he didn't know them. "You'll get your goddamn Game-Boy. Why the hell you would even want a GameBoy is beyond me. Only ignoramuses play with GameBoys."

"Grandma called me an ignoramus," I heard him tell my father. "And she swore, too."

"Where's your girlfriend the tramp?" The King had located us. "I bet she's getting plenty of action. That's why people join cults."

"Let's try to keep the conversation above the waist," replied my other brother. "We're in public." Fortunately, new prey arrived in the form of Sam, and the King was distracted.

Having dispensed of the GameBoys, my parents were ready to get back on the road, and I led them out. The dealer motioned me over and told me that he was so sorry, but he had to go to a bene-fit down the street, he was late already, he'd tried to get out of it but he couldn't. He'd speak to me next week, oh, no, not next week but the week after. He had to go to Europe. Oh, maybe it would be the week after that. At any rate we'd talk before the show came down. That was not a good sign. It was only a summer group show, not a top priority, and I understood, but it was not a good sign at all. Even worse, I was going to have to rely solely on Ditzgirl.

Ditzgirl was the kind of gallery director who liked to estab-lish a parent-child relationship with her artists. I had plenty of mother; I didn't need another, especially one with poor social and cognitive skills. I was willing to excuse the wrong date on the invitation—we all make mistakes. It took some time to cross out each and every one of them with a thick Magic Marker, and it did not look professional, but okay, mistakes happen. So she hung two paintings upside down. Big deal, she wasn't familiar with the work yet. It took some time to get familiar with the work, and anyone could miss the huge black arrows on the back of the paintings pointing "this side up." But it did not bode well. And neither did the look on the face of the collector she was still shuttling about.

The crowd was thinning. There was a choice of four or five openings to attend tonight, so it was a hit-and-run deal for people in the business and for the younger artists. The neophytes and the hangers-on no longer provided crowd-fill because they had lost their taste for art openings. Glamour follows big money, and there was no more big money, so things weren't looking too glamorous. The older artists who had crashed along with the market were too bitter or tired to desert the safety of their studios (or kitchen tables) for an opening. And the artists who'd already hit the jackpot had no reason to attend. But Ditzgirl didn't show any signs of dimming the lights. She was still going in circles.

I saw Rachel in the corner in an intense discussion with Perry. They were partners in the publishing company and practiced a peculiar dynamic. Rachel played the wise motherly gentile, and Perry played the kooky Jew who was never going to grow up. Perry was assisting Rachel with the dinner party, which meant that she'd plant herself in whatever chair would still handle her girth and hold forth while loyal Rachel slaved. I could predict that she'd hold forth on the indignities and untold sacrifices of pregnancy, childbirth, and motherhood until Rachel, incensed that the indignities and sacrifices weren't yet hers, exploded. I hoped to miss the explosion.

It was steamy under the lights and even steamier outside. I wanted to get the intimate dinner party over and done with, go home, stand vigil until Thursday, get the termination over and done with, and start all over again.

CHAPTER

6

RACHEL WAS BETWEEN APARTMENTS—SHE ALWAYS KEPT ONE STEP AHEAD of her demons by establishing new residences—so she held the party at an apartment belonging to a friend of mine from another giant-brother-inundated family.

Aaron was a California girl with an East Coast–tainted soul. We made the giant-family connection instantly. We referred to her family as the Addams Family and mine as the Munsters. Aaron had done her time in the art business—as a dealer. She quit soon after having an epiphany, during which she realized that the only good artist was a dead artist. I guess the view wasn't so great from either angle. Aaron's apartment was dark and dramatic and tasteful, like her. She had Northern Californian taste, soft sculptural couches in earth colors, king-sized ruby velvet pillows, and low wooden tables covered with candles—she had candles before everybody else did. Her rooms were graciously strewn with ethnic objects and fabrics. It was a far more soothing environment than an incandescent art gallery.

Rachel had outdone herself. The long oak table was artfully laid out and crowded with delicacies. But I couldn't eat much. I was there, but not really. Or rather I was there but my friends weren't. I was with ghosts instead: the ghost inside me, the ghost of Joseph Pendleton, and the ghost of Jack, the last-straw death who always turned up at such occasions.

After swigging down two glasses of wine I felt more drowsy than I should have, even with the hormones. I asked Victor whether it would be considered impolite if I lay down for a moment before the salad was served, and he assured me that it wouldn't. He was a little preoccupied because he was leaving shortly for an assignation with the wan Eastern European breasts-and-dresses artist. I headed toward the bathroom, then took a sharp right up the stairs to the bedroom, where I lay down under an ethnic cashmere throw on the king-sized bed.

My last conversation with Jack, he'd been in a rapidly escalating bad mood and I'd wanted to get off the phone before it was too late. He'd launched into a tirade about the woman in the news who'd lopped off her husband's penis, and I'd half-listened until he yelled, "How would you like it if I took a chainsaw to someone's vagina?"

"Well, it was just hanging there," I'd pointed out.

He'd hung up on me. He was that type. Talk about fury. Jack's fury was the kind of ethnic fury—Semitic, in this case—that simmers and is usually siphoned out in humor. I didn't call him back. I had my pride. Two days later his fury imploded and he was dead. Granted, this was an unlikely turn of events, but it made me reevaluate. I could no longer discount unlikely turns of events.

In the aftermath I promised myself that I would never let pride obstruct seeing a wavelength through to its conclusion, whatever kind of conclusion it might be. Death makes you dramatic—and promises to yourself don't always hold. Jack was trouble, no doubt about it, but a kind of trouble I was familiar with, a kind that could probably have been handled with courage and time, but we didn't have the time, and who knows if we would have had the courage.

I let my eyes close, and as I began to drift Jack joined me. He sat down on the edge of the bed and began a long grumbly monologue about the dinner party. He was feeling too bitter, too sorry for himself tonight, to be around these people, he told me. What a waste of time—he would rather be home working.

"Stay," I said. "I'm stuck here. Have pity."

He sighed and lay down beside me. When I once asked Jack what he meant by a narcissist (the term wasn't nearly as fashionable then as it is now), he said unapologetically, "You're looking at one." But when he said it, his mouth, a thin line of insolence, curved up ever so slightly—never all the way. His eyes smiled all the time though, with sly innuendo when a joke was brewing, right up until the delivery, when they turned opaque—watching for a response. Jack was another case of damaged merchandise. He was almost too good-looking, dark with a stony face, a cool character, but inside he was always quaking, so he was drawn to females who were more screwed-up than he was—tortured actresses, exotic dilettantes. He was also a member of the only-child species, but he didn't lack fathers; he'd had a surplus, four or five along the way—I can't remember—only one mother, though, and she was some mother.

For years we'd been strictly social acquaintances. Then, as we found each other more and more often hiding in corners at parties, we developed an antisocial kinship. Often we were the first to arrive in festive living rooms. Later, when we started to see each other alone, Jack would pick me up at least half an hour ahead of time. His punctuality didn't bother me—on the contrary, I was always ready—but sometimes I teased him. "Do you want me to leave? I could walk around the block a couple of times and then come back," he'd say, quite sincerely. "See, if I hadn't gotten out of the house now, I never would have."

Jack had a sterling set of personal moral standards, but he carried it like a shield. I'd always harbored a mild crush on him, but it seemed like a long shot. He regarded me, I thought, as a fellow black cloud and nothing more. I think it was at one of Rachel's soirées that he accused me of flirting with him. I walked away. The next time I saw him was at a garden party out of the city. We pulled a couple of wrought-iron chairs into the sun and sat there for the duration. I think he was seeing a tortured actress at the time, and he rambled and raged. When we left we agreed to get together soon, but when I called him he was evasive. Then one summer day he called. It had been a fiscally advantageous year, so I was about to leave on a trip. Jack's finances weren't in great shape, and the tortured actress had jumped ship. We stayed on the phone for an hour.

When I came home from my trip it was almost fall, the time of year when the sun starts to set at six-thirty and the bleak, raw light makes you wish you were on a sailboat somewhere. It was still light when Jack came over—it must have been around five-thirty, although he wasn't due until much later. Jack thought the ideal date should start at four so that you could end up in bed by seven-thirty, at the latest. We sat on the couches until I got nervous. It was pitch black outside when we left to go to the restaurant down the street. The restaurant was in an uncool phase, but Jack was so out of it he thought it was still cool. Having reached the stage when you can hardly get out of the house, he liked to go to a cool restaurant when he did, so he could see what was going on with the young people. The evening went by so quickly and easily that we both went home puzzled.

A week later I learned about my heart problem. The damaged valve was revealed through the chest pain I'd ignored for a week. The doctors in the emergency room decided that I would have to have open-heart surgery immediately to replace the valve. Jack happened to call the next evening when I was on some very effective sedatives. He was uncharacteristically upbeat: He had to come downtown for a drink, so he wondered what I was doing—maybe he could stop by? "Sure," I said, and told him what had happened.

"Oh, God," he said. "Jesus . . . I actually have tears in my eyes." He paused. "Well, are you sure you want me to come over?"

"Sure," I repeated. "I'm not doing anything. My parents are here, but I sent them to dinner with my brothers. I couldn't handle going out."

So he came over and he ended up ditching his drink date. My father insisted I have the surgery at his hospital or, at the very least, get a second opinion from his cardiologist. After some initial balking, I agreed to go a couple of weeks later. In the meantime I lingered in New York in a sedated limbo while all my friends competed to be the most solicitous. Jack won and I showed my appreciation. We neglected to posture and play coy because time seemed short.

He was still Jack though. The night before I left for my parents' he was supposed to come over, but at the last minute he called to cancel; he was too depressed.

"Depressed about what?" I asked.

"That's the thing," he said. "There's no real reason to be depressed, so I'm even more depressed."

"I guess I'm lucky," I said. "At least I have a real reason to be depressed." That got him, so he came over.

The surgery threat turned out to be a false alarm. The condition would have to be monitored, but surgery probably wouldn't be needed for at least a few years. When I got back I called Jack, but someone else had told him first, so he was nonchalant.

"Thank God. Now I won't have to take care of your cat. I was sure she'd jump out the window and I'd have to replace her and you'd notice," he joked. His voice sounded distant. "Oh, listen, I have another call. Can I call you later?"

Without the crisis, we had to backtrack, and our retreat

was awkward. There was a series of dates canceled without any convincing excuses. "I guess I must be busy," Jack would say, and then he'd laugh derisively. Well, it was fall, the busy season—anyone worth his salt was making plans and canceling plans feverishly. One time I said, "No, you just don't want to get together," and his response, a weak laugh, didn't argue very convincingly either. I took it in stride. Trust your first instincts, I told myself. Jack was always a long shot. But who can remember their real first instincts?

Then he called one night, pretty drunk—Jack was ethnically inclined toward pharmaceuticals, but he did like his evening cocktails. I actually had been busy, no doubt to ease the void left from the crisis, and I made myself sound even more busy and cool to get back at him. It worked. He sounded so impressed that I couldn't keep it up.

"Oh, please," I said. "I'm at the age where I can still fake it. Barely though." And then I took pity—he really didn't sound so good. "You're cracking, aren't you?"

"Cabin fever, I guess," he replied. "I should probably do something, go out, but I can't think of what to do or anyone I want to call."

"C'mon, you have a lot of friends."

"Yeah, sure . . . friends." We were in the middle of analyzing this problem when he interrupted urgently: "Well, what am I to you?" I sputtered in reply.

He came over the next night, and since I still had friends, I took him along to some early-Saturday-night social events, openings and such. The night felt as easy as had all the other nights—maybe even a little bit more. When we were walking back from the restaurant, Jack said, "Slow down, you're going to lose me." He hated how fast I walked.

"Oh, God, I always forget. Forgive me, I wasn't thinking. Sorry, I just got going, I thought you were next to me."

"You sound just like your mother."

"How do you know? You've never met her."

"I can just tell." That did me in. At the subway we were paralyzed. "I should go home," he said.

"Okay, but you know, well, my neighbor did tell me about a party, later . . ."

"A party?" For a second his eyes flickered interest. "But why would we go to a party? What would we do? How much later? What time is it now?"

"I don't know, a couple of hours later. We could read the paper at my house till then."

"Well . . . no, I should just go home tonight . . . I should get up early . . . no, I have to work tomorrow."

"Okay, then. Well, bye." He kissed me quickly and started toward the subway, but then he turned around.

"Oh, could I have the sports section?"

"Oh, sure, here."

"Oh, and maybe the 'Week in Review'?"

"Here, take it."

"Oh, never mind, I'll just take the sports. Good night." He kissed me again, with more vigor, and started to walk away again, so I did, too. "Hey!" he yelled.

"Yeah?"

"You said you'd come uptown."

"Yeah?"

"Well, when?"

"When you invite me." He gave me a shy look then, and I remember it well because it was the last look I got. I remember shivering, too, even though it was warm for fall.

Dead artists are traditionally raised to mythical, heroic heights, and Jack was no exception. At the funeral he became Saint Jack. His "best friends" talked about his "struggle with intimacy" in halting voices that didn't make sense to me—if they were his best friends, what could be more intimate? His colleagues spoke of his "uncompromising integrity," and all illustrated it with the same five folksy anecdotes. On the way out, I ran into Jack's neighbor, Dick, a gentle soul with big, eager eyes. When Dick whispered, "You know, Jack had a real thing for you—in case you hadn't noticed," it jump-started my first public.

When I woke up, Jack was gone. So were all the other guests. I went downstairs and found Aaron asleep by the glow of the TV on a soft sculptural couch, surrounded by ashtrays stuffed with half-smoked cigarettes and half-empty glasses of wine.

The next two days were as cloudy as I could possibly make them. I would like to say that I went about my business on Wednesday. But I didn't. I waited for a call from Joseph Pendleton. That pride I'd sworn off so solemnly forbade calling him. By dusk, with some help from a couple of pharmaceuticals, at least I wasn't angry anymore. Pharmaceuticals are less sloppy and more predictable than drink, especially when your intention is just to get past angry. I got way past angry. I was stunned. Obviously narcissists hadn't lost their appeal for me, but it was becoming more and more apparent that they did not foster equanimity.

While Joseph Pendleton didn't exactly inspire trust, I'd glimpsed signs of compassion; obscured tough-guy compassion that was not unfamiliar. Nothing had indicated behavior this aberrant. Nothing had prepared me for a cruel streak. This behavior had serious implications. A perpetrator concerned with incriminating leakage should not risk crossing a potential leaker, especially one with fluctuating hormones. Joseph Pendleton did not add up. I was sure he was the one who'd suggested getting together, having a drink.

I lay in a stupor, waiting. I was exhausted by waiting. My neighbor stopped by late. His face was uncommonly severe and his eyes narrowed. "I wouldn't treat a dog like this." He spat it out. That was all. We went through my old records together, searching for some neglected classics for Deejay Night. We assumed our positions on the couches and listened to the records loud enough so that we couldn't hear each other. If I could have, I would have said, "The hell with Joseph Pendleton" then. The hell with Joseph Pendleton and his rotten set of personal standards.

7

"How are you?" Rachel got in the cab, her old self, motherly in a businesslike manner.

"Okay, I guess."

"You never heard from him?"

It was seven in the morning, and the air in the cab was thick and sticky. Only the end of May and the city already resembled the tropics—with staccato rainstorms puncturing the monotony of swollen heat. The sun was still out when we got to the clinic, which was hidden in an insipid skyscraper in the East Forties—directly across town from the father-to-have-been's lair, come to think of it.

We had enough time to stall a bit in the outdoor plaza, a midtown version of the eyesore in my neighborhood with its own midtown bums sitting on cement cubes. We shared a cube in the shade of a mangled-steel sculpture. My doctor had arranged to meet me at the clinic because she couldn't perform general anesthesia in her office. Local wasn't going to do it. I needed to be knocked out for the duration. Rachel kept up a sweet steady prattle. Her brow was creased as she chattered; her face was pale, her hair was wet and combed back severely, and her eyes, blue eyes you could see right through, were even more transparent. All I had to do was nod encouragingly. There were several hapless-looking women in the seventeenth-floor waiting room, and a few helpless-looking men. All the women were young. We were among the common people. I don't believe Rachel had been among the common people before. Her face took on a stricken expression that almost made me laugh. I had to fill out several long forms, and Rachel continued prattling. Every time she paused to glance around furtively, I'd look up from my papers and wave her on: "Keep talking. Don't stop, whatever you do." I listened gratefully to every minuscule detail of why Jean had refused to go to last night's cocktail party and what he had said to her when he'd come to her apartment later in a fit of pique. I heard that he'd been a mess, sweaty, unshaven, drunk, in dirty jeans. I egged her on: "How'd he leave?"

"Oh, a dirty look. And he slammed the door—hard."

"Did you go after him?"

But I went cold when she confessed that she had begun working on a new book a few weeks ago, a photo book of jazz legends, and guess who was cooperating by lending his collection. She'd barely known who he was then—someone had suggested him. Then she hadn't known whether to tell me or not.

"He seems like a really nice guy, though, I mean he's doing it for nothing."

I didn't reply.

"Maybe this isn't the best timing," she said.

"Don't worry," I reassured her. "It's not your fault. I'm the one whose specialty is bad timing."

The woman behind the glass had a kind face, and when she

motioned me in I tried to look back kindly, but I couldn't form a kindly expression. It wasn't so bad going through more paperwork, but it began to get bad when she handed me a packet of abortion accessories and ushered me into a stuffy stall to change. When I shuffled out in my paper slippers, she motioned me over to a bench in the dingy gray hallway, where I slumped next to three young women flipping through copies of teen magazines. Young women do not have a clue—that's a walk in the park despite what they may think. The woman told me to wait there to be called for my sonogram.

I'd been under the impression that I was coming here to meet my doctor and to be whisked in and out. Hospitals were the only places—except for the hip art restaurant down the street—where I knew how to get royal treatment. This was not what I'd signed up for, not what I was paying extra for. I didn't understand the need for a sonogram. I didn't need to witness concrete proof that it looked big and healthy, that it might even make the ninety-eighth percentile one day. I was able to avoid looking at the screen, but the nurse said "six weeks" loud enough so that I couldn't not hear it. I struggled to stifle the public that was brewing.

CNN was swinging on a pole high up, or maybe it was MTV, in the mini airport lounge I was ushered into next, with the rest of my listless group in our matching paper gowns and slippers. A woman came in and said it was time for my counseling session, and my dignity failed me. I snarled that I didn't need any fucking counseling. She was understanding and gently prodded me into another dingy room, where I sat with my eyes closed and wet while she counseled me quickly. They moved me into a private room with carpeting, where the pile of magazines included the issue containing my liposuction article. It didn't divert my attention.

When the doctor came to get me, she apologized for the delay. I could barely mumble a reply. My vision was blurry with unfo-

cused rage. I followed her slowly. Under the lights I finally had the
public and the doctor patted my arm. By the time I stumbled out
into the waiting room, with my vision still blurry, the room was
packed with hordes of common people, and poor Rachel looked
beyond stricken. I motioned to her to follow me and kept walking.

•

Once Rachel had escorted me home from the clinic, I thanked her
profusely and told her we could discuss the jazz book and its con-
tributor later—it was just an unlikely turn of events, nobody's
fault. I changed into the most pristine virginal white cotton nightgown in my possession. I was a little light-headed but didn't feel
the least bit physically impaired. I threw down a sleeping potion
and got right into bed—under the covers, not on top of the bed in
my normal sign-of-the-cross nap position. Not long after making
the termination decision, I had purchased the air conditioner I
couldn't afford. A hot and soggy post-termination session could
very well have put me over the top. I turned it on high and luxurious, and soon it was loud and frigid and surreal enough in the
pinkness to silence any ghosts.

When I resurfaced, I showered and took out a short, festive,
melon-colored dress. My beauty editor had told me that the color
melon stirred up emotions, and mine were numb. I wasn't sure if
numbness was a good or bad sign, but I put the dress on anyway.
I saw that it was tight across the chest, a reminder that the hormones would continue to dance their ugly dance a little while
longer.

I met my brother and neighbor for dinner at the usual spot
down the street. A cold front had come in from Canada; it was
comfortable and breezy, so we sat at a table outside. At the next
table sat a group of art people with the current hot art dealer posed
like a Greek statue at the center, a steady procession of artists,

most of them art-world casualties, paying homage. I nudged my neighbor and pointed, and he said, "Oh, not him. Let's move down a table. I can't eat dinner and watch middle-aged artists grovel at the same time. I'll get indigestion."

We moved down a table. It was a lovely summer evening. You could see the World Trade Center planted solidly and protectively in one direction and the Empire State Building planted solidly and protectively in the other. There were people out strolling, and two thirds of them knew my neighbor. It was consoling, listening to them say hello, the breeze on my face, not having to say much, and I was not without some relief that the ordeal was over. I did say, "I'm not going to let him get away with it."

"You're nuts," my brother grumbled. The concubine was still ensconced in the cult overseas, and he was in the process of exerting all his willpower to stay away. "You're just going to start it up again. You're asking for more trouble." He turned to my neighbor.

"I'm behind her one hundred fifty percent whatever she wants to do," my neighbor said in his singsong liar's voice, without looking up from his plate.

•

When I got home I swallowed another medley of sleeping pills to squelch any imprudent dreams, and the next morning I marched like a robot into my windowless studio. My studio looked like a cross between a space capsule and an early cave dwelling. It was crammed with junk, the overflow from the rest of the loft, and it had reached its limit. I got right down to business. I gessoed some small canvases, and then I began to throw away empty paint tubes. I stapled a fresh white drop cloth onto the grimy, paint-encrusted wall. I scrubbed the floor, mottled with paint and greasy with linseed oil. I filled four bags with garbage using my favorite kind of garbage bag—the huge industrial three-ply kind—and lugged them downstairs.

By the time I was done cleaning up, the canvases were dry—and white and clean and fresh, and I was damp and filthy. I left a message with his new secretary to call me. Then I put on my headphones, turned the volume up high and painted. I almost didn't hear the buzzer when it rang. It was a delivery and at first I thought, Oh, maybe. It was a basket filled with flaccid fruit, cheap chocolates, ornamental cookies. There was a note from a plastic surgeon I'd interviewed for the liposuction piece: "Great job—loved the piece. Thanks." I rescued a box of plain hard biscuits and threw the rest out.

An hour later the phone rang. He was the last person I expected it to be. It was so soon. I wasn't prepared. "It's Joseph Pendleton," he said in a guarded tone. "I had a message you called."

"Why did you ditch me?" No rehearsal, and I screeched like a fishwife.

"What are you talking about?" He was incredulous, no longer guarded, but venomous. Maybe he didn't understand slang.

"Why didn't you call me?" I didn't like how I sounded—who likes to sound like a fishwife?—but it couldn't be helped. Apparently, he had had to go out of town for business. That was his initial excuse. He didn't preface it with an apology. Instead he became polite and distant with intricate details. He had had a business meeting with some investors regarding the record company. Oh, yes, and while he was there he had picked up some photos at a gallery. Not that he was doing much collecting anymore, but these were rare shots of Coltrane. The details didn't register. All that registered was polite, and it fueled my rage. I told my neighbor once, "I see right through your disdainfully polite," and he'd shot back, "We may have just hit on one of those traits you're so fond of. Name me one polite Jew." I came up with one but he really had me there.

"Why couldn't you just call me? Oh, I guess they don't have phones in Chicago. You could at least have called yesterday. You

made it so much worse. You were nice the other day. I wasn't prepared. How could you turn around and be so awful?"

"Awful? What do you mean so awful?" he hissed. "You never
once made me feel a part of this. And yesterday, I couldn't call you
yesterday, how could I call you yesterday? I thought I was the last
person you wanted to hear from. I had no idea you cared. I was
under the impression that you never wanted to see me again."

I was dumbfounded. It was so preposterous that it made
sense.

"Really?" I barely squeaked it out.

"Look, maybe it was because I was in the middle of a business meeting when we spoke and I was distracted, but I had no
idea how you felt. You have my deepest apologies." He used the
voice.

"Oh" was all I could manage, and we rested in our corners like
fighters in a ring.

"Well, do you still want to get together?"

•

I was still sitting there when she called.

"Honey, are you busy?"

"No, no, no, not at all." I played extra cheerful.

"Well, I was just making some calls, attending to some business, and I thought I'd check in."

"Great, great. What's new?" It wasn't near five o'clock. She
smelled a rat.

"I've been doing some research. I've been looking into funerals. These days it's eleven or twelve thousand for burial alone. Can
you imagine? You know the prices are going up." She paused. "As
we speak." She paused again. I could hear her calculating. "How
much do you think it's going to cost to bury Grandma?" Grandma
was closing in on a hundred and had been willing her own demise
ever since Penn Central went bankrupt twenty-five years ago, di-

minishing the meager inheritance I was still eagerly awaiting. Causing an inheritance to diminish was one of the worst sins an elderly Jew could commit. "Well, I just locked in the price. And I checked on the reserved plots. Thirty-four of them. They're all still there."

"Hey, that's great news!"

"If you know anyone who needs one, let me know. There's going to be a lot of extras. With any luck, Grandma won't be around to find out."

Trying to keep Grandma, well, not alive, because clearly she was going nowhere, but in relative peace, had taken its toll on my mother. At six A.M. the phone would ring and a tremulous voice would announce: "Guess who left last night," and the voice would add the name of a nursing-home crony (or more likely an enemy). "Oh, where she'd go?" my mother would reply. "You know where." "No, I don't. Tell me. Where'd she go?" Vindictive silence and a dial tone. And that was only the beginning. Needless to say, Grandma was not a cherished member of the nursing-home community. In order to placate the staff, who struggled to meet her six-foot, 250-pound shrill demands, my mother had become a voluntary member of the staff. The second she entered the home on her daily visits, cursing under her breath, the entire elderly front line would wheel over to stroke her and be stroked.

"Apparently, the ground is rising. Nothing's for sure—don't make any rash promises—we could lose some. Listen, honey, when Daddy and I go, cremate us and just throw the ashes anywhere. It's got to be cheaper. I don't want you kids to spend the money. Don't even bother with an urn."

"Fine, I'll keep that in mind."

"One more thing, honey, I just want you to know. Grandma's in plot number twenty. Just in case I drop dead tomorrow."

"Okay, I'll remember."

"Honey, write it down."

"I've got it, plot number twenty, right? Now, what else is going on?"

"Not much. We made it home in five hours flat. We loved the show. Any action?"

"There are reserves on two paintings, but that doesn't mean anything until the check is in the mail."

"Any reviews?"

"It's only been a week. Take it easy."

"Oh, honey, don't be silly. It's the last thing on my mind. Are you depressed?"

"No, I am not depressed."

"Don't be."

"I wasn't—until you called."

"Oh, honey, that's not even funny. The show looked wonderful. You'll get reviewed and you'll make some sales. Did Perry have the baby yet? She looked terrible."

"Not as far as I know. Oh, Mom, I just got another call. Can you hold on?"

"Take the call, don't be silly, take the call."

"Just hold on for two seconds."

"No, no, please God, take the call."

"Just hold on for two fucking seconds. It might be my editor—let me just get this. I'll call you back."

"No, no, don't waste your money. Take the call, hurry, take the goddamn call."

Ordinarily I would not welcome a call from a magazine editor, but at this moment, on this day, I did. Initially.

"How are you? Good, good. Well, we've got some glitches. Brown lipstick is not doing as well as we expected. By the time this is on the stands brown lipstick will be history and red will be back. Maybe burgundy. And pink, you know what? We don't know where pink will be."

"Oh. Couldn't you just replace the word *brown* with the word *red* and *pink* with *burgundy*? For the time being?"

"You know what? I wish it were so easy. We're on deadline, darling. And frankly, the piece is not your best. Can I be honest? You didn't hit a grand slam."

"I didn't?"

"You know what? There's nothing new, nothing hot. Do you hear me? It's got to be new, it's got to be hot."

"Any suggestions on how to make lipstick hot?"

"If I had any, I would not hold back. I give you my word. I'll tell you what I'll do. Are you listening?"

"Uh-huh."

"If something should change, I'll tell you what—I'll call you. In the meantime, if you come up with any ideas, you call me."

"Sounds good. I'll try to think of some."

I shuffled back into the studio and put the headphones on earsplitting loud, loud enough not to hear any kind of buzz or ring.

CHAPTER

8

On Monday I received a familiar kind of phone call. Curt and impersonal—the kind you'd expect from a secret agent on a mission. I no longer took umbrage. On the contrary. The caller identified himself as Joseph. No surname; we'd made progress. He suggested a bar in midtown. It was fine with me as long as I didn't have to participate in making a plan or a decision.

I waited on a wooden bench at the entrance of the bar. It was a weathered hotel bar with its own history and some of mine, too. I frequented hotel bars, and there weren't many in town that didn't hold some of my history, not necessarily of the heart, but history all the same. In our youth, Perry and I had made regular pilgrimages to this bar before my Sunday graveyard shift at a law firm where I proofread to support my painting habit. We'd begin the evening with a movie in Times Square—arguing the whole time whether Times Square was more southern or northern when it was really neither; it was just garish and gnarled-with-romance

Times Square. After the movie we'd go to the same Chinese restaurant for inedible food, which prevented me from indulging at four A.M. when the other proofreaders ordered their Chinese. Then we'd saunter over to the swanky (in those days) hotel bar a block or two away and join the sad sacks out late on a Sunday night for a beverage and a couple of bowls of free cashews, and at eleven I'd head up to the law firm with a swanky afterglow, which would vanish by eleven-thirty.

Just yesterday I'd visited Perry, tangle-haired and swollen, stuffed in her new Mission rocking chair unable to rock, wallowing in misery. I'd steeled myself but had to avert my eyes nonetheless. I didn't react to her litany sufficiently, so she turned on me. "Where is your dignity?" she ranted. "What's happened to your morals? This guy, whoever he is, this scourge to humanity—what could you possibly see in him?"

I started to explain that it wasn't just what I'd seen in him, it was what he'd seen in me, but Perry wasn't listening. She was sure my lapsed morals had caused her first contraction.

He arrived at the bar looking extremely impatient. He couldn't miss me at the entrance, tan and summery in my light linen shift, affecting nonchalance. Joseph Pendleton hesitated briefly in acknowledgment and continued rapidly across the plush golden carpet. I rose and followed, to a dark room that was not so comely. It was more sleazy, sleazy with loud tourists. We settled into our habitual positions. He posed imperiously in his taupe summer suit on the hard chair at the end of the table, while I wreaked havoc on the light linen dress by slithering back and forth on my trusty banquette, a weathered brown one this time with historical cracks in the leather.

"How are you feeling?" he said, stony-faced.

"I'm trying not to. I've been painting." No response. "I wrote a lot of articles last month, so hopefully I can just paint for a while. You know, to regain my sanity."

His eyes were empty. I rambled about lipstick and liposuction and the beauty editor and the art world until he suc-
cumbed and we were off and running like two city slickers on a
highly successful third, or maybe fourth, date. I told him my hero
and his band were coming to town soon and it would make my
twenty-sixth concert.

"Can they still play?" He smirked. "Anyway, how did a nice
East Coast Jewish girl happen to pick such a fellow as her hero?" I
glared. "I might know somebody. Maybe I can get tickets for you."
He added, "Hey, why didn't you tell me about your show?"

"When was I supposed to tell you?"

He ignored me. "I had a drink with your dealer last week."

"You know my dealer?"

"From Paris. We used to do business. He's not a bad guy.
Just watch him—he's tricky." He would try to get down to the
show soon. He might be able to get so-and-so to review it—if so-
and-so would still take his calls. He still knew a few collectors,
too; maybe he'd send them down. Try, maybe, and might. Not
that I was complaining. I was content to banter evasively all night.
He was the one who steered us over to the unpleasantness of
the past.

"I think we have some things to talk about," he said. I gri-
maced. "You were nasty that afternoon at the bar."

"I'm sorry. I had no idea what I sounded like."

"You were hostile. Why were you so angry at me?"

"I was just trying not to like you. I thought you could tell."
When I raised my head he had his chin up and he was looking sideways. I took his hand. It was just lying there on the table,
and I saw no other way. "I thought you knew I wouldn't, that I
couldn't keep it."

"How would I know? You began by goading me about my alleged past. Then you casually mentioned a blackmail plan that
you'd concocted with your little friend—and added that the two

of you found the evening you and I spent together very humorous. You told me you couldn't recall what I looked like. You said I had everything. You were so dismissive. You acted as if I'd engineered the entire situation on purpose. And then you stopped speaking altogether. How would I know anything? Was I supposed to read your mind?"

"I guess I left some things out. I forgot that you didn't know me."

"Know you? How would you draw that conclusion when you didn't even remember what I looked like?"

"I did remember. I just said that."

"How could I possibly know that? By the time we left I was convinced you were a psychopath who engaged in endless sexual encounters with strangers." That comment was beyond my sphere of reference. It hardly registered. "I spent that weekend convinced you were going to have the baby without any regard for my feelings."

My defense was poorly constructed. I feinted and swerved, using the same thin excuses, gripping his hand instead of gripping the arms of chairs or stripping labels off bottles of olive oil.

"You kept insisting I was going to be mean and shrugging it off—laughing—when I asked for an explanation."

"Did I? Did I do all that?"

"Yes, you did all that. Why were you so angry at me?"

"I don't know. I had no idea I was. I guess I didn't think you cared one way or the other. I don't know. You're the man, you're supposed to be the bad guy. They said you were the bad guy—and I fell for it."

"They? This they—there never should have been a they. What do *they* have to do with us? Why didn't you tell me first? Wouldn't that have been the most logical way to proceed?"

I had never thought of us as *us*, and what did logic have to do with any of this? I lapsed into a silent attack, and he bristled. "That's what you did before. Don't."

"I don't know why. I mean, I do know why. I hardly knew you, but I felt like I did. I knew that you wouldn't want me to keep it—I had to make up my own mind first—and I had to tell somebody. Then when I did tell you, I felt like you knew me, you'd get it somehow. I was pregnant. The hormones. I don't know."

I gave up and looked over to the loud tourists at the next table to see if they could give me an answer. They had to avert their eyes quickly to pretend they weren't watching and listening.

"Aren't you aware that you're not allowed to say 'I don't know' after the age of thirty?" he said slyly, with just enough of the momentous smile to make me crumple. "You're a highly intelligent woman."

"What does that have to do with anything?"

"Everything you say is interesting," he said intently, leaning toward me.

"Yeah?"

"Well, don't be afraid to talk. I know you have things to say. That kind of behavior, it's infuriating. It brings out the worst in me. You have to tell me things."

"What's the point in telling you anything? You're married. You're married and I'm not."

"You're married and I'm not." He repeated it again and laughed. I didn't see why it was so funny. But I didn't ask, since one why might lead to another why and another and another and veer out of control. Or perhaps bring us back under control, which might be less desirable. He extricated his hand from my deadlock grip. He took both of mine in both of his and stared at me with the muddy eyes. There was an almost imperceptible crack of shyness across his face—the sharp, worn planes that didn't quite connect.

"Would you like to start fresh?"

I'd had plans to start fresh, but they didn't include him. Then his eyes made my eyes go as weak as my body, and I said okay. He meant this instant and stood up to make the necessary plan reversals. "I need to make a phone call. I'm supposed to have dinner with a possible investor, Richard Eberle. You know Richard." The art dealer. I didn't exactly know him, although I surely wouldn't have minded knowing him. It occurred to me that he was trying to impress me. He ignored the hard chair when he returned and slid into the booth next to me. Expertly. I refused to look at him.

"What did you tell him?"

"That I was sick."

"What kind of sick?"

"Never," he chided, "never specify an illness."

My will dissolved, and I turned to face him. Released from the hard chair at last, pressed close to me on the banquette, it seemed his will dissolved, too, and our depleted brains went out the window. We started fresh right then and there. In the booth with the tourists next to us, no longer modestly averting their eyes, but staring unabashed. I can't remember who started it. With others, I was able to keep track. I tried, I tried valiantly to keep track with him, but I never could remember. It always came on like a card trick and you couldn't tell who was dealing. He recovered his presence of mind first and had us upright and gliding over the golden carpet, through the bar with its history, now finished for me with our history, and he guided me into a cab, where we took right up where we left off. Starting fresh.

It was a long ride downtown, and there was traffic. I wriggled away from him just once, apologizing, "I have to make sure this guy knows what he's doing," and he repeated my words, laughing until I went back to him. On my corner people were raucous and crazy, spilling out of the bar. The goatlike hippie was gloating on his bench, and our eyes met. The grizzled potbellied painter was on his stool, and my super was next to him on his. I hustled Joseph Pendleton out of the cab, my own presence of mind returning.

We started up the stairs and my presence of mind made up for lost time. My memory returned, too, and I remembered the last time and the consequences and what had transpired on Thursday and I remembered what I wasn't supposed to do until I healed medically, and I hadn't healed medically or in any other respect. I didn't mention it. I fixed us cold drinks. It was hot and we were thirsty. I sat on the pink couch and he joined me. I swallowed what I should have been remembering because I liked remembering what he felt like more and I liked remembering the way he whispered and I whispered back. When I whispered back what I'd remembered medically, he whispered back he'd forgotten, and I could have gotten outraged but I wasn't outraged, and it wasn't going to change the course of things for either of us no matter who'd remembered or who'd forgotten. He whispered: "I'll be gentle, I'll be gentle," and he was gentle, though neither of us was feeling just gentle. He opened me up urgently, and later when he put me back together again, gently, fear returned.

The seedy loft looked its best at this time of night with the sun going down in school colors, maroon and gold, behind the river. It was peaceful lying there wrapped in the illusions of the present, and I hadn't had peace in a while so my fears subsided. We didn't engage in combat. We exchanged small confidences, just talking aimlessly. Until we stumbled into the future.

"Are book parties as bad as art openings?" he asked. "I have to go to one for a book about the eighties art scene. It was unfortunate enough that we had to live through it, but to prolong it by writing a book about it? Why would anyone do such a thing?"

"Money, I would wager." He smiled and I continued. "You mean Rachel's party, don't you?"

"Rachel—you know Rachel Miller?" He was no longer smiling.

"She's one of my closest friends."

"Really."

"She went with me . . . on Thursday."

"She knows about this . . . us?"

"Yes."

"And she knows about tonight?"

"Well, she knew I was seeing you tonight. But she understands. She's completely discreet."

"You don't know that for certain."

"Yes I do."

"No. You don't. You're being naïve."

"No, I'm not. I've known Rachel since I was fourteen, and I know that she's discreet."

"Oh, I see. Did you also know I'm lending her photographs, and doing some consulting, for a book she's doing?"

"Consulting? No . . . but yeah, I knew about the photographs."

"Oh, Christ. And you didn't tell me?"

"When was I supposed to tell you, when you didn't show up—"

"Tell me again. Who else knows?"

"I told you. My neighbor."

"And who else?"

"I told you. No one."

"How do I know you're not lying to me?"

"Look I've told you—I can't lie. I'm a terrible liar. You'd see right through me."

He saw right through me but let it go for now. Every deception, self-deception included, requires a deceptor and a willing deceptee, and the roles are interchangeable. We alternated roles seamlessly. Sure I was telling lies. It wasn't so difficult. I even believed my lies as they rolled off my tongue. So someone else knew who he was. It was only Victor, who didn't register gossip as anything but theater with anonymous players serving as fodder for his convoluted theories. Oh, and my brother. Well, he didn't count. I felt sick about it now, but I would feel worse if Joseph Pendleton got upset, too. It was just as well that he didn't know, especially if he was going to get all riled up. It didn't feel like I was lying. Not at all. I was just sparing him. It was already becoming a habit—sparing him.

"What should I do at this party when I see you?" I asked.

"Don't worry about it. It's not for a while."

"No. Really." I closed his eyes with my fingers.

"Run up and kiss me," he said flatly as he removed my fingers.

I started to giggle, but he cut me off in the same flat tone.

"I'm hungry. Let's get something to eat."

We went to a dive, an adulterer's safe haven, and we kept it light. When I got home, guilt came home with me. The guilt was not your proper adulterer's guilt. It was the guilt of an inept criminal who couldn't play by the rules, who had never expected to need the rules. It was guilt that I had not been discreet, that I was going to ruin his life. Not my life, strangely enough, but his life. There was another guilt, one that ate at me. A pointed, serves-you-right guilt. Guilt that I'd behaved so carelessly, so childishly, again and so soon. Just asking for it, making light of it.

I carried my guilt straight to the sanctuary, where I put on my chaste nightgown and got into bed. The guilt consumed me, but at the same time I couldn't help feeling light and really good. I berated myself, and the guilt joined in. I woke at two not feeling light or very good. I called on my medical genes to rescue me. Risk of infection—that must be it. I rifled through my store of pills in the refrigerator, found the antibiotics, and began gobbling down a carefully chosen selection. In bed I resumed rationalizing. So I was embarking on a casual affair. No one would have to get hurt. People did it all the time. It wasn't a criminal act. Except that nothing about this affair thus far had been casual. My feelings about what had transpired on Thursday were not casual, my feelings about Joseph Pendleton didn't feel casual. In fact, they could have been considered criminal. Joseph Pendleton and I, we could play at casual, but it never lasted long. The loose emotions from Thursday would be funneled into this not-so-casual affair, this distraction. And postponed. Postponed indefinitely.

As I embarked, I knew all this. I knew who would pay later. I knew who would pay much more. Later. After Try, Maybe, and Might became Forget It, So Long Sucker. Somebody should take action immediately. Somehow I knew who it wasn't going to be. That left only one other candidate—one whose former steely will was shot—not a very promising one.

9

I HADN'T QUITE RECUPERATED WHEN JOSEPH PENDLETON STRUCK AGAIN, two nights later. It was almost impossible to hear him on the phone. He was in the neighborhood; would I like to meet?

"Yes," I replied automatically, but I harbored reservations. I'd been on edge for the past forty-eight hours, never knowing if or when he'd strike or how I'd respond. In order to paint, you can't be on edge—you have to lose yourself. I was having trouble losing myself entirely, in my own home. If you can't hide from the elements of the city, both man-made and mankind, in your own home, you're at a distinct disadvantage.

Hurricane season had begun, so every night the weathermen would get all lathered up, describing the disasters that were in store. And no doubt there was a real hurricane down in North Carolina, but there were no trees going down here in town. It was windy and unusually sultry for early evening, but I had my mother's sixth sense and I did not detect danger when I leaned out to the fire escape and took a sniff.

I met Joseph Pendleton in the alley adjacent to the restaurant down the street, and we walked a few blocks to another charm-less safe haven. Suburban-Italian with a colonial seafaring theme. The neighborhood still had a few suburban restaurants, but the only people who went to them worked in the token skyscrapers, and even they only stayed for happy hour. There was no one at the bar when we arrived, and only one silent couple staring bleakly at each other in the restaurant. We sat on bar stools with ship steering wheels for backs.

At first I didn't notice he was drunk. I'd never seen a drunk Joseph Pendleton.

"I just came from the most inane party," he said.

"Oh."

"You seem nervous."

I confessed I hadn't been prepared for his call.

"Would you have been more prepared if I'd called you yester-day?"

"I didn't mean it that way. I'm glad you called. I just meant I panicked after the other night. After what we did."

"You mean what we did."

"I said what we did. Calm down." I told him I'd assumed that the risk was infection and that I hadn't slept much the last couple of nights.

He interrupted. "We didn't really talk the other night. It was more of a physical thing. Your behavior the afternoon when you first told me. You have to explain."

Again, I said I really felt terrible about it, that I hadn't realized how angry I was, but remember the situation, and yes, he had got the brunt of it, and yes, I had been enormously defensive and I was aware that that was a problem. He said he could relate to that, but that I'd been worse than defensive.

"You belittled me. You acted like a spoiled bitch. You said you couldn't afford to have a baby, but your family had money. You looked at me like I was beneath you."

"I wouldn't have said that, or if I did, I didn't mean it the way you took it. Believe me, you have much more money than I do."

"Oh, yes. You said all of that. I remember it very clearly. I haven't told you this, but I was planning to try to get custody. When you said you couldn't afford a child I thought maybe I had a chance. I was going to tell my wife, tell her, you know, these things happen." His voice was low and deliberate. I didn't tell him that my Brother the Lawyer would have ripped him to shreds before it even reached the courts. That might have been belittling.

"These things happen?"

"I was wondering how my son would feel about a baby and what I'd tell our child about his mother, about you. I'd tell him you were a brilliant painter."

"You haven't even seen my work."

"Yes, I have."

"When?"

"Yesterday. I saw the show. I got it but I had to look. For a long time. Layers, all those layers. Your layers—I know your layers. You don't think so . . ."

It almost worked. "Wait a minute. You were going to try to take my baby? Are you out of your mind?"

"Our baby," he said, looking at me more vindictively. "Our baby." Then he looked away and I moved in closer to hear. "Did you ever think about what it would look like? I did. It would have been pretty attractive. Don't you think?"

"I didn't get that far. No, I just worried it would know too much for its own good—you know, between the two of us—and be doomed."

"Yeah . . . yeah, I guess . . . I guess we're cut from the same cloth, you and I."

A drunk and unleashed Joseph Pendleton caused too many conflicting sensations and tied up my vocal cords. He tried to coax me out of my silence with words, without touching me. Finally he said fiercely, "You're doing it to me again. Like that first time."

"I'm not doing it to you. You're doing it to me." I tried to take his hand, but he clenched his fist. "I told you exactly what was going through my mind that first time. Look, this was a terrible thing for me. Why are you torturing me? I'm sorry. I told you I feel really bad. I thought you understood. You're better than I am at these kinds of conversations."

"You're wrong there. I can just fake it better—it's your job not to let me get away with it." He laughed without smiling and took a long swallow of his drink. "Maybe we are too alike. This thing, the two of us, it's never going to work. This woman, back in Paris, she'd do the silent routine. I haven't told you about her."

"Oh, yes, you did."

"I did?"

"Liars don't have good memories."

"When?"

"The first time we met. You told me the whole thing. How you never saw her again and about the kid and how she never told you about him until he was gone. Remember? You said you hadn't told many people—that's why I knew you'd react so strongly when I told you, and that's why I was scared to."

"Why didn't you say that?"

"Why did you do the 'I'll call you tomorrow' act?"

"I meant it. But then you were so . . . well, I assumed I was just another one of the men you were sleeping with, and—"

"You thought I sleep with just anyone?" He didn't say no and I laughed. "That's so wrong it's funny. I just figured you'd forgotten me."

"I tried, but I couldn't forget your voice." He said it in a low voice. "I tried, I really did try . . . but . . ." Then his tone changed and his clenched fists tightened. "Did I also tell you why I quit playing? Marriage," he said derisively. "A condition of marriage. I'd just found out about the kid, that he'd died. My wife, she got me through it, big-time. She—well, that's between us—it's of no concern to you." His face was empty when he turned back to me. "When you said I'd made it worse, after I stood you up"—he half-smiled here, as if he were congratulating himself on a victory—"it was the first time I thought, Oh, this might really be something." I was uncomfortably mesmerized, so I didn't say anything. "I wanted to go with you on Thursday, but I couldn't. When I was in Chicago, I wanted to call and tell you I'd take you on Thursday. But I couldn't. I just couldn't."

He said it so softly, in cadences so lulling, that I was unable to say, Well, why couldn't you? Instead I said, "It was so awful. Those places." When I described Rachel's stricken expression, we couldn't help laughing, and that provided some relief.

We kept at it, huddled over the bar, bravely clearing up mysteries without touching. But for every mystery that was cleared up, another, deeper one was created. We were cowards at base. When I mentioned Rachel again, he became certifiably paranoid and constructed a whole scenario about how she was going to blackmail him and how my neighbor was in on the scheme. In reality Rachel and my neighbor could never get past "Hello, how are you?" and I informed him of that. He continued ranting.

"But you said you trusted me," I reminded him.

"I do trust you," he said, and resumed ranting. That was when it became clear that he'd reached the far side of drunk, and that he hadn't been there in quite some time.

I was just trying to change the subject when I mentioned my latest job offer, writing an in-house educational film, whatever that was, for a cosmetics company. "What cosmetics company? How long have you known about this?" He got the message across—the message concerning you-know-who just happening to work there. Neither of us used the term *wife*, we used *she*. Luckily we were rescued by an old soul tune on the jukebox and his face cleared. He wasn't in the restaurant anymore and I wasn't either, and because we didn't have to explain our flights to each other, it led to an eruption of public pawing, and he said, "C'mon. Let's go."

On the way out, I said, "I feel so guilty. Now why am I the one who's feeling so guilty?"

"It can be summed up in one word: Judaism."

"As if I didn't know. You can do better than that. You never feel guilty?"

"Guilt never absolves anything. It's just another way to rationalize, an exercise in futility. We'll talk about guilt later."

The streets were oddly forsaken, probably because of the hurricane alert. We argued on the corner over taking a cab. Cabs were verboten by the genes for less than twenty blocks. We were only seven blocks away from my loft and I said, "It's silly. Taking cabs everywhere is a black thing. That's what my neighbor says. Jews walk."

"Not the ones I know," he said, and hailed a cab.

When we got to the loft, he said, "Show me what you did today," so we went into the studio. That was a ruse. "We're depraved," he murmured with a real smile and half-closed eyes.

"You are," I said, just to rile him up.

"We are." He took his hands away and was about to start in on me, so I suggested we go to my room.

"It's so pretty," he ventured. "Have I been here before?"

I didn't tell him he'd been barred. I just said, "Liars don't have good memories."

"That painting—it's beautiful. Innocent. It's from a while ago, I can tell."

He stared at pictures of Jack on the dead-people wall and looked at me.

"A dead friend."

"He looks familiar, what did he—" he started, and I diverted him.

The sanctuary served as a combat-free zone. He fell asleep in the sign-of-the-cross position and I curled up rigidly next to him and didn't fall asleep. Maybe he regretted saying too much already, but I didn't: I had more to say, so I held imaginary noncombative conversations in my head. I told him I was well aware that he was no solution to the Big Picture, but it was okay for the time being because he gave me more than he took away, because he didn't shrink from the black cloud—he could get behind it and even see behind it—which provided sustenance and a relief that I just could not deny myself. And I told him not to worry; I knew he was hanging by a thread—in more ways than one—but I wouldn't pull too hard. Unless of course he said, "No . . . pull. Pull hard."

Then I began to worry because it was getting late. Then I wondered why he wasn't worrying. I tried to get him up, but he didn't want to get up. For several hours I worried and he slept.

When he woke up, he got back into his suit and went into the kitchen to get a glass of water, and when he came back he perched far away from me at the end of the bed and said in a hard voice, "I have to go."

"We never talked about guilt like you said we would." I made him lie back down, and we whispered a little. "I wish you could stay," I whispered.

"Don't say that." But his voice wasn't gruff anymore.

"It just slipped out," I whispered, and we lay there for a while longer.

10

THOSE WEEKS WERE TEEMING WITH CALLS; NO SET PATTERN, BUT CALLS, calls, calls: Meet me here, meet me there, what are you doing, what about later. Sometimes we'd meet in the late afternoon near his office in Times Square and go to some out-of-the-way dump, pretending it was just for a quick cup of coffee but always ending up back at the loft with the sun going down, listening to music, looking at paintings. Eventually I'd have to nudge him gently off the couch and out the door. He'd mumble, "Are you okay?" before he got up, looking away, and I'd reply, "uh-huh," and steer him toward the door. The night before Rachel's party he took me to see some band no one else would have heard of, or would have wanted to see, except the two of us—well, maybe my brother. That night it was harder than usual to get him out the door.

When Rachel called at seven the next morning I was asleep, so she knew something was up. I confessed and she was merciless.

"What about his wife, his kid? Where do they think he is at three A.M.?"

"I doubt the kid notices. I don't know about the wife. She probably thinks he's at the club. I didn't ask."

"You haven't talked about his marriage yet? Don't you want to know?"

"It's come up, but, well, no."

"Tu est folle!"

"Rachel, please speak English. She works for a cosmetics company. They have a big office in Paris, so I guess she goes back and forth, I don't know."

"You asked him?"

"No, no, I just—"

"Is she in Paris now?"

"How should I know? He's not the type who would leave—"

"Did he tell you that?"

"No, I just know, and anyway, I don't want—"

"What do you want, for God's sake?"

"Nothing. It's casual. I have to go."

"Well, you're coming to my party tonight, right?"

"I don't know. Maybe."

"You have to come. You have a show up and you should be seen. There'll be people there you should talk to."

"But I think he's—"

"He is coming because we have to talk over specifics."

"Let's not discuss tonight now, okay? Let me just get through this morning."

"You don't sound very happy."

"No, I'm happy. I'm ecstatic."

Rachel had grown up privileged and sheltered enough to believe that happiness, clear and unsullied, was an inalienable right for each and every one of us. I wasn't going to be the first to inform her otherwise.

•

I spilled my tea on the way to the TV for the morning news shows. At the progressive boarding school, intimate clusters of girls sipped tea at four o'clock while they listened to Vivaldi. To me, four o'clock had meant *Return to Peyton Place.* Never in my life had I sipped tea or listened to Vivaldi, or any other classical music, for that matter. For some reason, we didn't have a record player until the King turned sixteen and demanded one, and then he reared us exclusively on soul. As for tea, I'd only turned to it as a last resort due to the nervous stomach.

The morning shows were juicy because a celebrity had dropped dead earlier in the week: a famous shoe designer. Also a celebrity adulterer, a senator, was being publicly flogged, one of several public celebrity-adulterer floggings this summer that weren't helping my own foray into the field, especially with this particular partner. I was personally acquainted with ethnic paranoia, but mine seemed almost frivolous next to the life-or-death nature of Joseph Pendleton's. It was only logical, but logic didn't make it any less daunting. I turned off the TV before the how-to-have-a-healthy-pregnancy segment began and got ready to face a day of meetings.

The first was with my beauty editor. The shoe designer's death had thrown the magazine world into a miasma of grief and postponed deadlines. Everything had to be shifted to make way for the accolades, the personal tributes—and for the ads displaying the shoe designer's posthumous wares. I had been enlisted to write a how-to-deal-with-your-grief piece. I didn't want an assignment on grief and how to deal with it. Not only did I prefer to grieve in the privacy of my own home, I wasn't grieving for the shoe designer. I liked his shoes but I didn't know him. But you'd better believe all the magazine editors were pretending they knew him, and were grieving, grieving hard.

The weathermen had wised up and changed their tune to multiple hair-raising heat-wave warnings. It was almost as bad as a winter-storm watch. Winter and summer are not unalike in the city. They're both seasons where you create your own imaginary indoor climate, batten down the hatches, draw the curtains, and wait it out. I slogged along Forty-second Street in my air-conditioning-appropriate corporate layers. My well-preened editor led me into her office and confided that the lipstick piece had been transformed into a chart. No doubt the ayatollah editor in chief, who entertained grand Wizard of Oz delusions, had bellowed a proclamation from behind the curtain. The piece read like a Nielsen ratings chart written by a Las Vegas card shark.

I didn't raise any objections. Vulnerability had no place at magazines or art galleries, even though painting and writing did induce vulnerability. But both were about commerce, impersonal commerce, and you were just a sitting duck if you let feelings get in the way. It was hard to remember that personal life was about vulnerability and even harder to switch back and forth.

When my editor started in on the how-to-deal-with-your-grief piece, I interrupted. "Um, I'm not really grieving."

"You'll grieve. You're in the denial stage—you should be in the anger stage to write this piece. In the meantime, make some calls. Learn how to grieve. I've got a list right here of about ten hot women who are grieving. They'll tell you how to do it right."

The meeting was cut off abruptly because my beauty editor had to make an appearance on a dead-shoe-designer special. There was a large cranky crowd milling about on the subway platform when I got to Grand Central. When an announcement came over the loud speaker like a skipping forty-five, I balked and went back up the stairs to hail the verboten to take me to my next meeting— a strategy session with Ditzgirl. When I arrived at the gallery, she was in the back room, feverishly showing a collector some of her wares: life-sized photographs of naked coupling lesbians in beige living rooms, which brought to mind illustrations from a teenage lesbian romance novel.

"A very complicated process is involved," she was saying, gesturing wildly. "A very complex, complicated, conceptual—extremely conceptual—process. The artist Draws the Figure, Photographs the Drawing, and Throws the Drawing Away."

"Fascinating," murmured the collector.

She could smell the money. "I'd also like to show you some paintings," she added, half shoving the collector into the main gallery, bless her heart. I got up to follow like an insatiable puppy, but she shooed me away—and I applauded her instincts. Unfortunately the collector had a voice that carried, and the news wasn't good. He left after writing a check for two coupling photographs.

"He seemed very interested," she said.

"Oh, absolutely."

It could have been worse. Some dealers hid in the bathroom when they heard the footsteps of an artist approaching in the distance. Ditzgirl meant well, and she had some promising news. A dealer from Paris was interested in meeting with me, and the two reserves were still holding. Our strategy session ended with a discussion of the dead shoe designer and how much his shoes from the seventies would be worth.

I couldn't concentrate at my third meeting—with the cosmetics-company honchos—because I was too busy peering up and down hallways looking for *her*. I was experiencing some of my own frivolous but quite possibly medically certifiable paranoia. I was also struggling to hide my sun-speckled face and chest because cosmetics-company honchos all have flawless freckleless skin and they might not hire someone sun-speckled. It was a feat to hide and crane and appear involved all at the same time. By the time the two filmmakers arrived, I was contorted and twitching in my white leather chair under the fluorescent light. The filmmakers were downtown scruffy and brash in a thirty-years-old kind of way. They were too smart not to know they'd made compromises early on that might backfire later and had developed scornful wits that challenged anyone to hint as much. One was British so he sounded even wittier. We got on pretty well, all the same, sharing snide, world-weary comments. They told me they would let me know soon, and we went our separate ways.

I took a circuitous route through the endless white hallways, ostensibly gazing at the art on the walls but really searching for someone who looked as I imagined her. I think I half expected her forehead to be branded with his initials. Then I saw her name on a door and flashed quickly on what must have been her: a delicately sculpted woman with 1940s marceled hair, formidably tailored with tight, trampish undertones. It was like the climactic scene in a horror movie, and I almost covered my face with my hands.

•

Rachel's new home was packed with guests who all appeared to relish the opportunity to celebrate an eighties revival. I didn't spot the one person I knew would not be relishing such a celebration, but then, I was trying not to. I wasn't sure that I could master the necessary skills to greet my fellow adulterer at a social gathering. I wasn't even sure what those skills were. The faint trail of moist air drifting in from the floor-to-ceiling windows, not to be confused with a breeze, wasn't sufficient to cool down the sweltering guests who were everywhere, standing woodenly or slumped against what little wall space was bare, crammed together on spindly French couches, sitting precariously on thin wicker chairs, or sprawled on large floor pillows.

Rachel was manning the party alone because Perry was home in the throes of an awkward adjustment to motherhood. When Perry was not adjusting well she shared her maladjustments with the world—too generously—so we were better off without her.

Jean was standing, grimy, sullen, and alone, in the farthest corner of the living room. I hid in the next-farthest corner with Victor. Victor had made a grand total of six, or maybe it was seven, subway trips up and down the island that day and had encountered the same technical difficulties at Grand Central. Only he hadn't jumped bail and had ridden out the storm, so to speak. Either Victor was the exception to the rule or my neighbor's ethnics-and-cabs theory was a fallacy.

"So I went to get my portfolio at the magazine," Victor told me, expressionless. "They'd requested these pictures, right? Then some lackey calls me to pick it up. Three days ago. No mention of the pictures they'd requested, right? I call before I go up there to make sure it's there. Well, big surprise—it wasn't there, and of course I was supposed to bring it to a record company today, as in it would be too late if I didn't bring it in today. I went to midtown three times today in the middle of a heat wave, right? I didn't get one gig out of it. In fact I even lost a gig." Victor was in a very bad mood. I couldn't decide what to change the subject to—perhaps the breasts-and-dresses artist. Victor didn't respond to direct prying, innocent or otherwise, so you had to be crafty. His answer would most likely have no bearing on the original question, but it would sound like it made sense until you thought about it later.

When Sam appeared, his top-dog nasty girl was moping beside him. She was dark, petite, and aloof, like all the others, and she had a burgundy-tinted sneer. None of us ever took to Sam's girls. It was hard to tell whether Sam even took to his girls. This one might stick as top dog though. What did it really matter, he'd told me recently, once you get used to a certain set of problems, whether it's a brunette or a blond set of problems? Was it really worth the trouble to embark on a new set? Might as well stick with what you know, he'd concluded with a shrug.

"I just found out I had my third million-dollar idea stolen out from under me," he said. "At least I know I'm on the right track."

Sam was always coming up with peculiar inventions and not quite following through on them. Victor was eager to discuss someone else's bad luck, and they immediately became engrossed.

I affected a listening pose so that I could scan the crowd surreptitiously, but the floating sensation had returned and my scanning technique was rather slipshod. A few semicircle neck maneuvers were all I could swing before I became dizzy. I did notice various notable people in the business whom I should have been talking to, but none looked terribly enticing. Mobility was a problem—I was wearing delicate princess heels, and the combination of the floating sensation, the heels, and the sweltering crowd in the midst of an excessive amount of spindly French furniture might result in an awkward spill.

Fortunately Rachel swooped in, with an art person on her arm and my neighbor plodding stoically behind. The art person was a collector and behaved like one: blundering, earnest, and goofy, traits filtered through the ineffable air of confidence that emanates from rich people. We had a short conversation, which ended with him assuring me that he would see my show tomorrow. Rachel was delighted. Victor rolled his eyes.

I was rather enjoying the lewd commentary Sam had begun with Rachel when I saw Joseph Pendleton. I could tell he was looking somewhere beyond me or he wouldn't have been proceeding at such a furious pace right toward us. Rachel lunged for him, causing him to step back in alarm. I stepped back in alarm, too, or rather I tripped backward in my shoes. She got him in a neck lock and planted effusive kisses on both cheeks. He told Rachel he had some business to take care of but would get back to her, looked right through me, and moved on. A look right through me from someone who'd been wrapped around me less than twenty-four hours prior caused distress that proceeded directly to my internal organs. I would have liked to move as regally as possible right out the door. Instead my bound feet and I rose to the challenge and minced painfully around the party with a renewed gregariousness built on a foundation of nerves and despair.

I talked to the art people, including a critic my good pal Joseph Pendleton had mentioned, when was it, a day or two ago? Then I teetered over to the farthest corner and, under the circumstances, found Jean's sloppy pretentiousness endearing. He rewarded me with an introduction to a fellow countryman who turned out to be the dealer Ditzgirl had mentioned, David Mendelsohn. He was slight and wiry with a big brainy forehead and bulging eyes. He said all the right things; he even said he found my paintings serene. The only other person who had described my paintings as serene was Jack. Then my neighbor appeared like clockwork to sweep David Mendelsohn—he was just balding enough—right off his feet. I backed away to leave room for potential sparks to ignite, but my neighbor turned around: "Victor and I are leaving. Do you want to come?"

The hormones, I hope it was the hormones, or the shoes, maybe, or the word *serene*—that had to be it—made me exit abruptly.

I sat on Rachel's stoop taking deep gulps of summer air so dense it could hardly be called air. Her block was lined with one quaint brownstone after another, each equipped with large enough parlor windows so that you could spy on the seemingly tranquil lives proceeding within their sparse elegance. By the time my neighbor and Victor joined me, they were already involved in a convoluted discourse about Victor's apartment eviction and subsequent move—to where nobody quite knew. I trailed behind and at the corner I told my neighbor I didn't care where we went as long as we could go in a cab.

"Oh, now there's a switch," he began, but after one glance at my face he stopped.

"My feet," I began.

"Oh, sure, it's your feet," he said sharply.

We headed down Seventh Avenue through the gridlock traffic and festering swarms of club kids. Clubs were opening and closing so fast that not even the club kids could keep up, judging by the crowds outside even the clubs that were boarded up. We went to the restaurant on my neighbor's block, a cutesy yuppie restaurant we held in contempt under more solvent circumstances. This block—just an average city block clogged with buses and cabs and jeeps and sports cars wending their way uptown or taking the tunnel to New Jersey—served as our village green, and it wasn't long before I recognized a voice.

My brothers were always turning up at the wrong time. This brother's long body, unwieldy with middle age, was crammed into a table designed for a trim up-and-coming yuppie. Crammed across the table from him was his drummer, Hank. Hank and I had more than a slight acquaintance, and there was something in the air between the two of us—he had a rakish, street-kid element that reminded me of Jack—except the timing was never right. Actually, I had a sneaking suspicion that bad timing was really saving us both some wasted time.

"You're all dressed up," my brother said. "Where were you?"

"A party at Rachel's."

"Ooooh, lots of celebrities? Doesn't Rachel always stoke her parties with celebrities?"

"I guess."

"A little down tonight? Wouldn't you agree, Hank?" Hank didn't look up. "Dr. Doom?"

"Who's Dr. Doom?" This time Hank looked up with interest, interest that was simply a manifestation of the human condition.

"Don't ask." My brother smiled a superior smile.

It had been leaked through the family members that the concubine had deserted the cult, and there were rumors that she might be considering joining ours, legitimately, that is. But privacy was at a limited premium within our ranks, and a precious commodity, so I remained mum.

"What are you guys doing tonight?" I said instead.

"We're doing a hang, going to some clubs. Not the club you're thinking of."

"Why don't you come with us?" Hank had perked right up.

"No, I can't, maybe—"

"Off to more parties with your rich friends?" Hank's bluster was becoming tainted by bitterness as he aged, a process that is always most devastating for the vain. He also had a blue-collar chip on his shoulder that required one to buoy his ego far beyond the call of duty. After some desultory buoying, I went back to my neighbor and Victor.

"Why don't you go out with him?" my neighbor whispered.

"I've told you. Bad timing. And the blue-collar chip on his shoulder."

"Oh, yes, I forgot." He nodded. "You're into the black boulder these days."

"I'm not into chips or boulders," I snapped.

"Speaking of boulders, we won't mention any names, but that was cold," my neighbor said. "That was really cold."

"What are you talking about?"

"You know what I'm talking about."

I turned to Victor. "Listen," I said, "if you need any help moving . . ."

Victor accepted my offer but warned me that it would mean clearing out twenty years of debris—although he was pretty sure he could find another shovel—and then he said, "That David Mendelsohn didn't seem so bad, especially for a dealer."

"I'm not sure he's even gay," my neighbor said. "I don't know, I've done the nebbishy Jew so many times. I may be over it."

"But you've never tried a French one," I said.

"That might be worse."

"Much worse," said Victor.

When I got home I turned up the air conditioner and drew the curtains tighter. My favorite ten o'clock show was on. I wasn't ordinarily a cop-show fan, but on this one I'd discovered a tortured Irish cop version of Joseph Pendleton. I was just settling in when the phone rang.

"Perry, what are you doing up so late?"

"Up late, up early, what exactly does that mean? I wouldn't know. Who sleeps? You might recall, I am a delicate flower who was raised in a tropical hothouse, so I need my sleep. And I need a life." She paused. "I vaguely remember life." The next pause was more dramatic. "Of course, you wouldn't understand. You're care-free, you have your cherished solitude, no responsibilities . . ."

"For Christ's sake, Perry, you wanted the baby, at least you pretended you did, and you have live-in help and a maid. If the baby cries, the nurse takes her. If the bottle spills, the maid cleans it up. You're not even breast-feeding. It can't be that bad, can it?" Condescending behavior from the new breed of parents was unpleasant at the best of times, and this was clearly not the best of times.

"It can be that bad," Perry snapped. "I've lost my identity."

"No, believe me, you haven't. I've seen you twice since the miracle of her birth. You're identical. You haven't changed one bit."

"I haven't?" Her voice lost its hard edge and turned helplessly southern again. "You're so kind, you're so sweet. We've enjoyed your visits so, Melanie and I."

"Perry, get to the point. My cop show is on."

"Well, how was the party?"

"It was fine."

"Poor dear Rachel, handling it all by her lonesome. Was I missed desperately?"

"I don't think anyone even noticed, least of all Rachel."

"You don't mean that."

"Oh, Perry, I'm sure I'll think of someone who missed you, but can we talk in the morning? I know you'll be up and I'm tired."

"You don't know what tired means."

I had just enough time to watch the nasty cop get shot in the head and be attached to a respirator before Rachel called.

"You didn't go to Deejay Night. Are you okay?"

"I wanted to watch my cop show. Why's the party over so early?"

"I'm glad it's over. Jean went home all bent out of shape—he hates these parties."

"I'm not so keen on them either."

"Well?"

"Well, what?"

"Did you talk to him?"

"No. What was there to say?"

"You should call him."

"No."

"You should call him. First thing in the morning."

"No," I repeated, and then I couldn't resist. "Did you talk to him?"

"Well, yes. We're supposed to get together next week to finalize some things. He said he'd picked up some new photos. I guess he was just in Chicago. What's that guy's name? You know, that saxophone player, really famous? John . . . you know his name—"

"Coltrane. Oh, thanks for introducing me to that collector. And thank Jean, too, for introducing me to David Mendelsohn. Was the party a success?"

"You should call him. He could have at least given you a sign."

"Rachel, I can't think straight right now."

"You deserve to be treated with respect."

"I don't feel like talking about it right now, I'm sorry. Why don't you call Perry? She can't sleep."

"One more thing. She came at the end—did he tell you she . . ."

"Rachel, I really have to go. Can I call you in the morning?"

It appeared that the nasty cop was going to survive, so I could rest easy on that front. I was rather proud of myself, no prying questions concerning her attributes, or perhaps her flaws. But pride is more debilitating than anything else, so I hid in the chilled sanctuary, slid under the down comforter, and pretended it was last winter, back when I was reasonably comfortably frozen.

Perhaps consideration or compassion are not among the guiding principles of adultery. Certainly Joseph Pendleton had made no promises and I had no expectations; I had no idea what to expect. I would have liked an idea of what to expect, if only a ballpark figure. Rachel always expected. At this very moment she was in the process of training Jean to be what she expected. I marveled at her skill. I never even knew you were supposed to train. I had grown up with male royalty—mama's boys—who did not necessarily obey or serve, although they were full of good intentions and certainly trainable. I'm not saying the Jews had the market cornered on mama's boys. No, they came in all colors and classes. I'd mentioned this to Victor recently. He became visibly agitated, a rarity, and offered a theory in such a low voice that I couldn't hear it and I'm certain I wouldn't have understood it even if I had.

When the phone rang much later, I didn't answer. In the morning I listened to the machine and had no trouble recognizing the voice, the two weak hellos. And then the click.

11

TIME WENT BY FASTER THAN IT HAD IN A LONG WHILE; THERE WAS NO time to think. After Rachel's party the calls stopped and time stopped. But I made sure there was still no time to think.

I painted doggedly and I researched grief. I attended concept meetings with the young filmmakers, where we got cozy trading caustic remarks. There were calls from Ditzgirl or calls to make to Ditzgirl; a promising studio visit with David Mendelsohn. I made plans for the evenings, although I couldn't always execute them. On the evenings that I did I was home by a nine o'clock curfew set by wishes and dreams. From nine to eleven I sat on the couch, as alert as a cat listening to rats scuffling in the walls. At eleven I moved into the sanctuary with the phone and the air conditioner turned up and lay there bewildered but determined not to think.

I spent a stoical evening with Hank, who no doubt had his suspicions. He retaliated by observing strict date protocol, hoping against hope, I imagine, that the proper role-playing might vault us over the formidable wall that guarded the possibility of romance between us.

"Let's have an adventure," he decreed. "Let's go to Chinatown."

Chinatown had long since lost any sense of adventure for me. Chinatown meant crowds, narrow, sweaty streets, and loud gleaming restaurants with glaring lights. He ignored my pleas and it was pretty hopeless by the time we were seated. When he handed me the long, complicated menu, I tried to turn the tide by suggesting cheerfully that he order for us: Whatever he wanted was fine, since he knew me well enough to know that I didn't really care about food, didn't he? (Rachel admonished me later: Any accomplished dater knew to feign interest in food foreplay. Jack and I hadn't needed it, I argued. We knew it was just a formality, a means to an end. She reminded me that Jack hadn't been an accomplished dater either.) When Hank delivered a biting lecture on how my lack of interest in food was a serious "issue" that I should "deal" with, I didn't bother to mount a defense. He had only just begun therapy, and really, I could have been any female sitting across the table in enemy position receiving any number of lectures. I tried valiantly to salvage the evening by devouring his carefully selected noodles and dumplings with the proper gusto, but it was no use. Once again, we accepted defeat in mutual maudlin silence.

•

"It's Joseph returning your call."

"Returning your call" was not a warm greeting. Perhaps he was confusing me with a potential investor.

"Hi."

"What a busy week. Excruciating. It's been hellish, really."

"Oh."

"I just got back. I had to go to Chicago again, to deal with investors—no, to kiss their asses is more like it. We're getting closer—the record company is going to happen, I think. I'll know in a little—"

"You didn't just get back."

"Pardon me?"

"Well, Rachel said you two were having a meeting."

The silence that followed made any mention of Rachel's party moot. It was unfinished business that had been left out too long and grown rancid.

"Is that so? Your friend Rachel told you she and I were having a meeting?"

"I haven't talked to her in a few days. I mean, she mentioned that she was going to see you, she didn't tell me—"

"That I canceled our appointment? That this project is nothing but a nuisance, a regrettable obligation that's just bullshit? I'll bet she didn't tell you that. But it doesn't matter what she told you, now, does it? Because I'm telling you now. Yes, I have been back for a few days. I've also had friends from Paris here in town. Did Rachel tell you that? I've also had to be at the club every night. The big boys were playing, and I had to grease the wheels. They had to be baby-sat. Entertained in style. Dinners, parties. Only the best. Every night. Did she forget to mention that? Did she explain that this is the crush before everyone splits for the Fourth, or for the whole fucking summer, for that matter, and I've got to be a million places at once?" His voice was frigid with displaced shame.

"No, I guess she couldn't get it all in." My chuckle came out hoarse and shaky. "Well, anyway, I was just calling you back—you called the other night . . . that was you the other night on the phone . . ."

"What night are you referring to?"

"Um, the night of . . . ah, let's see. Thursday night."

"No, that wasn't me. What time was it?"

"Oh, I don't remember." Twelve thirty-three on Thursday night, to be precise, but who cared what time it was or wasn't, or what night it was or wasn't, if it wasn't him who called—or was it? We both knew the answer. I welcomed the complicity, our short-cut to intimacy. His lies were like gauzy curtains we could both hide behind, which helped maintain our alliance as casual, not so criminal.

"I guess there must be a Joseph Pendleton clone out there somewhere." His voice became softer. "Now, that's a scary thought." It was his turn to force a laugh.

"Very scary." There were midtown office sounds in the background: beeps and rings and buzzes. This call was unexpected, jarring, as long-expected calls always are when they finally come. "Well I guess that's it, then."

"What do you mean?"

"I mean it wasn't you on the phone and you've been busy and you're still busy. I get the picture."

"So tell me what you've been doing."

"Nothing. Painting. Trying to write another article. I told you. 'Death of a Shoe Designer.' "

"Oh, right, I forgot." A laugh that wasn't forced at all. "How's it going?"

"Fine."

"And what are your plans for the Fourth?"

"Which day is it?"

"It's the day when people roast hot dogs, toast marshmallows, light firecrackers."

"Come on. You know what I mean. What day are people in offices celebrating?" I was getting rattled.

"I've heard rumors that it's going to be held on Friday this year. That's what people in offices are saying. I'm told some people in offices will be taking Thursday off, too."

"I'm going to that concert. I thought I told you about it," I mumbled sullenly. "So I guess I'll be here for the Fourth. And then I'm going away for a couple of days."

"I forgot about that concert."

I didn't respond.

"The next few weeks are going to be crazy sewing up this deal," he said. "I'm going upstate for the holiday, and then I've got business in Paris. But listen, I'll call you when I get back."

"Oh, sure."

•

The call had come and gone so quickly and I didn't know much more than I knew before. I knew he still wanted me trapped in the web of his life, but now I knew that the wanting was actually quite capricious and I should not expect inner-circle treatment all the time.

Technically, I could claim to have had a reasonable amount of busy city life myself, but not enough to fend off the delayed reaction that stabbed my empty gut or the longing that trickled in to close the wound.

But now I'd been given fair warning: I had a reprieve! I was on furlough until, at the very least, after the Fourth. The heat wave had abated; the tropical storms were less frequent. I opened the windows and waved away the dull ache. The new air felt fresh and clean.

When the phone rang, I knew it would be a mistake to answer.

"Your voice. Oh Jesus. What's wrong with your voice?"

I had to think fast. "I'm sick."

"You're what?"

"Sick."

"Spell it."

"S-I-C-K."

"Oh Mother of God. Why, honey? How could you get sick?"

"People get sick."

"Oh, God in heaven, she's sick."

"It's just a cold."

"Oh, honey, have you taken the Tylenol?"

"I took one."

"One? Son of a bitch. One? Why would she just take one?"

"I don't know why I would even take one—it's only a cold. I'm fine, really, I'm fine. How are you?"

"Oh, you know. Little Lord Fauntleroy's neck is bad so he's in traction and I can't even get in there to make the bed. Yesterday it was the fucker's lower back. And did I tell you Grandma's gained nine pounds? She is the only one—I swear, I've done a poll—in the goddamn nursing home who's not withering away. They tried to confiscate the chocolates I brought her, and I said, Hell no! Let her have a little pleasure. Elaine's mother died last week, did I tell you? Do you realize I am the only one of my friends who still has a mother? What if I go first? I know you kids won't take care of her. Honey, I can't take much more." She sighed. Then her voice became low and conspiratorial. "Well, we've done a pretty goddamn good job of holding back, haven't we? What's your verdict?"

"About what?"

"You haven't heard? Oh, hell. I was sure he'd have told you by now. He's turned into a snake in the grass, your brother."

"Told me what? Oh, I did get a message from him, but I haven't had time to call back yet."

"Oh, boy. I'm screwed. Just screwed. You know you kids can always trust me, don't you? You know you can tell me anything. Have I ever breathed a word? Of everyone in this family, who is it that you can trust? Who? Tell me. I was sure that sneak had told you. I said to myself, I wonder why I haven't heard from her. I said to myself, Okay, maybe she's busy—"

"Just tell me!"

"Aw, honey, I can't. I promised."

"I'll pretend I don't know. He was going to tell me anyway. What is it? Uh-oh. I think I know. He's going to marry the foreigner."

"Oh, honey, don't call her the foreigner. I'm sure she's a nice girl. Why don't you like her? If she makes him happy, then who are we—"

"Oh, Christ. I like her, I like her. I've only met her once. Is she still with the cult?"

"Let's not discuss the fucking cult. I don't like to ask. We're better off not knowing. Although I guess we'll know soon enough."

"What do you mean?"

"The foreigner's coming to meet us. We're all going to Florida. To get to know each other, to welcome her into the family."

"We?"

"Yes, we."

This was unprecedented. My family did not get together to welcome interlopers into the fold. I guess at this point my mother was willing to do anything to procure one of her sons a reasonable facsimile of herself, even if it meant going to the condo in Florida that she loathed ("What the hell, honey, Daddy loves it—who am I to ruin his pleasure?") to finalize the deal.

"What do you mean, 'Oh, hell'? You vicious rat," she said.

"Florida in the summer?"

"Don't give me this 'Florida in the summer' shit. I hate when you get like this. You know who you remind me of when you get like this? Her."

"Her?"

"You know goddamn well who 'her' is. His mother. The bitch of Buchenwald."

"Oh, Mom, please. I like the foreigner. I'll try to come. I just hate group get-togethers."

"This isn't a group! It's your goddamn family!"

"It's just that I have a lot of work to do, and I'm not feeling well. Remember? I'm sick."

"What's this 'I'm not feeling well, I'm sick'? I'm not buying it. You liked the foreigner before. You were on his side. What is wrong with you? Oh, wait a minute. Wait, just a goddamn minute . . . oh, Jesus. She's depressed."

"No, I am not depressed. Do we have to go through this? I'll come, I'll come."

"You are depressed. You've been depressed since the show, even before the show."

"Okay, okay, I am a little depressed. Happy now?"

"Oh, honey, don't make jokes. Is it the painting? Oh, Jesus, is it the writing?" The hysteria was mounting.

"No, it is not the painting. And no, it is not the writing. It's sort of personal."

"Oh, for Christ's sakes, you know you can tell me anything. When have you ever ever not been able to tell me anything?"

"But I can't. Really I can't."

"When? Tell me when! What have I done to deserve this?"

"Mom, I would if I could. I just can't."

"You vicious rat. I'm going to have to hang up now. King Faisal is calling from his fucking headquarters. If I have to lift him up with my own two hands, I'll make that bed. Good-bye."

"Mom? Wait . . ."

Silence.

When was the last time I'd told her anything personal that would cause her to worry? Too long ago to remember. Maybe she'd forgotten, too.

I went back to work. I called a griever, a German fashion photographer with a thick accent. Was he ever grieving! After a brief conversation exchanging mutual condolences and bemoaning the tragedy of a young life snuffed out, the griever paused for a moment. Then he continued brightly, "Ah, ya know wot. Dot's da way da cookie crumble."

•

The summons came in the next day around two-thirty, while I was on the phone with my groom-to-be sibling. I eased into the obvious subject at hand by way of shop talk.

"Did you watch yesterday?" I said casually.

"Kelly's really gained, hasn't she?"

"Funny, I was thinking the same thing."

"Yeah, she's fat. Her face is puffy like a crackhead's. Her days are limited if she doesn't act fast."

The groom-to-be was slightly abashed to be running with the pack he had denigrated for so many years. To make it easier for him, I tried to express boundless enthusiasm over the upcoming nuptials, but I couldn't keep it completely boundless.

"What actually happened with the cult?" I tried to be delicate. "Are we just going to put that behind us, pretend it didn't happen?"

"Well, she was just screwed up about us, and I think her father's a drug addict—don't say anything—and she'd just gotten fired from her job. It wasn't her fault."

"Of course not."

"And it wasn't really a cult—" If the other line hadn't rung, the excuses would have continued. It was clear that my brother shared my attraction to damaged merchandise, and I welcomed his company.

"It's me," Joseph Pendleton cooed. Me who? In less than twenty-four hours we'd gone from a cold "Returning your call" to a cooing "It's me."

"Oh, hold on," I squeaked, and to my brother I said, "Listen, it's Dr. Doom."

"Oh, no, not Doom. Oh, Jesus, I thought we were over that. You're crazy—"

"Could I call you back during the show?"

"It's going to be a damn good episode, but I have a sneaking suspicion we won't be in communication."

•

Why are you still in town? I'm on furlough! I wanted to assault him with this when he arrived at my door. Instead I stuttered and squeaked. He was all disheveled. His shirt was coming untucked, everything was creased in all the wrong places, and his khaki suit jacket was crumpled under his arm along with the tabloid, so it was spotted with faint blurred ink stains. "I thought you were out of town."

I didn't hear his reply but nodded, pretending I had. We stood for a shy moment yards apart in the kitchen, the most unsightly room in the loft. Then I stumbled back and forth trying to be a hostess until he looked me into submission and we leaned together for a moment of relief and I asked him, muffled, what we should do, where we should go.

"I'm just tired," he whispered, "sick of it all . . . tired of pretending. It was so relentless today." He lifted his head. "You know what I mean." I continued to hide. "Let's not go anywhere. Let's just stay here. It's nice here."

He made his preemptive strike as soon as we sat down.

"So you're mad at me. Really mad, right? Isn't that right?" He was spread out on his side on the couch, and what I could glimpse of his face revealed a perverse pleasure.

"Mad at you? God forbid . . ."

"You're not getting religious on me now, are you?"

"Oh, yeah, I forgot to tell you. You've finally driven me to it."

"See. You are mad at me."

"No, not really. No, I'm more mad at myself."

He straightened up to look at me. A deviation in the script always titillated him. I continued to look straight ahead, uncomfortably erect in the demarcation zone between my side and his side of the couch. It was loud outside on the streets: honking and beeping and cursing from the backed-up mess outside the tunnel to the west and the backed-up mess on Canal Street to the north. But the streets in the enclave were empty. Even the loser musicians downstairs had mercifully decamped. I'd planned to spend the day in the studio. There was nothing more satisfying than working in the studio while the rest of the city was out groaning and grunting and struggling to a destination where they would continue to grunt and groan and struggle in their efforts to have fun on a holiday.

"Why are you mad at yourself?" Joseph Pendleton was intrigued. He moved closer to the demarcation zone.

"Well, you're the way you are and why would you change? Besides, you're too old to change."

"The other day you told me I wasn't old." He cackled, but his eyes didn't let up.

"I was just trying to be nice. Look, I know you're not going to call if you don't feel like it. I'm mad at myself for imagining otherwise. It's not even worth bringing up. I accept it, or I—"

"Your tone on that message. I didn't call you back sooner because of that tone. God, I hate guilt."

I'd been operating under the assumption that guilt was my department. Why would I presume to have the power to instill guilt when he had strongly suggested that he didn't indulge in such foolishness?

"Then you asked me when we'd see each other again that last time. Just as I was leaving." He sounded like a little boy unjustly accused of stealing candy. "It can't be that way."

"Oh, Christ, don't you think I know that by now? I said it because it was getting late; I figured you'd run screaming for the door. I was just kidding. I couldn't resist torturing you."

"And then that message. That freaked-out message. I played it back a few times."

"I had a bad week. I had time to think, a delayed reaction. You know, the baby thing. It doesn't just go away."

"So why didn't you just call me and we could discuss it like adults?" He'd switched into his professorial mode, earnest and morally invincible.

"Since when have we behaved like adults? And how was I supposed to know I sounded freaked-out? Anyway, I hate calling you at that office. Maybe you haven't noticed, but I try not to call you. Ever."

"That's crazy. It makes no sense!" He stayed on his side of the couch but he couldn't keep still. "This involves two people."

He used my name when he said that. He only used my name when he was extremely agitated or there was no alternative, which was something I tried not to dwell on; still I couldn't help noticing it when he did.

"You're this guy who's doing eight billion things and you're busy and—"

"You're not making sense! Look, here's the story. I really . . . I like you. But I can't do this . . . this isn't going to work between us if you can't keep it between us." Joseph Pendleton made clichés sound like sonnets. He had an uncanny ability to stun me into silence through his audacity. "I understand. It's only natural. I mean, of course you would confide in your best friends. But your friend Rachel. I mean, she fucking leapt into my arms. I just met the woman, I'm doing her a favor—I can't live like that, with my private life under scrutiny."

"I don't blame you. I won't talk about it anymore. I had to before. I wish I hadn't. You know how I feel about that. In fact we've been over it a million times, just so we can avoid talking about anything real—"

The phone rang. I ignored it.

"Answer your phone," he ordered. Mama's boys, especially only sons, are a specific, dangerous, bossy breed; they expect obedience and they have no shame. I obeyed.

"I was just calling you back," said my neighbor. "What are you doing?"

"Oh, oh, nothing," I squeaked.

"What's wrong?"

"Nothing, nothing. How about you? How are you?"

"Calm down, cracker, we talked an hour ago. I'm still in a bad mood, why wouldn't I be? What's wrong? You sound tense. Which reminds me—I got a message from another tense Jew, David Mendelsohn. I don't know if I can handle it. It might be time to retire as a homosexual."

"Maybe you need to investigate a new ethnic group instead. Anyway, let me think about it and call you back."

"What is wrong with you? Oh, wait a minute. I get it. The black boulder has landed. He's there, isn't he?"

"I'll call you later."

Joseph Pendleton was just revving up. "That's not enough. If this is going to continue between us, you have to tell your friend Rachel and your neighbor—when you call him back later, perhaps—that it's over, finished, that we split up."

"Okay, okay, I will."

"Can you do that? Don't say it unless you really can. I understand if you can't."

"I can."

"I don't believe you."

"I said I can. I have incredible discipline, and it'll be better that way—"

"It has nothing to do with discipline. You have to be comfortable with it, or it's not going to work."

"I am fucking comfortable with it. I am not a big mouth. You caught me at a weak moment. But you can't go off brooding and sulking, you'll have to talk to me. Wait a minute, why am I even trying to convince you?"

"I just . . . I don't think you're cut out for this . . . at all." He clasped his hands on his knees and leaned forward on his side of the couch.

"Look, if I can't do it, we'll just stop."

"You don't know; it's not that easy to control."

"But you can't keep bringing this up over and over because it's really miserable. You make me feel like a criminal."

"You are a criminal."

"Look who's talking."

When the phone rang I grabbed it on the first ring.

"I hear you decided to make an appearance in Florida," said the King. "You fucking spoiled brat. What's she doing, flying you down in a Lear jet?"

"I thought you were out of town. I haven't decided if I'm going yet, but listen, I can't talk now—"

"What the fuck do you mean you haven't decided yet? Too busy writing that crap? How long can it take? The kids want to see you. Don't be an asshole. Hey, what's the story on the foreigner—does she have a brain, or is she all tits and ass?"

"She's nice, but I can't talk now."

"Hey, did you hear, Audrey won her tennis tournament, fourteen and under, and she's only eleven. She's unreal. Do you want to talk to her? Hey, Audrey, your snotty aunt is on the phone."

"Now listen, try to listen. Try your best. Ready? I can't talk now, do you hear me? Tell Audrey I'll call her later. I have a friend over. Good-bye."

"My brother," I said, and before he could speak, hurriedly, without fanfare, I crossed the demarcation zone.

"You're close to your family," he murmured.

"Too close. My mother suspects something, but I can't tell her, so she's upset."

"Your parents have morals. How come you don't have morals?" he said softly, and I struggled to get up.

"Me?! That's the pot calling the kettle black, wouldn't you say?"

He cackled and then he used his mouth insistently, wordlessly, to make his point, and I guess I was immoral because I didn't argue. The sounds of the storm provided a cushion that smothered the street noise, but when I opened my eyes I saw the rain was coming in and got up to close the fire-escape door.

"No, no, it's nice with the rain coming down. Don't close it."

I sat right back down like a dazed robot. The gray mist floated into the room and hung over the couch like solace.

"How long can you stay?"

He looked at his watch. "Another forty-five minutes." He closed his eyes. I pinned him down with my arms until he had to open them.

"What are you doing still in town anyway?"

"I told you, I'm going to that concert."

"What?"

"I told you when I came in."

"I didn't hear you."

"Someone sent me comps."

"I'm the one who should have the comps. You hardly even like them. Why are you going? To ruin it for me?" I forced him to keep looking at me. "Who are you going with?"

"I'm going with . . . well . . . my wife." We locked eyes. "We haven't talked about my wife yet. Talk about miserable; that's going to be miserable."

"I was looking forward to that concert." I started to move toward the demarcation zone, but he wouldn't let me. He diverted me with stories, some that I'd already heard secondhand. I moved closer to search his face for the subtle flickerings that heralded his deceit. He really wasn't a very good liar. His was a skittish conscience, but it was a conscience. His real expertise lay in lie detection. Eventually he rendered every story I'd heard inconsequential or slanderous. I'm not sure what prompted Joseph Pendleton to choose the truth, but more often than not, the truth he chose to tell was the truth I was as loath to hear as he was to tell.

"My mother and I, we moved to Paris when I was fourteen. She got a teaching gig, and she wanted to get away from her family. At fourteen, Paris was your worst nightmare—there was no action. I went back to Chicago as soon as I could. That's when I really started playing. I quit school . . . my mother never let me live it down. Everybody was in Chicago then. But the singer, you know, the singer—God, we met when we were so young, babies really—she was the only person who had a pulse in that town. And my mother, well, she was alone, and when she gets low, it's bad, you know, she wouldn't ever say so, but I knew she was in bad shape. So I went back then and I stayed. In the States jazz musicians aren't shit. In Europe they're gods.

"Anyway, the singer, she flipped out, and I met my ex-wife. She got pregnant . . . we were cursed, cursed from the start. She came from money, a real princess. Still is, but we get along now. I was on the road, she had the gallery, and she never really wanted our kid. Then I got this record deal, you know, I thought I had it made, I still believed what they said. I should have known—bass players just don't get big record deals. It was amazing. Too amazing. When it fell through, my marriage was a mess, and the singer, she showed up again. Incredible timing, that woman did have incredible timing.

"But the music was good in Paris then. It was before . . . but you probably know all this from your brother. Or maybe he's too young—"

"No, I know all about—"

"Hey, what does he really think about my place?" He didn't look at me.

"You know, I've only been to Paris once. I never really got the appeal."

He picked up my cue easily, relieved. "You just don't know the town. It's a silly town if you don't know it. I'll show you sometime. So after my marriage broke up, the princess—she got really angry and high and mighty—we'd gone through a lot of money, a *lot* of money. Anyway, I had to support my son. My son . . . he'll barely speak to me now. I blew it."

"How old is he?"

"Early twenties."

"Oh, he'll get over it. It's just that age."

"It's been 'that age' for a pretty long time."

"No, no, really—that age will end. It happens all of a sudden. It'll end. I remember, with my father and my brothers. I promise."

"You promise?"

"Well, yeah . . ."

"That's sweet. You promise. That is too damn sweet; you are just too damn sweet."

The thought went through my mind that I could sit here listening forever, and I reprimanded myself. I did keep listening though. I listened until he told me how the club in New York had fallen in his lap around that time and he took it as a sign to get the hell out of Paris. He never said *we.* He always said *I.* "I did this," "I did that," "I'm doing this." And the way he said it sounded natural.

"Last month when I was in Paris, you know, I started thinking about playing again; I talked to some people . . ." He was looking toward the fire escape, and I could hardly hear him. "Yeah, I was thinking . . ." Then he closed his eyes and I assumed he was falling asleep until I heard him whisper more softly, "You know, right? You know you don't deserve this."

•

It was no forty-five minutes when he finally left. It was dark, and he got up to go reluctantly. During the ten o'clock cop show, I tried not to focus on what he'd whispered and tried not to again when I woke up at two A.M. While I fumbled around for a sleeping potion at four, something else occurred to me. He envied how I lived, where I lived—he imagined it was glamorous, romantic, the real thing. His gilded perception of my life intruded on what he was fighting so hard to forget and what he was fighting so hard to be. I guess it was a relief to be with someone who'd bailed out early on. But I was starting to look back, too, and I was entertaining some regrets. I didn't bring them up, though, and he didn't dare inquire. I never got around to asking about her, either.

12

No doubt the train windows had originally been clear glass, but now they were covered with a silver-gray sheen. It didn't bother me. I preferred the train to the haughty buses that traveled caravan-style to Long Island. I liked to stand between the cars where the wind propelled you forward with promise and hope even when the train was just inching along. The city can shrink into a four- or five-block cage if you don't get out in time. Sometimes you lose the ability to see beyond those bars, so that even simple errands become major hurdles. Lately, if I hadn't gathered my daily provisions by early morning when I could still see beyond the bars, I'd just as soon go without nutrition. I could see more clearly through the silver-gray sheen of the train windows than I could through the illusory bars in the city.

Aaron's house was near the end of the island. It was not a gleaming white, sunny beach house but a dark, tacky ranch house deep in the woods. It was square, with only a few pieces of oversized bamboo furniture strategically placed inside it, so that what little light did get in had room to move around. The pièce de résistance was the grand bamboo canopy bed in the living room, piled with sumptuous fabrics, that was just crying out for a collapsed body. Aaron enjoyed the finer things in life. She didn't consider food an inconvenience, and she drank good wine, more than enough good wine.

Since I usually charged blindly past the finer things in life, visiting her was sometimes a challenge. But we could always drive over to Sam's ranch house, which sat on a plot of land cluttered with gray sheds, red chicken houses, and ragged greenery that resembled a miniature golf course in Appalachia. His house was always a work-in-progress, and recently he'd covered the windows with tar paper, so now you couldn't see the discarded nasty girls arranged on the couches inside. Sam was blindly loyal to his discarded girls.

I knew about blind loyalty and often wondered if it was a blessing or another curse. I'd followed Joseph Pendleton's orders regarding Rachel and my neighbor posthaste, that same evening. My neighbor and I had gone down to the hip art restaurant, where the staff always greeted him like he was the messiah. He'd recently developed a crush on one of the balding members of the staff and he confessed that he had always been drawn to members of the service industry.

"You just like to be waited on," I'd said.

"No, no," he'd insisted. "There's something else." As a former member of the industry, I wasn't at all convinced that there was something else but I hadn't pushed it. My orders were weighing on me. The name Joseph Pendleton had barely left my mouth before my neighbor's face turned long-suffering.

"I can't discuss it with you anymore." My words had come fast. "And I'm supposed to tell you it's over. I mean it probably will be momentarily anyhow."

"With me? You can't discuss it with me anymore?" His eyes had been livid for an instant. "I don't even know the guy. I've talked to him, what, maybe twice in my life."

"I think he's right. I mean, I understand how he feels. And it's not going to last much longer, I guarantee," I'd pleaded. "You hated hearing about it anyway."

"Fine," he'd said. "I have to go home and work. Let's get the check."

I'd followed the same formula with Rachel.

"Fine," she'd echoed briskly. "As long as that's what you want." I'd muttered an assent and there'd been a pause. "Do you remember what happened to Patty Hearst? What did they call it? You know, when hostages initially identify with their kidnappers and then they empathize with them. God, what did they call it? Do you remember?"

"No, I don't recall," I'd replied stonily.

I'd spent the next day, the Fourth, with Victor. Victor was not much of a celebrator either—he only really noticed holidays when he came across long movie lines on weekday afternoons— so we'd worked all morning shoveling out his apartment. I'd been wrong to be skeptical about the need for shovels. His two rooms were filled with magazines and books and photographs, though they weren't immediately recognizable as such. Molded in stiff, awkward shapes, some were so crusty they could hardly fit onto my shovel. We had to sneak the garbage bags out to the curb because the evil landlord was on Victor's trail for some reason—it was just one of those things. Victor's credit card had recently been revoked—it was another one of those things—so we used mine to rent the moving van. There was another group of volunteers stationed elsewhere in the city to unpack the van. I didn't ask for any of the particulars, and he didn't offer them.

After he was done unpacking, we met up again for the concert. We arrived late because we knew what to expect: There was no telling when the funk would really start, and once it did, there was no telling when it would end. But we knew how to pace ourselves, and at least it wasn't crowded. Certainly not too crowded to see Joseph Pendleton, and her, from just about any spot in the house. There was practically a receiving line paying homage to him; he'd say a few words to each, and every so often reach over and touch her lightly on the small of her back. I tried not to look. When I glanced up furtively, he was looking at me. It was not quite his standard reproachful look; it was also blatantly lascivious. I started to smile involuntarily and ducked, clutching Victor's arm to steady myself, but I remained queasy. So I fled after giving Victor a sketchy explanation. He just shrugged.

I was still queasy when I got home, so I called Aaron. She responded to the sound of my voice instantly: "Just get your ass out here." The brush with the mouse in the water glass the next morning only hastened my departure.

•

Aaron met me at the train, and we went straight to the beach after a stop at her house to change and get supplies. On the way there she updated me on her current saga. She had met Jerry at the bank. He looked like Kojak and sounded like Billy Graham. At first she couldn't be bothered, but he'd been a dogged suitor—and he had plenty of cash. What he actually did to procure the cash was a mystery, since his daily life seemed to revolve around psychotherapy appointments, massage appointments, dentist appointments, and acupuncture appointments—a full schedule by anyone's standards. Gradually Aaron came around because, after all, she did appreciate the finer things in life and that meant cash. At dinner the night before, there had been a row between Jerry and Frankie, a dashing South American homosexual who supported Aaron's business and her luxurious habits. Once we settled on the beach she poured the wine into picnic-sized red plastic cups.

"I don't really remember much—I was pretty loaded—but I do remember Jerry screaming about my support issues with Frankie. If I hear the word *issue* one more time, I'm going to be the one doing the screaming."

I lay inert, half listening, heavy-headed and drowsy, more from the relief of finally being out of the city than from the gargantuan cup of wine I could hardly lift my arm to drink. The beach was at the end of a long lane lined with stone walls and foreboding hedges hiding ostentatious mansions, and it was always deserted. I could never figure out why; it certainly was as dazzling as any other.

"Frankie will come around," I told Aaron. "And Jerry, you know he'll just sulk for a few days. He doesn't have anything else to do. He'll come back for more."

She shrugged and refilled her cup for the third time. I cringed and closed my eyes. I was still somewhat drowsy when we got in the car but not too drowsy to miss the savage look on Aaron's face. When she slammed down on the gas, I reflexively slammed on an imaginary brake. I was no longer drowsy when the car went into reverse instead of forward and we landed deep in the hedge, only inches away from a stone wall. I wasn't surprised, though, because Aaron, drunk or sober, attracted crises. Apparently some sort of technical malfunction had caused the car to shoot backward. Now it wouldn't go in either direction. As we began our silent trek, I ventured, "This isn't so bad. It's not that far." Aaron didn't answer. There was really nothing to discuss. When Jerry pulled up in his truck, even I was glad to see him.

Aaron and I didn't speak as we entered the house. She headed for the bath, and I headed for the canopy bed. Bad luck is easier to endure alone. I endured dinner at a restaurant, where another brawl ensued. This one concerned Aaron's drinking, a frequent source of discord between the two of them. When I suggested my presence as a third-party witness wasn't really required, they glared at me. I endured the ride back in Aaron's jeep on country roads where you could go ninety angry miles per hour and no one cared, and I pumped my imaginary brake until I had cramps in my leg.

I went back to the city early the next morning. The train ride and the beach and the canopy bed had revived me sufficiently. There was no need to explain my sudden departure because Aaron had grown up with silent communication, too.

•

"Hello, dear. How are you? Good, good. You got my fax?"

"Oh yeah, thanks. I'm working on the piece right now."

The grief piece was in front of me—that is, the ravaged version of it, which I was still struggling to decipher.

"And the message, darling. You got my message?"

"Yes, yes, I got your message." It had gone something like this: "Darling, I just loved the piece. And loved your voice, loved your voice. But you know what? We need a really fun piece, and this piece is just not fun. Period. And while grief may not have been fun five years ago, oh, I don't know, maybe ten years ago, grief is hot now. And it's everywhere, and we've got to make it fun."

At least it was a response. There'd been no word from Ditzgirl lately, and I feared we were at the stage where art dealers, even motherly art dealers, stop returning the artist's calls because the news is not good. Concealing desperation was key at this stage with both her and my editor.

"Maybe you can give me suggestions about how to make it fun."

"Suggestions? I've got nothing but suggestions. Number one, we don't really want to know about grieving; that's just a big bore. We want to know about the grieving process. Investigate funeral homes! Who's going where? Are there waiting lists? Who gets in and who doesn't? What's the deal? How long do you have to plan in advance? Weeks? Months? Days?"

"Um, I'm not sure this is a situation where you can always plan in advance . . ."

"Darling, darling, you writers are so damn literal. You get my gist, you get my gist. Who's getting cremated and who's going for the casket, the procession, the burial, the whole nine yards? Ashes ashes ashes—who's spreading them and where? Urns—what's hot? Are we talking gold? Are we talking brass? For Christ's sake, are we talking clay? And how much? Price range, price range! What's cost-effective? Where are the bargains? I want to know the ten hottest funerals and the ten hottest caskets in the last six months. Who gets in? Who sits where? I want to know the peak funeral season. And do you know what? I want you to tell me just how long our readers should expect to grieve! Who's grieving for how long? I want to feel the grieving process—without the grief. You get the gist? And Jesus, shoes, don't forget about the shoes. This man designed shoes, he *was* shoes. Shoes, let's see, shoes . . . stilettos . . . he was stilettos . . . stilettos as a metaphor for death! Are you with me, darling?"

"I guess so. I'll try my best. I don't know if it'll be exactly fun, but I'll try."

I'd never presumed to write a serious treatise on death or grieving, nor was I capable of such a thing, but I had expected to maintain a modicum of dignity. Expectations can never sink low enough.

I'd encountered death when I was young, before it was fashionable, before there was such a thing as the grieving process. Yes, I was familiar with nervous breakdowns and mental hospitals, which were much more fashionable back then, but death I was familiar with only tangentially. Much later the deaths came fast, sometimes a couple at a time. Each on its own wasn't significant enough to form the kind of death bubble that causes paralysis—

until Jack died. I never knew I was in the death bubble because it's hard to recognize until it's gone. These days it felt like I might be in the paralysis kind of bubble, but you can't very well mourn the death of something that never was. Or can you? Can you mourn the death of dreams?

•

Summer's torpor was lingering for days at a time. Almost everybody left in town was either not up to par or in hiding. Even the downstairs establishment was gloomy, empty except for the two scruffy regulars splayed on their stools under the hippie's morose gaze. Seasonal shifts cause corresponding mood shifts in the city. It was always comforting to discover you were never alone in your current mood shift; it was usually quite the contrary—everyone was up or everyone was down.

Perry was depressed because she'd risen from her "maternal bed" too early. She was convinced that that was why she and Rachel weren't getting along. She was right, in a sense. The maternal bed was part of the problem—more specifically, the fact that she was still blathering on about it—ad nauseum. Even Rachel, ordinarily blind to the concept that Perry might be overdue for a lesson in tact, was exasperated. Rachel wasn't up to par, either. Jean had gone abruptly and sullenly back to Paris for a break, and she was attending to the problem with systematic dating, which kept her in a cranky state of superficial intrigue and upheaval.

Perry and I were having our own difficulties. The idea that Rachel had been privy to more intimate details of my saga than she had made her bristle. In turn, I was tormented with guilt by the fact that I'd let his identity slip out—not to mention that the maternal-bed soliloquy was grating on me, too. More often than not, I was unable to contain my ire. Only certain people had the talent to trigger my ire—Perry happened to be one of the most talented—and she knew it as well as I did. I was careful when I explained to her that there was nothing to be privy to anymore.

"Oh, well, we should all be thankful for that," she replied smugly.

"What do you mean?" I took the bait wearily.

"Oh, just something I heard," she countered breezily.

"Elaborate, please."

"Oh, never mind. I probably shouldn't tell you."

"It's a little too late for that, isn't it?"

"Okay. First of all, are you aware that this fellow may be disturbed, severely disturbed? Pathologically disturbed. Has he ever been hospitalized? When I told my cherished Richard—never fear, no names, no names—he said it was a clear case of bipolar disorder with classic misogynist elements rooted in an inflated sense of self based on self-loathing—and he should know, it is his field— and he also said in the case of the black male . . . now, would you say he's more black or white, I mean, I know he looks—?"

"Perry, don't start this."

"All right, then. Answer me this. Is his wife white or black?"

"Jesus, Perry, what does that have to do with anything?"

She sighed an anguished sigh. Perry's northerners-are-the-real-racists attitude allowed her the liberty, under the guise of sophisticated irony, to indulge in cute racist slurs, but they were neither cute nor sophisticated enough. No, they sounded just a little too real.

"All right. Are you prepared? He was seen at an art opening."

"So?"

"Well, I wasn't a direct witness. Of course, I was unable to attend. Rita had the night off, so I was chained to the crib of my beloved. It's of the utmost importance to treat help as you would a member of your family, I firmly believe, but Richard says that up here class and race are sensitive issues deeply imbedded in structures from the—"

"Perry."

"All right, all right. He displayed very disturbing behavior."
She whispered, "I believe he could very well be classified as a
sexual deviant."

"How would you know what a sexual deviant is? Do you even
remember sex?"

"Yes, I do. Well, vaguely. But allow me to say this. He did not
display the behavior of a gentleman who is taken, who has responsibilities back at the hearth. He did not behave honorably. If
you understand what I mean."

"Oh, yes, I think I've got an inkling."

"He was observed lavishing attention on a fashionable young
lady."

Perry's definition of "lavishing attention" was bound to be en-
lightening, but I could do without. Perry was bent on revenge. Her
information wasn't for my benefit. That kind of information never
is. In this case, it was a vehicle to proselytize turgid morality—and
to help lay to rest whatever doubts, insecurities, or regrets Perry
was nursing over her own situation. The fashionable young lady
didn't disturb me—there were those who liked to be validated by
the opposite sex on a frequent basis, those who enjoyed playing
the game, a game that I didn't enjoy playing, but it didn't bother
me if he liked to play. That was the least of my problems.

•

When he called a half hour later, my brain had miraculously shut
down for the night and my hello came out soft and slurry.

"Is that you?" he said. I was startled to hear his voice. "You
sound spaced-out."

"I was just watching my cop show."

"You mean with the Irish guy? He's your favorite character,
right?"

"No, he's not! Well, maybe he is."

He wanted to get together, and he cooed until I surrendered. It didn't take long.

"So where would you like to meet?" he asked.

"You might as well just come over."

"You want me to come by to get you?"

"I don't really want to go out."

"Of course, if that's what you'd prefer."

The show of gallantry didn't fool me. Best to prepare myself for a state of siege. I was lying inert on the bed, naked and sweaty, with the sheet half draped over me, and I stayed there for a few moments, contemplating. I couldn't very well get all dolled up, now, could I? What would I be doing all dolled up at home at midnight? On the other hand, we weren't at the all-scuzzy-in-a-nightgown stage yet. It was stifling, and the new air conditioner wasn't up to par either. By the time he showed up, I'd sweated through dress number one and transferred into dress number two.

He was shifty, uneasy, at the door: "Are you sure you don't want to go out?" I had to physically pull him inside, and I noticed that he was soaked.

"I didn't realize it was raining. Was it hard to get a cab?"

"Oh, ah, no, it just took me longer than I thought. I had some obligations, uptown, a dinner. It's not important. What have you been up to this evening?"

"Oh, this and that. Maybe the rain will cool things off."

"Maybe." He was way ahead of me, taking long strides toward the couch. In midstep, he asked offhand, "So what about that concert?"

"What about it?"

He stopped and turned: "What's that supposed to mean?"

"It's supposed to mean 'What about it?' "

"Well, the band, of course. What'd you think?"

"I thought they were great, especially—"

"I thought they were terrible."

"You did?"

"Too many jams—pure self-indulgence, endless and indiscriminate. Just some over-the-hill musicians doing bad covers. It was incoherent at best. Sophomoric."

I was crushed like a teenager. "You've been away too long—you've forgotten what those concerts are like."

"Okay, I guess I don't go see as much music anymore, but come on, they sounded like a bunch of old geezers up there."

"Guess I'm a more loyal fan," I said blithely.

"It was pathetic."

"Guess I'm a more loyal fan," I repeated.

"No, you're indiscriminate. That's all, you're no longer capable of discriminating." He couldn't help smiling, and I couldn't either. Our system of checks and balances had kicked into gear, smoothly bypassing any discussion of the more delicate aspects of that evening. When we went into the studio, he didn't say much. He usually said just enough. He didn't say he saw wombs or eggs—Rachel always saw wombs or eggs. He didn't say he saw scary faces—Aaron insisted on scary faces. Or penises—my neighbor was adamant about penises. As was my father, who also pointed out internal organs I didn't know existed, with great excitement, extrapolating with medical terminology I couldn't pronounce. Joseph Pendleton didn't need to tell me what he saw. Instead he turned to me in the way that always made me look away, and I turned off the bright lights in a hurry, a signal toward the couch, where words could mean anything. I never knew how much time we had, so I was always in a hurry. He slowed me down with a powerful tenderness.

"What were you thinking?" he whispered. "Just then."

"Nothing."

"Don't say nothing, it wasn't nothing."

"Maybe it was. I try not to think when I'm with you."

He became less tender and less lazy, and I became more so, until we both lay sweaty and tired. I whispered into his cheek that I'd followed orders, and while he didn't exactly tense up, his reply was less husky and more considered.

"So what did you tell them?"

"I said it was practically over and I didn't want to talk about it anymore."

"They believed you?"

"Why wouldn't they?"

I got up to open the fire-escape door. It felt so close inside. I shut off the air conditioner and struggled to open whatever windows weren't stuck permanently shut. He watched me.

"So what's the latest on the show?"

"Two paintings on reserve; I think one will sell. He's in Europe hustling the secondary market—you know, the summer—so Ditz-girl's in charge. I sure wouldn't buy a painting from her."

"Maybe I'll buy something, but wouldn't I get a better deal direct from the studio? What about that drawing over there? How much?"

"Which one?" There was a whole wall of drawings, not all of them mine.

"Um . . . the one on the far right." He smiled to himself. "That's yours, isn't it?"

"You lucked out." I couldn't keep a straight face, either. "I'll think about it and let you know. Hey, I listened to one of your records tonight. I took it from my brother the other day."

"You're sure it was mine?"

"Pretty sure. I think it was the live one in Stockholm, or was it Copenhagen? I never look at titles. I liked it, I thought—"

He interrupted. "Did I tell you about the club I opened in Paris? Well, it's just starting to get somewhere. There've been some happening gigs, with guys who can play, you know. There's no money in it yet, but it's cool. I hired this stiff to run it so I don't have to deal with too much. No one knows I'm behind it." He turned abruptly to give me the warning look.

I ignored it. Joseph Pendleton was more comfortable when I played the bad girl sharing duplicity—the good girl was getting under his skin. His duplicity was instinctive, and usually I excused it because he would never have what I took for granted—the privilege of not living on a daily diet of digesting rude insults and spitting back polite lies. I knew he trusted me as much as he probably trusted anyone—almost as well as I knew the last thing he wanted was the grim responsibility of my trust reciprocated.

"You know, I think my brother . . ."

"Yeah, last winter, his trio. They weren't too bad."

"Not too bad? You're not allowed to insult my family."

He pulled me back. "You're too easy to tease. It's cute. You're still a baby."

"No I'm not." Flushed, I continued. "So why did you come back?"

"My son." He cackled derisively. "He hated it—he was eleven years old—a New York eleven, not a Paris eleven—and I knew how that felt . . ." Proper names for present-day intimates were not allowed—and allowed only occasionally for spirits from the past. Proper names risked upsetting the increasingly precarious system of checks and balances.

"I went there originally because my mother died," he continued. "I had to take care of things, and I finished, so—"

"Oh, I didn't know . . ."

"See, there are still some things you don't know about me. Yeah, I could breathe in Paris; this city can strangle you, it's so fucking tight."

"This dealer from Paris just offered me a show."

"Who?"

"David Mendelsohn."

"I've never heard of him."

"Well, he hasn't been around long. He came over the other night. It was fun. We had a good studio visit."

"He came over here? Most of the paintings are at the gallery, aren't they? Are you sure he's interested in the art?"

"Don't be ridiculous. He's a kid. Well, it was a little weird. We thought he was gay at first, but it turns out he's not. Oh, he wouldn't be interested in me."

"Why wouldn't he be interested in you?"

I was mute.

"Don't pull that—answer me."

"Anyway, he is smart and I think he might actually have integrity. I mean, it always seems that way at first . . ."

"Whatever integrity means. You didn't answer my question."

"You do so know what integrity means."

"You still didn't answer my question." When I didn't say anything, he spoke softly. "Hey, I don't know what you're thinking. I'm not one of your brothers. Come on, you should know not to listen to me by now. A show in Paris—that's great! You should be excited."

"I'm trying not to be. It's safer."

"I have to go to Paris next week."

"Oh."

"Why don't you come along?"

"Huh?"

"It's only for a few days. I have some things to take care of."

"Okay, yeah, I mean I'd love to go, but I have to be back by next Sunday. I have to go to Florida."

"Florida in the summer?"

"Family."

"Your parents—they must be pretty out there . . . to come up with you, I mean."

"Well . . ."

160 • Betsy Berne

"In a good way, naturally."

"Naturally."

"We'd have you back by Sunday. We'll talk more about it later."

We'll talk more about it later could mean anything.

"It's getting really late," I said. "You should probably go."

"I know," he said, but he didn't get up and it gave me courage. "Joseph?"

"Yes?"

"I always think it's the last time, every time I see you," I whispered to his back. "It's not you, anything you've done, it's just me, and experiences, the accumulation of the years."

He whipped his head around, and his eyes were small and cold. "Why would you say something like that?"

"I don't know, it just feels that way. Circumstances, fate, the past. You can't intellectualize all your emotions. At least I can't."

He shot up. "You're being ridiculous. Christ, you're so melodramatic. What do you think is going to happen? I'm not going to die!" He started walking toward the kitchen.

"I told you, it's not you—don't take it so personally!"

He turned around. "What am I supposed to take personally? Is our . . . is this, are we something to take personally?"

"I'm not sure yet."

"Don't start that! Tell me, what *do* you take personally?"

"I guess I'm not sure about that either."

He shrugged, half smiling to himself, but his eyes remained small and cold, and he strutted toward the door while I trailed behind. Usually we'd stand there for a few minutes, I'd say good-bye—never good night—a few times as I pushed him out the door and he'd kiss me. Tonight there was barely time for one good-bye and no time for a kiss.

Even with the windows open, it still felt close inside, so I climbed out to the fire escape. I looked around, but I didn't see him. He must have gone the other way. The corner was quiet, almost peaceful. I think I saw Victor hunkered down at one of the establishments across the street, engrossed in a big, thick book. At least it looked like Victor, and who else would be sitting at a bar engrossed in a big, thick book? The evening had been so lovely—until one of us had the foresight to stab the lovely evening in its dark, unlovely heart before it became too lovely, and the other had the good sense to oblige.

I shivered; it was almost chilly. The weather had gone awry somewhere along the way, just as our fail-safe system had. I wasn't exactly sure when or how. Just as I wasn't exactly sure when or how Joseph Pendleton had been twisted and turned around—or if it went straight to his core. My soft spot had been gripped by this puzzle from the start, and quite often it skewed reason.

•

In the morning, on the way to a meeting at the cosmetics company, I ran into a friend with her baby. It was one of my favorite neighborhood babies—it was dark-haired, and I was sick of blond babies. Even my niece and nephew had the nerve to be blond, and how much could you take? I listened while the friend rambled on about how exhausted she was—the baby had kept her up all night. I didn't tell her that a baby had kept me up all night, too.

13

"THE CASTING CALL SAYS REAL PEOPLE—IT SOUNDS SO SIMPLE, DOESN'T IT?" The head honcho spoke in a rapid upper-class drone, low and whiny, and her frequent sighs were accompanied by a couple of slender figures running through sleek beige hair. Her face was sleek and beige, too—I had to squint to detect crow's feet—and she wore a matching sleek beige suit. "Well, it's not. We've seen some twenty girls, and, oh, I don't know how many guys. How many guys, Janet?" Janet, her secretary—no, her assistant—seemed a little too eager to please, judging by the beads of sweat on her forehead.

"They all start to look alike," she continued. "You know what I mean? We need two girls. One has got to be blond—not a Connecticut blonde or a feminist blonde—an Ohio blonde, a blonde with some padding, just a few extra pounds in the right places, you know, a blonde bordering on mousy. But not mousy. For the second girl, we're going to need an ethnic. When I say ethnic, I mean ethnic but not ethnic. Let's be honest. Dark hair but the skin—we're going to want to go dark but not too dark. What I'd like to call a tint as opposed to a hue, you know—a lip gloss as opposed to a lipstick." She flashed an in-the-know smile.

I was able to respond only with a weak grin, but the film-makers managed something a little more substantial. "The girl from Barbados, she was almost there—she had good hair, good teeth, good muscle tone. You know what I mean—and she had curves. But the voice, my God, the voice. Ethnic can be exotic, but please—not immigrant." She paused. "Now I think we're onto something. We've got a lead on an Asian—mixed parentage, you know—not too Oriental. This girl can pass for just about anything; she's got some range. And she's educated, so the voice doesn't present a problem—you get the picture. To tell you the truth, it's the blonde that's keeping me up at night. We can't afford to alienate the fat girl changing diapers in Queens."

The conference room gleamed whiter, shinier than I'd remembered. I was afraid to lift my coffee cup to my lips, lest a dribble sully a white surface. My eyes drifted to the walls. The paintings were part of one of the most important corporate art collections in the city. Primarily white or beige, they were each rationed a portion of color—circles, squares, stripes, an occasional scribble. I had some paintings in important corporate collections, and I had a feeling they were not hanging in a conference room, more likely they were stacked in cool, stark storage rooms.

When the head honcho paused, Janet, who exhibited a distinctly ethnic pallor, took up the slack eagerly: "You know, seriously, I think, like, our real challenge lies with the guys—you know, whether to go ethnic or not. You don't want to end up with one of those guys who wear the baggy jeans and that weird headgear. I mean, I guess they're real, but yuck." She wrinkled her long, distinctly ethnic nose in disgust. "You know the kind when they come near you on the street, like you're just praying to God, they're not going to pull out a gun. I think, you know, like it would be in our best interests to go with, like, regular guys."

There is a thin line between "acceptable" and "unacceptable" bigotry, especially in cosmopolitan beige-and-white circles, but even the head honcho could see that Janet had crossed it. She interrupted hastily: "Why don't I show you a promo film we did a few years ago? It'll give you an idea of what we're about, get us on the same track. We want the laughs, but we also need the tears. No tears coursing down cheeks, God forbid—but tears in the eyes, you know, welling up in the eyes."

We were discussing a five-minute history of a cosmetics company here. It shouldn't be dull, that was understood, but to evoke tears? I studied the promo film for clues. It was white, too, spotted with all kinds of females in tints, not hues, all speaking in educated voices, one big happy family of females, diving into aquamarine swimming pools with big white splashes, dwarfed behind blond wood desks with big white smiles, leaning against sparkling white sinks clutching clean, plump babies. My eyes remained dry, but the filmmakers' faces had become solemn. The Brit broke the hush.

"I was very moved," he spoke slowly and carefully. "To be frank I wasn't expecting it. I quite liked it. It was quite brilliant, wasn't it? I'm thinking I'd like to work primarily with water in our film. I think water as a sort of key element could cover all the bases. Water dripping, sort of bubbling, streaming. Quite modern, really. Clean, fresh, cool, crisp. Very minimalist, isn't it . . . and abstract . . . sort of . . . but concise."

I scrutinized the Brit, trying to figure out whether he could possibly mean what he was saying, while simultaneously trying to imagine what kind of script would include water dripping, streaming, and bubbling. Some cold coffee dribbled down my chin—it was inevitable—and when I turned to grope for a napkin I saw her. She'd slipped in unobtrusively. She seemed taller. Talk about sleek. I lurched back in my chair and choked on the rest of the coffee, which caused an even more conspicuous chin dribble. Up close, she didn't look much older than me. She was as sharp and angular as he was, with eyes that were large and expressionless, eyes that were directed decidedly outward. The coughing spasm that followed my initial choking episode was brief but audible.

"Are you okay?" the Brit whispered. "Do you need some water?"

"No, no, fine, fine," I wheezed, gesturing with my hands. "Just went down the wrong hole."

She was charming. She engaged in a short personal chat with each of us. When it was my turn, she looked me up and down appraisingly but so skillfully that a less wary target would hardly have noticed.

"You look like you've had a great summer," she remarked. "What a gorgeous tan!" Oh, sin of sins, the tan! I'd dressed so carefully this morning, choosing a pair of long pants and a prim jacket, in an evidently useless ploy to cover the scandalous tan, which was now deepened by a head-to-toe blush. I uttered some disavowals in conjunction with pointed references to the company's high-quality self-tanning products. She responded favorably: "So tell me about yourself."

I sallied forth with a recitation of my writing credentials, and again, she went for it. The filmmakers looked relieved. "Oh, who do you work with? I may know your editor. I've worked with fashion magazines in some capacity or another for years, although I've been overseas for the past several."

"Well, there's a high turnover, as you're probably aware," I began, and she laughed, a deep, throaty, and, well, charming laugh, so I told her my editor's name.

"Oh, she's wonderful. I know her well. Well, not all that well, but as well as can be expected when you work out at the same gym. I guess that is pretty well, isn't it?" Another throaty laugh escaped, and everybody joined in—almost everybody. I was too busy studying her to join in. Judging by the shape she was in, she knew my good friend the beauty editor quite well. And spiked heels during the day—that indicated a formidable capacity for pain. "I understand you're a painter?"

"Well, yes, I guess you could—"

"That's fabulous! Do you show?"

"Yeah, in fact, I'm in a group show now downtown."

"How absolutely remarkable! So you have both verbal and visual skills. How unique. You must be either very levelheaded or virtually insane, to be able to deal with both worlds. I know the art world very well. You see, my husband collects. Maybe you know him? Joseph Pendleton."

"Hmmm . . . I've heard the name."

"Of course—Joseph Pendleton!" Saved by the Brit. "I used to see him play when I was just a kid. He was quite brilliant! I was into that sort of thing in the seventies—he played a lot in London. Or was it the early eighties?"

"Well, he's not playing or doing much collecting these days. You know, family life—"

"Oh, sure." I smiled.

"Anyway, my husband, he's into photography primarily, or I'd send him right down. Not that I want to tempt him."

"Oh, well . . ." I shrugged.

"At any rate, I imagine we know a lot of people in common."

"Um, probably, I mean I'm sure we do . . ."

"But we'd better not even get started. In the interest of getting this film in the can, right?"

"Right."

"We need a rough idea of where we're going, a first draft by the end of next week. Does that sound feasible?"

"Oh, I think so. I'll certainly try. I'll need to get more of an idea of the visuals, but I think I can handle it."

"Listen, do what you can. If you need a few more days, go ahead, take them. Why don't we say the Monday after next—is that fair? I think we can work with that."

Tough but fair. I'd envisioned a pussycat, meek and mild, not a cold, clever lioness who clearly had plenty of fight left. The Monday deadline would work, I thought, unless something came up—like a sudden trip to Paris. I had trouble focusing during the filmmakers' presentation. The Brit glanced over and whispered, "You know, you don't have to stick around for this."

I headed toward the nearest exit, which wasn't near enough. I was still shivering when I got outside, and the asphyxiating air was welcoming. I took off the prim jacket and stood for a few moments among the midtown late-lunch crowds. My favorite department store was across the street, beckoning like a giant bottle of painkillers. Inside, the walls were warm and creamy and the displays were lavish, and I would have been content to ride the escalator all day. Instead I went directly to the shoe department so I could grieve—in style. A salesman crammed my feet into a pair of the dead shoe designer's frisky red patent-leather heels. I approximated a corporate strut and nearly knocked down an old lady in suede oxfords. The second pair was more sedate—a drab, sulky almost-pink. I was able to get across the floor to the cash register without too much trouble, so I made the grieving process more fun with a purchase.

"Thanks, I'll just wear them," I told the salesman, and made my way down Fifth with a high-heeled bravado. At Broadway I ducked under the nearest theater marquis and stared at the tall brazen building across the street, the one squeezed between a forlorn ex–pinball parlor and a spanking-new sports bar, where Joseph Pendleton had his office. Leaning against the wall, I lifted a foot to study the blisters and when I glanced up I thought I saw him go inside. At least it looked like him.

A verboten cab ride later, I kicked off the shoes at the entrance of my building, climbed up the filthy stairs barefoot, limped inside, and called him.

"Hello?"

"Joseph?"

"Yes?" He sounded remote.

"Did you mean that last night about Paris? Because I have work. I just got this new assignment, it has to be done quickly, so I have to have an idea—"

"I'll know more in a few days. Why don't we talk then?"

"Oh, okay, great . . . so . . ."

"We'll talk soon."

•

"Let's not get excited, honey, but it was a little late to get you a nonstop flight. There's going to be a layover. Not too bad. Really, it's nothing. Two and a half hours in Washington . . . okay, maybe closer to three. Let's not discuss it."

"Oh, Jesus, why don't I just take the train . . . oh, never mind, it's fine, it's fine."

"And honey, please, enough of 'Florida in the summer.' You may hate us, but the rest of the family members, we still like each other. We're all looking forward to Florida." She sighed.

I sighed, too, but I had no right to. I'd learned from the master and initiated the call this evening—my preemptive strike—before she had a chance to place a desperate call and before I lost the ability to disguise my voice. He'd slipped away again, and chances that he'd touch down before the alleged date of departure for Paris, that is, in two days' time, were slim.

"Well, if you keep insisting that I hate you then I probably will start to hate you."

"Oh, honey, you're right. Forgive me. I didn't mean it. But we'll have fun, won't we have fun?"

"Yes, we'll have fun."

I was only going for thirty-six hours, my usual trip limit. The rest of them were signed up for the full ten days—except for my middle brother, who never committed himself to more than a tense forty-eight.

"Hey, how are we all going to fit?" I asked. "There's no way there's going to be enough room for all of us in the condo, is there?"

"Hell, no, there's barely room for Royalty, Ellen, and the kids. The rest of you are going to be in a hotel. Won't that be fun?"

"Great. What hotel?"

"The Days Inn down the beach. I'm getting the groom-to-be and his concubine a suite—I'm just hoping they can keep their hands off each other in front of the kids. When they visited they were practically humping on the couch in front of Daddy and me—not that we care, but we didn't know where to look. You and your brother will be sharing—"

"Oh no. Oh no, we won't. I draw the line. I am not going to share a room with my brother—we are grown adults! We are middle-aged people! You've already put us in the sleaziest chain hotel in the country—how cheap can a Jew be? How fucking much can a Days Inn room cost?"

"Thirty-seven fifty, if I'm not mistaken." She stage-whispered: "And, honey, don't say *Jew.* I am not a cheap Jew. The suite is going to run forty-eight ninety-nine."

"Thirty-seven fifty? Forty-eight ninety-nine? That's insane—you have a husband who has a six-figure income!"

"Honey, he's only teaching now—we're on half-income. I've told you. I am not a cheap Jew."

"I'll pay for it. I think I can rustle up the thirty-seven fifty."

"All right, all right, goddamn it to hell, I'll look into it. Now, how are you?"

"Oh, fine. There's really nothing new. The show came down."

"I won't bother to ask how it went. You don't tell me anything anymore anyway."

"Maybe you and Dad should just fly this time. It's for such a short time."

"Honey, it's not a bad drive. Hell, it's the only good part of that damn Florida, I've told you. I just strap him in the front seat and step on it. Who needs the hassle of airports when you can just get in the car and go? Last time we made it in twenty-six and a half hours—only six stops—and if it weren't for his goddamn prostate, it would have been less than twenty-four. You know, I've been thinking lately, when he goes, it may not be such a bad idea, I'm thinking I may become a trucker."

"Is there something you haven't told me that indicates he's going to go soon? How is his health? Where is Dad, anyway?"

"I hope he's okay. I mean, I think he is."

"What do you mean? Are his organs functioning?"

"I think the kidneys are worse, but, honey, who listens anymore? All I know is he lines up thirty-six bottles of pills every morning."

"Well, where is he now? I haven't talked to him in a while."

"He's glued to the news. You know, watching the latest on the senator who was caught shtupping the slut—they're both commoners, honey, lowlife. He's fucking glued to the TV all day. You know how Daddy feels about men who play around—he thinks it's just despicable. And he's right, too. Goddamn right."

"Hmmm. Well, can you get him? I should probably say a few words before he goes."

"Oh, the son of a bitch is gonna outlive all of us, believe me. Besides, I'm not speaking to him."

"What'd he do?"

"Every goddamn morning. He always talks to me with his back turned while I still have the earplugs in and before I have time to put the hearing aid in. Anyway, I say to Daddy, 'Excuse me?' And he says, in that spoiled son-of-his-mother voice, that vicious voice, 'Can't you hear me?' I'm still not speaking to him."

"Oh, well, could I talk to him?"

"Where the hell is he? Honey, do you promise you won't be like her, his mother the bitch, in Florida?"

"If you get me my own room. Let's splurge."

"Hello?" He was giggling. "It's not my fault. She won't wear the hearing aid."

"I know, I know, I heard all about it. So Mom said the kidneys are worse."

"Herb adjusted the medication. It's going to be fine."

"Are you depressed?"

"Do you mean do I think I'm going to drop dead?" he snapped. "Are you waiting for me to die?"

"Not really. Sorry. I just thought—"

"So what do you think of the senator?" He was still petulant. My father, like most members of his sex, was most scathing when he was really just hurt or scared.

"Dad, that's what people do, men and women. It's none of our business."

"That's a cliché. That's New York bullshit."

"Maybe it is New York bullshit and I talk in clichés. I can't help it, that's where I live, what can I do? Anyway, what else is going on?"

"Your mother and I had to go to a party. Maryann Adams's eightieth birthday party." He was giggling again. "She's been underground for a year, but her husband threw it anyway. She loved your mother. The WASPs, they all love your mother."

"They had a party and she's dead?"

"I think it's a WASP thing. No cake, though . . . no one to blow out the candles."

"Damn, I could've used that for my grief article . . . Dad? I have to go. I'm meeting your son for dinner."

I had to get out of the loft fast. When the phone rang, I took measured breaths before I answered.

"I've never been so despondent."

"What happened? You were fine yesterday. Oh, was the date a nightmare?"

"*Comme çi, comme ça.* I really thought he had potential. He seemed okay . . . the first two dates. He even has a job. With an income. I mean, he's nobody anyone would know, but he's starting to get around. But he talks nonstop about his feelings. You know, he's in therapy."

"I'd rather go out with an alcoholic than with someone who's in therapy."

"It's not funny."

"I'm sorry, but, Rachel, you admitted you didn't even really like the guy. Why waste time tearing your hair out?"

"It's not just that. Jean hasn't called."

"Oh, that's different. I'm meeting my brother tonight if you want some distraction. And my neighbor and Victor said they might show up."

"Really?" Rachel thought my neighbor and Victor were exotic. "Oh, maybe I will. I have a little work left to do. On guess what? The jazz book. Actually I have to call him about something. Maybe it would be better if I have Perry deal with him."

"Oh, no, that would be even more of a disaster. So, are you coming?"

"I have to have a drink with Jacqueline first. She's here from London; I told you about her. She's really cool, she only goes out with black men."

"Rachel, that's not cool, that's sick!"

"Why is that sick? Oh, forget it. Where should I meet you guys?"

"We're just going down the street."

"I'll meet you at eight-thirty. Are you sure Victor's going to be there?"

"As sure as you can be with Victor."

I ran out of the house. It was a premature departure, but I could count on my brother to match it. It was better to keep moving. Movement prevented flashbacks. Summer had become the season for flashbacks. One hit me on the way down the street. I guess I wasn't moving fast enough. Dwelling on things, it was a terrible habit, a terrible curse. I started walking faster, almost running. I could see my brother slumped on the bench outside waiting.

14

YOU COULD FEEL THE HOT CRANKY SUMMER NIGHT INFILTRATE THE RES-taurant even though it was quite frigid inside. Determinedly styl-ish women of all ages were crammed in groups of five or six at tables for two or three, while the bar area was flooded with men in suits, of all ages, too, I suppose—it was harder to tell. I conducted my search by rote, the search for a man, slight but im-perious, in khaki or navy-blue linen.

My brother muttered a ritual of weak protests: Why did I in-sist on coming here every single time? It was freezing! Why was it so crowded tonight? What if we missed the cop show? I reminded him that I always got free drinks here—and that my neighbor might stop by.

"Oh, really?"

"And Rachel's coming."

"That should be good."

"And Victor."

"Even better. How do those two get along?"

"Rachel gets off on Victor, and she could really help him. Just relax." He was usually the one telling me to relax. There was definitely something wrong. His brown eyes, usually semi-murky like mine, were much murkier tonight.

"So how about Demi and Bruce?" he said. "They're history."

"Oh, I know, I heard. I don't care, I hate them both. But they're still good friends."

"Yeah, right. You know Tom and Nicole could be headed for trouble."

"Do you think so? Do you believe that?"

"I believe everything. I mean, they've been cooped up in fucking England for a year."

"Ummm, maybe. So when is Ramona coming?"

"She's still not sure. Yesterday she told me tomorrow night. Today she said she didn't know. It's hard to tell." His voice became guarded, almost unintelligible.

"Is work keeping her there?"

"Not exactly."

"Can't get a flight?"

"Well, no . . . at least I don't think so. I'm not sure what it is. It doesn't really matter. She'll get here." He wouldn't meet my eyes.

I hesitated. "The cult didn't resurface, did it?"

His mouth barely moved when he finally spoke. "I'm afraid to ask."

"Oops. Now we're in real trouble. What makes you think so?"

"She's got that weird sound in her voice—it's a little too light and lively for my taste. Those long-distance phone calls are deadly. All you can hear are the dollars ticking away. I don't know, I kind of think she may be seeing someone else, maybe a cult member. She even, well, not exactly, but she brought up, just mentioned it, real offhand, the wedding, postponing it. Not canceling it, I mean, she just mentioned it, it was casual, very casual. Don't breathe a word of this to them. Dad already hates her, I'm sure."

"Oh, no, he doesn't," I lied. "He told me tonight that he liked her. I talked to them right before I came. He said she was sweet and—"

"Bullshit. He wouldn't have used that word. Who wouldn't he hate? You don't like her, either, do you?"

"I do, I do . . ."

"What about Mom, what did she say?"

"She said be grateful that I won't have to pimp for you anymore. Oh, she's thrilled. Are you kidding? No, actually, Mom is so mad at me she won't notice anyone else. I have to have fun on that stupid trip if it kills me."

"If you don't, we might be able to get you by on a technicality." His eyes were clearing. "Do you want another drink? Are you sure they're going to be free?"

"At least one'll be free."

"So why's she pissed at you?"

"I admitted I was depressed and I wouldn't tell her why."

"Oh, big mistake. Well, what *is* going on?"

"It's too humiliating. He invited me to Paris. We were supposed to go in a few days, and I haven't even heard from him. And I actually believed him."

"Oh. Hmmmm. Paris. I'm going to be there next month. That's where the tour starts—remember I told you about that new club? The one that pays." He didn't notice my expression. "You never heard from him again after he invited you? Wow, that's bizarre."

"It's pathetic."

"Jesus. Well, why don't you tell him to fuck off?"

"I will, I'm just immobilized. I haven't been myself . . ."

"You're not in love with him, are you? You're not that stupid."

"Of course not. Don't even use that expression. The baby thing, I think that makes it seem—"

"God, I'm getting drunk. Maybe you are and you don't know it. Well, do you care more about what happens to him than to you?" It was such an innocent, prepsychology question that I couldn't comprehend it at first, and then I couldn't answer.

"Here comes the waiter. You sure you don't want another drink? Oh, there's Rachel." He couldn't hide his relief. Silent communication had its pluses. "That was quick."

Rachel was looking saucy, in tight pants and a low-cut T-shirt. By the time she had negotiated her way through the crowd, I was ready. There is nothing like a common gene pool for renewal of the spirits. She threw her arms around my brother, delivered the double kiss, and turned to me.

"I came straight here; I couldn't wait to tell you. Jean called before I left and we talked for a long time, and don't tell a soul, but we're talking about . . . you know."

"Why?" flew out of my mouth before I could catch it.

"What do you mean why?" My brother got up hastily and headed for the bathroom. "We're in love, of course."

"But you've been together for less than six months and you were in huge fights most of that time. I mean, it's great, but maybe you should wait a little longer."

"For what? If it doesn't work out, at least I can say I've been married."

I reached for my drink.

"I know we're late." My neighbor was out of breath, rumpled shirttails flying out of his khaki shorts. Victor couldn't have been more collected, debonair in his pale gray pedal pushers and a lavender vest. He almost looked normal, except that his forelocks were nearly to his shoulders. Rachel cozied right up to him, fondling his vast array of necklaces with one hand, the other fluttering at her breast.

My neighbor looked drained. "We couldn't get out of that party; it was hell. What a crowd. There was this slutty publicist who kept talking about ten-million-dollar deals and fifteen-million-dollar deals . . . and that artist, that fat Jewish one with the uptight bend-over-and-kiss-my-ass husband, they were there. I talked to the old doctor who didn't seem to know anyone, and then I watched the white people get drunk. You know how their faces get all red and splotchy? Then they were off to some new restaurant in Brooklyn that I'd never even heard of, and they were all freaked out that I hadn't been there. What do they think, I'm running back to Brooklyn every chance I get to commune with my people? Fuck no. There's plenty here. As if they'd let my ashy black ass into that restaurant anyway."

My brother had returned sheepishly, and he and my neighbor began baiting each other immediately. I'd put more than a little forethought into choreographing this dinner, and it seemed to be working out beautifully. I leaned back to stake out new arrivals. Neighborhood relics were beginning to stumble in, grumbling about the heat. Among them was Sam, who directed his first remark at Rachel: "Hey, you're dressed like you're looking to score tonight."

Before she could retort, I interjected, "What are you doing here?"

"I'm gonna meet the schoolteacher. She wants me to pay her for sex."

"You're really hitting bottom. How much?"

"Two-fifty."

"Wow."

"I thought it sounded interesting. Who knows? She might not even show up."

"If she doesn't, you can always come to Deejay Night."

"Maybe. I'm supposed to meet up with my girlfriend later."

Sam was a big talker. I left him to Victor, who looked like he

wanted to hear more, and as soon as we'd eaten, I said my good-
byes. My neighbor followed me to the door and said nonchalantly,
"Don't come to Deejay Night if you've got other plans."

I tripped through the door. How could I fool anyone else if I
could no longer fool myself?

●

There were a couple of breathy hang-ups on the machine. I went
straight to the chilled sanctuary, took a minor sleeping potion, and
set the alarm for eleven-thirty. With the proper sedation, I could
get in an hour's nap before Deejay Night. Fifteen minutes later I
followed up with a major potion. By the time the phone rang I was
almost there.

"Hey, I'm downtown."

"Huh?"

"It's me. Am I disturbing you? You sound like you're asleep."

"Oh, no . . . I was kind of trying to take a nap, but I don't think
it's going to work. I'm going out later—it's Deejay Night."

"What the hell is Deejay Night?"

"Oh, my neighbor deejays on Thursday nights. It doesn't start
till later, so I was just trying to rest."

"How late?"

"Midnight."

"Oh. I was calling to see if you'd like to go out for a drink, but
it sounds like you're busy—maybe some other time."

"No, no, I don't have to go out till later."

"No, you're busy. Another time, perhaps."

"No, really. I can go there as late as I want. I don't have to get
there until . . . I have time to see you, it's fine."

"All right then. How should we do this?"

"You could come down here, I mean, all those bars downstairs. Where are you exactly?"

"Thirteenth Street. I'll come by to pick you up."

I stumbled over one of the pink shoes on the way to the bathroom. I was discombobulated but in a speedy way. You would think I'd have been slowed down by the evening's accumulation of alcohol and sleeping potions. But the truth was I couldn't remember the last time I'd been slowed down. I took a quick shower to calm myself and got dressed.

•

"You're all dressed up for Deejay Night." The idea that I might have dressed for him was too risky to consider; instead he tried to hide his pleasure with a look of amusement.

"No, I'm not. I've had this on all day. Business in midtown. Do I have everything? Where are my keys? Do you see my keys?"

I kept busy moving around the kitchen, and he shifted back when I came close. I'd never seen him in a T-shirt and jeans before, like he was trying to be cool.

"What are you listening to?" He pointed to the Walkman on the kitchen table.

"Oh, you know, my favorite tunes. All my hits."

"No, I don't know. What are your hits?"

"Do you see my keys?"

"You're so cryptic."

"Oh, here they are. Should we go?"

"Who's this?" He pointed to a picture on the refrigerator.

"Should we go?"

"So what kind of music does your neighbor spin?"

"You go first so I can lock the door. Oh, good stuff mostly."

"Big crowd?"

"It's a tiny bar. I don't really know who goes there. I just know the regulars, my neighbors' friends. They're my Thursday-night friends."

He laughed—it was a little forced—and paused on the landing. I stepped around him and kept going.

"Do you have Friday-night friends?"

"Nope. Position's open. Which bar should we go to? It's so crowded out here tonight. It's awful."

"How about here?" We were in front of the downstairs bar, and I said, "No, I hate that place, the guy who owns it is disgusting. He's opened three bars on this corner. I think they started as drug fronts. He used to be a drug dealer. He probably still is."

"So what if he's a drug dealer? You sound like a tight-ass yuppie."

I followed him into the bar. "It's just that his dealers used to live in my building and I heard them all night; they drove me crazy. No, I don't want to stay here. I hate this place."

I was all red and sweaty, and it wasn't from the heat. Yuppie! I wasn't the one with a couple of nightclubs, the fashionable wife, and the kid, an ex-wife and another kid, and who knows, miscellaneous progeny scattered around the globe, and no doubt a fleet of cars, and probably a country house or two.

"It's so stuffy. Let's just go to the place across the street, okay?"

There were two bars across the street. One was trying to be exclusive and sophisticated with a doorman and an opulent decor, but all the velvet loveseats and brocade curtains and ebony tables in the world didn't muffle the scream of crass money. The bar next door, which I had suggested, was large and barren like a cowboy bar you would imagine out West, but without the character. The walls were all window, and I could see all of three people inside.

We sat at the bar, and he ordered drinks for both of us. I looked over at him for clues, and he stared back empty-eyed.

"So where were you when you called?"

"At a stupid dinner."

"I went to a stupid dinner, too."

"Guess who's playing tonight? At that new club uptown." He wouldn't tell me, and when I grabbed his arm he pulled it away. It was only when I gave up that he told me.

"Oh, you're kidding! Really?"

"I have to check out the place, you know, competition. I was planning to take you, but you probably don't have enough time."

"That'd be great. Maybe we could even dance!"

"I'm too old to dance."

"You weren't too old to dance three months ago."

"Well, I am now. Anyway, you don't have enough time."

"I have enough time. I told you, I don't have to go till later."

"No, there's not enough time. And you told me your neighbor gets upset if you show up late. You don't want to hurt his feelings."

"Joseph, come on."

"And you don't want to be late for your Thursday-night friends."

"Joseph."

"All right, you can come. But you can only stay for two songs, maybe three."

"Four."

"If you're extra good, I'll let you stay for five."

We both looked down, sober again.

"What'd you have to do in midtown today?"

"The beauty editor wanted to see me, about the new assignment. Remember, I told you I got a new assignment."

"What's the new assignment?" He was real casual and took a long swallow of his drink.

"Oh, it's dumb, not worth going into."

"Tell me. I'm interested." He fixed the stare on me.

"Why was your dinner so bad?"

"You big liar."

"It takes one to know one." He didn't smile. "Okay. I wasn't in midtown today for business. I was in midtown yesterday for business. Business that is none of your business. I don't want to talk about it, all right?"

"Why didn't you tell me?"

"What does it matter? I told you I was doing this a long time ago. You just forgot. You have the ability to summon up memory loss at the drop of a hat. What's the point of talking about it? What's there to say? I never imagined that . . . that . . . I'd be remarked upon. Don't worry, you're safe. It . . . it was uncomfortable for me, all right? That's all."

Then the voice came out of nowhere. "I'm teasing you. Come on. Talk to me."

I couldn't. If I could have talked, I would have talked.

"Come on. Say something." I went blank, so he went on. "I don't know how you feel. If it weren't for the baby thing, you know, we never would have gotten . . . started with this . . . this . . . friendship. What about that? Look at me. Tell me something. Hey, don't do this . . ."

"I have a shy streak. I get tongue-tied."

"That's not it. No, that's not it at all. You talk. You talk plenty."

"No, really I do. Have a shy streak. I'm sorry. Just don't torture me about it. It's not on purpose." I wanted more than anything to tell him, to tell him what I was thinking—or feeling—but I still wasn't exactly sure what that was. Sure, at that very instant I was thinking, what is he getting at with this talk about a "friendship" that never would have happened? Sure, it disturbed me, made me feel diminished, perhaps irrationally, and sure, I would have liked to respond: "Oh, do you fuck all your friends?" But that wasn't what I wanted to say. I also knew better than to tell him what I was thinking or, worse, feeling, even if I knew exactly what that was. He didn't want to hear what I wasn't exactly sure I wanted to tell him. He just thought he did tonight.

In a predicament such as ours you needed one, at least one participant to be all starry-eyed, to harbor grand illusions. If you had at least one, it wouldn't be so hard to string the other along, to take the risks, to play it out. Oh, sure, we harbored some of the grand illusions—we wouldn't be here otherwise—but neither of us harbored enough.

"I'm scared."

"What?"

"I'm scared." I whispered a little louder.

"Scared of what, for God's sake?" If he had used the right voice, I would have been able to explain. I would have been able to explain that the grand illusions might escalate if this kept up—and that scared me.

"I . . . I . . . have secret thoughts. Look, don't you have secret thoughts? That you don't tell me? Don't you?" His nod was almost imperceptible.

"So I clam up. I can't help it. I just can't. It's not on purpose."

"It's okay." He was zipped up tight again. He finished his drink. "Do you want another one?"

"I don't know. Do you?"

"I don't want one. If you don't want one, don't have one—I'm not forcing you."

"No, I'll have one."

I put my hands on his knees beseechingly, but he didn't move forward, so I had to lean so far that I came partway off my bar stool. He gave in gratefully, and the bartender stared when he brought my drink. Joseph Pendleton stared right back at him with his most scathing I-dare-you expression, and I sat back on my stool.

"You're upset about the show."

"No. I'm just sick of being a failure."

"You're not a failure."

"I feel that way now."

"Listen, the trip to Paris is off. I'm not going."

"You're not as good as you think." I grinned.

"All right, it is happening." His shame came out low and husky. "It's just not . . . it's just not a good time."

"Okay." A scrupulously unrepentant liar, he respected a good detective and actually appreciated being caught, but I didn't want to know the truth and I looked down again.

"You're not a failure."

"I'm not saying it so you'll tell me I'm not. I know it's luck, but I'm sick of getting my hopes up. I'm sick of not having money. I'm completely broke right now."

"Then what were we talking about Paris for?" He hurled the words with venom. Joseph Pendleton, he was as explosive as a tropical storm, certainly as explosive as one that was then erupting in sheets of beaded curtains against the bar windows.

"Credit cards of course." I laughed into my new drink. "When did we talk about it? You must be confusing me with someone else. The other night you invited me, I said okay, and tonight you said it was off. Unless I've forgotten. Remind me, when did we talk?"

"Who pays for your fancy loft? Your parents?"

"You're the only person I know who considers it a fancy loft. I've told you, it's dirt cheap. You don't listen to me."

"I do listen to you."

"No, you don't, not when you don't want to hear it. You listen selectively. It's okay. Feel free to persist in your fantasy that I'm a princess. I'm just letting you know you're wrong."

"You're just spoiled."

"In a way I am. But you can be spoiled in different ways. I was spoiled with love, not money."

"Don't live beyond your means. It's stupid. You're not a kid anymore. You'll regret it." He spoke tersely. "What about the show in Paris? Your work is more European anyway—you could do well—you don't know."

"Yeah, maybe, but it's not a sure thing."

"You just need a good dealer who's behind the work and can really sell it. Why don't you try—"

"Don't tell me how to make it in the art world. I've been doing it for almost fifteen years, and I know what I'm doing. The problem is I just can't kiss ass anymore. I don't know . . . Don't you ever feel like you can't do it anymore?" We looked at each other for a while—as equals, for the first time—and that caused us both to look away abruptly.

"Well, all right, it is arbitrary, I agree, and there is a lot of luck involved, but you can help it happen."

"You've been in a position of power for too long. You've forgotten what it's like not to be. I didn't start out feeling this way, but it adds up . . . I mean, it's understandable that you—"

"No, I haven't forgotten. Look, it's gutsy—"

"It's not gutsy, it's dumb."

He reached his hand under the flimsy dress so deftly that I didn't notice until I felt his fleeting touch. I looked away.

"Well, do you want to go see this band?"

"I don't know. It's kind of late, don't you think?" The concert was no longer a priority. No, all I wanted now was to get us both back across the street and back up the stairs.

"You're the one who's going out till four in the morning."

"Joseph, I never stay that late, I told you. I do want to go, but . . . sometimes those concerts are only really fun for the first twenty minutes, you know? You never can tell if it's going to be depressing with these old bands—they might not be so good."

"Yeah, I guess." He was disappointed. He had wanted to take me out on a date—a date would make it all seem less criminal, less urgent.

"I have their records at my apartment. Maybe we should just go back there."

He nodded resignedly and paid the bill without so much as an I-dare-you look at the bartender, who didn't even attempt to hide his disgust for us. The tropical storm had petered out into something between a wet fog and a light drizzle. It didn't deter the delirious crowds, or me, for that matter. I floated across the street like it was noon on a spring day. He didn't. He looked like he was going to the devil.

"Joseph, do you think I'm a cliché?" That made him smile.

"Sure. You're a complexity of clichés. But that's all right, everybody's a cliché."

"Maybe I won't even go to Deejay Night."

"You have to go. You don't want to disappoint your neighbor. Or your Thursday-night friends. Won't they be disappointed?"

"I doubt it. Most of them won't even notice. Victor, he wouldn't notice."

"Is that the guy you were with the night . . . Who is that guy? What does he do?"

"Artist."

"Does he know about this—us?"

He sneaked it in real flip, and I was caught off guard because I was floating. "Um, well, yeah, I guess he does. He's actually a photographer, you might like . . ."

We were separated trying to get through the crowd on my corner, so I couldn't finish. Nor did we speak while I searched for my keys or walking up the stairs. The summer air accompanied us through the door in waves, devious waves. It trapped us in the kitchen until I couldn't stand anymore and I leaned against the refrigerator and then I grasped the door handle.

Once we were in my room, he said, "Talk to me," in the voice that I couldn't not obey, and I talked. He talked back. He murmured, "I want you to be my baby." His voice cracked on "baby"— it was hard for him to say it, and to make it easier so he'd say it again, I didn't say back, "I want you to be mine."

I whispered instead, "Oh, I am!"

It didn't feel like a phony cornball line the way he said it, and if it was, I didn't care. It didn't matter because he wasn't able to obey his rules tonight. Usually I could feel his rules holding him back. I could feel the weight of his rules just around the edges, a certain propriety, not for my benefit but for someone else's. Tonight there was not a trace of it. There was something else in the air that made it like the first night, except that it was more—

and it was less, but in a way that still felt like more—because there'd been too many nights in between that we couldn't ignore, no matter how hard we tried.

But the propriety returned. It was a shame because I knew what I wanted to tell him now and I was ready but he moved away and when I tried to keep some piece of him, whatever was available, he took it away and then he got up and left the room. I lay there for as long as I could. He was sitting in the bright kitchen with his face in his hands.

"What's wrong?" I whispered. When he didn't answer, I continued, "You're all sweaty," and gently brushed away the sweat on his back with my hands.

"Yeah. I'm just going to sit here for a few minutes and dry off." His voice was distant, and his hands remained over his face.

I went back and tried to close my eyes. He followed momentarily, assumed the sign-of-the-cross position, and fell asleep. He slept heavily, although not so heavily that he didn't shake me off like a bug each time I tried to touch him. I lay beside him like wood. My body was still and sated, but my mind was spinning fast, and my heart was racing. I got up and went out to the couch and sat in the dark. It wasn't pitch black. In fact there was an eerie amount of light for this time of night, a six-bars-on-one-corner light.

Everything would be fine once I got to Deejay Night. I just had to get there and everything would be okay. Rachel was probably waiting for me—what time was it?—and she would be worried. My neighbor would be wondering where I was. He wouldn't be worried but he would be wondering. My brother might actually be worried. I hated it when he fell asleep, and I hated even more waking him up. If only we'd made it to the couch. He never fell asleep on the couch. It was the bed that scared him to sleep.

Finally I got back in bed and whispered, "I have to go soon—to Deejay Night."

Eyes closed, he mumbled, "Yeah, yeah. Soon, soon, a few more minutes." So I reached over to the night table for a sleeping potion—sleep would really be my best bet. If only I could sleep, too. For once I wasn't even worried about whether he would get in trouble with her. If she got upset, she would just have to pedal extra hard at the gym tomorrow. I got out of bed again and stared out the window in the other room, considering my course of action.

I went back in for another half hour, and then I crawled onto his chest again: "Joseph, I have to go soon."

"Okay, I'll get up in a minute. Baby, go back to sleep."

I could take another shower. I'd be fresh for Deejay Night. Instead I got up and opened and shut the drawers loudly, stomping around the room. He didn't stir. No, he did stir. He sprawled out wider until he took up the whole bed. I squeezed back into position, in a clean white T-shirt and a pair of pants. What am I going to tell Rachel? Oh, she wouldn't care; she must have left by now anyway. Still, I had to get out of here, I thought. No, I had to get out of this. That was closer to the truth. I had to get out of this, and Deejay Night was a start.

The third time he tried to stave me off with his hands. "We'll get up in a little while. Why don't you start getting dressed?"

"I am dressed." I said it in a small voice. He didn't answer. I lay back down, and then I returned to the couch to wait the requisite half hour. It was so late there was really no point in going. There was no way Rachel would be there, she was home planning the wedding by now; my brother wasn't really going to worry; my neighbor would know, and he would look at me with disappointed, disapproving eyes, and Victor would be off in a blank daze. But I had to get there now, if only to prove to myself and him that I was still mine. That I never was or would be his.

"Joseph, I really have to go. It's late."

I stood at the foot of the bed and hardly got the words out before he snarled, a sleepy snarl, but what a snarl: "Just go then, if you have to go! Just leave me alone. Can't you leave me alone?"

I left him alone. I wasn't his, but I wasn't mine either. When I went back in, before I had time to speak, he whispered in a low voice I'd never heard before, "I'm sorry, I'm really sorry."

He lifted himself up, sat on the far side of the bed, and looked down, and instead of going to him, I panicked. He'd never actually said, "I'm sorry," at the moment when it would make a difference. Instead, he said, "My deepest apologies," politely, frostily, after the fact, if all else failed. For the same reason, perhaps, that I went mute at the moment when it would make a difference, when it might move us forward. But I didn't go to him. I stood frozen far away and whispered fast, "It's okay, it's okay. Do you want to be by yourself to wake up? I'll just leave you alone for a few minutes."

That's what he wanted, wasn't it? To be left alone? Only the faintest glow from the streetlights shone through the windows when I resumed position on the couch.

"Hello?"

I heard his hollow, weak voice—he didn't say my name—and I answered something.

"Joseph, I'm out here," or "Yeah," or "What?"—I can't remember. I didn't say it very loud, nor did I get up right away. I imagined he'd stop in the bathroom, and I wanted to give him some time to be alone. So I took my own time walking back through the pitch dark to the kitchen. It was empty when I got there, and at first I stood and stared. I looked in the bathroom, and then it hit me. He was gone. He'd left. He'd left without saying good-bye. I didn't necessarily need words, but tonight I needed to see his eyes. I grabbed my raincoat. Only a few moments had gone by. Or had it been more than a few? I jumped the stairs two, three at a time, and then I ran to the corner where he always got a cab.

It was still drizzling, and it was just me standing on the empty corner in the raincoat that had cost me time. A cab stopped instantly.

Only Victor and Sam were still at Deejay Night. My neighbor was packing up, and he couldn't help himself when he saw me.

"You look beautiful!" he said wide-eyed, not at all disapproving.

I sank between Victor and Sam, and they listened to me while I disobeyed the rules. I had no trouble disobeying the rules tonight because he'd disobeyed them first.

"Oh, he split because he thought you did," Victor said matter-of-factly. "He probably thought you were pissed-off. I wouldn't bring it up next time you see him. Just forget about it."

"He thought I left?"

"Of course, what did you think? He took the pussy and ran?" Sam yawned. "No one would do that, not at this stage of the game."

"He thought I left?"

They just looked at each other. My neighbor came over and said, "I'm ready. Let's go."

So it was my fault. Of course. In his eyes, it was always going to be my fault. That's the way it had to be. In his eyes, that is.

CHAPTER

15

"I GUESSED, SO IT DOESN'T COUNT."

"Well, if I'm struck down from above, or found dead in an alley, you'll know why. I don't even care anymore."

"You don't care about which: the black boulder or being struck down or found in an alley?"

"I don't care about any of it." Oh, I cared about Thursday night's debacle and the subsequent silent fallout, but my neighbor didn't need to know that. "It's over. I'm sick of it. You are, too. Tell me about you."

"I told you. The usual. That review I just slaved over, they killed it because I trashed the artist and she's the new colored messiah. She's bi, too—and a feminist. Could you ask for anything more?"

"Not that I can think of. They must've thought they hit the jackpot—and then you screwed them up."

"Yeah, they finally found themselves a colored messiah safe

enough for the advertisers, but I was uppity—and I betrayed my people. At least I got paid the full amount—I mean, I will get paid . . . what's your estimate as to when?"

"Three to four months. If you start now and call them every day."

"And I told you, didn't I? I think I've got a new deejay gig— one that actually pays at the end of the night. Whoring myself again. But dumbing down music is easier than dumbing down writing."

"I guess."

"It's that new club down here. It's pretty faggy."

"That place? Oh, yeah, my beauty editor's been there every night this week—where fags go, you know what follows. But I thought you'd never been there."

"I lied. Anyway, it starts even later than Deejay Night."

"I'll get there. I'll bring Hank. He's been calling lately. I thought he had a girlfriend, but it must have gone sour already."

"He's not so bad. Hey, your brother's finally broken me—I'm doing a piece on his band."

"You don't have to do that. I'll just make up some excuse—"

"I know I don't have to. I want to. Anyway, I've pitched the idea, and it might be fun—it would be a way to get out of this inferno. They'd pay for me to follow him on tour. We were talking about hooking up in Paris."

"Oh."

"Did I say something?"

"It's just that, it's just that I haven't heard a word and . . ."

"It's okay. You're allowed. Just . . . hey, are you there?"

". . . I can't explain, I mean I can't and I can't . . . oh, let's not get into that. I mean, he still thinks I just left, after that night. I left a message at his office, but . . . and then it was Saturday, I couldn't call, and he's out of town. Anyway, by now he's figured out a way to blame it on me, or he's feeling too guilty . . ."

"Guilty? Did you ever confirm the white blood? Maybe it's Jewish."

"The disappearance act sure isn't Jewish."

"Well, maybe he's Catholic. The blame thing is a black thing. I told you before. It's cultural."

"I'm sick of hearing about the black thing."

"Then find yourself a fat Jewish professor. What happened with David Mendelsohn? I told you he was interested in you, not me. He fooled me at first with the fag act, but I had a feeling."

"It's the art world; they'll go either way if it makes a sale."

"No, I think he just does the fag act because it's easier to pick up girls."

"Probably both. I have to have dinner with him before I go to Florida."

"Good luck. Anyway, blame and black men—it's survival."

"I know. Actually, though, I can think of several Jewish male blamers."

"With the Jews, the blame gets mixed in with their tedious guilt; it's harder to identify."

"Do WASPs blame? I don't think so."

"What's there to blame? What can go wrong? A stubbed toe? Couldn't get to Maine this summer? It's like when a black person says they have no money and they really don't, but when a white person says it, they actually have at least five thousand in the bank. I'm sure the boulder will touch down."

"No, he won't."

"Why? You never know."

"No. No, my feeling is you do know. You always know."

•

There was an unpleasant scene with the beauty editor over my grief piece before I left for Florida. Surely she meant well, but when she suggested that I include more details about the funeral home on Madison—did they accept credit cards, what was the average income bracket of the deceased, who was responsible for the fabulous urn that transported the ashes of the dead shoe designer—I snapped, "Who the hell cares?"

"Okay, forget it!" she hissed back. "Just forget it. If you don't want to write for the highest-profile women's magazine in the country, then don't. Do you know what? Seventy percent of our readers have six-figure incomes! Six-figure incomes! And Ivy League–educated—forty percent! Forty goddamn percent, does that mean anything to you? Does it?"

No, it didn't. But I backed down immediately, motivated by pure avarice: I wanted to get paid. I changed the subject. "By the way, I met a friend of yours, you know, through the film I'm doing, well, sort of a film," I explained.

"Oh, she's terrific."

"She seems terrific."

"Great-looking, too."

"Oh, yeah, great."

"I've missed her at the gym lately. You know what it's like getting to the gym—and she never usually misses a day. She's in great shape, isn't she in great shape? And those big beautiful eyes, you know?"

"Great shape. Beautiful eyes. So she hasn't been around?"

"Oh, no, she's been in Paris. She lived there for a few years—just moved back."

"Funny, she didn't say anything about leaving last week. And she seemed anxious for me to finish the script. Maybe I can take a few extra days."

"I'm trying to remember . . . we worked out together that morning, Thursday, I think. She was going to the airport after she picked up her kid—what a doll he is. I was in such pain through the weekend. Two massages I had to have."

•

I met David Mendelsohn for dinner right after the editing session. I encouraged him to choose the restaurant, so we sat outside in a greener-than-usual cement garden behind a new restaurant in Little Italy where young entrepreneurs were on a development binge, gobbling up properties faster than I could gobble up the oysters David Mendelsohn ordered. We talked business. I recited the results of the show: "Two paintings were sold—not bad for a dying art form. Paintings are so impossible to sell these days, aren't they?"

"I think we're about to see a change," he assured me. "Painting is coming back," he continued, leaning forward. "There's no doubt in my mind."

"They were sold to fairly decent collectors," I added, "and some large drawings were sold"—to friends of mine, but I left that detail out—"and now the dealer is back in town. You never know—a lot can happen in the month after a show." Except during the month of August, when everyone's out of town, but I left that part out, too.

"Absolutely," David Mendelsohn said with a dismissive wave of his hand. "That's not bad, not bad at all, why it's good, very good—for these days."

"Oh, and some decent reviews are due to come out in the art magazines, not that anyone reads them."

"Not true, not true, that's absolutely not the case. They read them in Europe," he assured me. A very reassuring fellow, David Mendelsohn. He refilled my wineglass for emphasis. "No, that's a definite plus."

"But no reviews in the paper. A disappointment."

David Mendelsohn agreed. He agreed with everything I said. "I know it's old-fashioned, but I personally believe it is a dealer's responsibility, his duty, to buy at least one painting from a gallery artist's show," he declared. The first bottle of wine was gone, and his speech was jumbled.

"That's nice to hear." I nodded enthusiastically, wondering

why, if that was the case, he hadn't purchased a painting, perhaps as a vote of confidence, from the show of a freshly anointed gallery artist—or at least scammed a good deal from her studio now that the show was down.

The second bottle of wine had arrived, and David Mendelsohn continued in a booming voice: "I pay my artists within days of a sale's conclusion, without fail. Any of my artists will tell you: I never ever wait until I receive payment from collectors—unlike some dealers." He glanced over at me after this speech and I gave an encouraging nod. "Collectors can be so impossible," he added, glancing at me again for confirmation.

"Right. Oh no, thank you, no more wine for me. I'll fall asleep. I've had a long day."

"And I want you to know up front that I'm responsible for all the costs of the show—ads, shipping, framing, what have you. You have my word. Travel expenses, your accommodations—you won't be responsible for a dime."

"Great."

Granted, David Mendelsohn had a pompous streak, and enhanced by drink it came perilously close to insufferable, but he really wasn't that bad for an art dealer. I would have liked to lap up his promises, and not so very long ago I might have, but tonight I suggested a contract, spelling out our mutual obligations in cold black ink.

"So there won't be any misunderstandings after the show—you know how things get confused after a show," I said, smiling. "It's always seemed odd to me that so few dealers believe in contracts."

"Isn't it?" he said, shaking his head. He beckoned to our waitress, who regarded him with a resigned just-another-asshole expression on her face. He whispered something in her ear, then after she fled, leaned in closer with a lewd grin: "Enough talk about business. Let's have champagne to celebrate."

He gulped down the champagne—I faked gulping—and said how fortunate it was that the heat wave had broken before he returned to Paris. The trip had been very productive, and there'd been some good times partying.

"Oh, that's nice."

"Reasonably good times," he repeated in a low voice. "Not quite the kind of partying I'm accustomed to. You understand, I'm sure."

"Afraid I don't party much." I searched frantically around the garden in an effort to avoid the face that was looming dangerously close to mine. "What a relief this weather is. In fact I'm a bit chilly—I could use a cup of coffee. Where is that waitress?"

"It's a perfect night," he murmured.

"Where is that waitress?" I repeated. Not that I could really blame her for hiding.

"Really a perfect night," he murmured again with a queer gleam in his eye. My smiles were becoming less tolerant—I couldn't believe this was happening. "A perfect night for . . . wouldn't you like to get laid tonight?"

What a peculiar technique, I thought. But maybe I had the wrong idea.

"Not really." I laughed nervously and added, "I mean, I'm kind of seeing someone, and he's away."

"Oh, I had no idea," he said. "Is it serious?"

"Serious trouble." I laughed again. "A long-distance relationship. I was up at the magazine closing a piece, and I'm exhausted. And you must be exhausted—all this running around. Aren't you exhausted? In fact, forget the coffee. I'm too exhausted."

I declined his offer to share a cab. "Oh, no, thanks, I don't want to take you out of your way. Besides, I need to walk, you know, walk off all that rich food."

As soon as the cab disappeared down Houston, I broke into a feverish trot. David Mendelsohn made Joseph Pendleton look like

Jimmy Stewart. But when he called the next day, I accepted his apology. Surely he meant well.

•

When I related David Mendelsohn's singular method of seduction to Hank, he smirked and said, "Have you ever watched a male dog piss on a fire hydrant?"

Hank and I had tried another evening, and since we were both involved in equally ludicrous alliances—the new girlfriend didn't speak English, and Hank wasn't exactly multilingual—we relaxed our defenses. I decided to take Rachel's advice and give him a chance. I acted like a girl, I looked him in the eye and reminisced about our more triumphant evenings. I even gamely agreed to go to his favorite bar after dinner and then raved over his juke-box selections. It was late and I'd just hailed a cab when we began kissing. This was unprecedented, and I flinched inside. As I got into the cab, he said, "What was that?"

"I have to go," I mumbled. There's more than one kind of deceit when you're dealing with the human condition, and who's to say which is more duplicitous?"

When we spoke the next morning, we agreed that it had been a flight of fancy.

•

"You have to take charge," Rachel scolded the next day. "You've never given him a proper chance."

"Last night I did," I pleaded. "I tried. But it was so fake for both of us."

She let it go, and we resumed the wedding discussion. Rachel had chosen Perry to be her maid of honor, and Perry had accepted gushingly, although she maligned the groom-to-be mercilessly to me on a daily basis. Before I left, Perry had suggested introducing me to a friend of Richard's. I listened until she said, "It's just perfect. He's black, too, except he's our age—" I hung up on her. It was no big deal—she was used to it.

•

The stewardess steamrolled up the aisle with her cart, and when she handed me the cardboard snack box I smiled. She had a voice like the beauty editor's, so it was a wan smile.

The plane was small, thirty passengers at the most. It was like an airborne submarine, so cramped that I couldn't stand up straight without knocking my head on the ceiling, and my knees were smashed nearly chest-level by the seat in front of me. But I didn't care because I was earthbound no longer. I tackled my cardboard snack box with gusto—plane food was one of my favorite forms of cuisine. If I'd been on a jumbo jet with a certain globetrotter, I might have feigned indifference toward a cardboard snack box, but the globetrotter would have seen right through me. And he was currently not alone. She'd left on Thursday with their son, what a doll. So no one had been home on Thursday night. Had he had special plans for us? The stubborn sprawl on the bed, the refusal to wake up, was that part of the plan? If only he'd let me in on it, I would have taken my cue. I would've said, "Yeah, let's go see the band. Let's stay out late, forget about Deejay Night." We would have had plenty of time. But Joseph Pendleton did not share plans or goals, nor did he even admit to having them.

My father looked so shrunken and frail I walked right past him at the gate. In fact I nearly tripped over him. We laughed, but I couldn't help venturing, "Are you sure you're okay?" He snapped back at me, so we shuffled together in silence.

I shuffled a few steps behind him, a habit I'd fallen into over the years, so I could catch him in case he stumbled and fell.

•

It was a two-lane road, lined with droopy tropical foliage and dotted with clusters of high-rises along the ocean side. The buildings within each cluster were indistinguishable, but the clusters themselves were wildly disparate and I would have been hard-pressed to identify the architectural style of any of them. Making their way down dirt paths were pairs of leathery old people, feisty in sweat suits, their arms swinging like privates in the army.

My father's facial expression was inherently grim, but today his lips were pursed tighter than ever. It wasn't until we were almost there that I noticed that the car's interior smelled new and that I was sitting on a red seat instead of a brown one. So he was forced to tell me about the accident.

"Why didn't anyone tell me?" My voice was shrill.

"You were coming down soon anyway. We're fine, we're fine. I think your mother may have a few broken ribs, but she won't have an X ray. I know a guy in town, too, and he's the best. I have some bruises, but I don't dare speak up. It was raining so hard, and the fog, there was a twenty-car pileup. It was just bad luck. It could have happened to anyone."

"You're crazy to keep driving all the way down here."

"She won't listen to me. Do you know the first thing she said after the accident?" He giggled. "She said, 'Oh, Mother of God, the dishes. The case of wine.' She got right out of the car with her broken ribs to check. Only one cup broke, and the wine was fine. Your mother would have had a breakdown—"

"Dad, she's crazy. She's going to kill you both."

"Don't tell her I said anything. Please don't make trouble." He paused to cough. "I've been coughing since we got here. It's strange, I don't have a cold."

"Isn't it just the cardiac cough?"

"That's not a hacking cough. This is a hacking cough. Anyway, I'm on different medication now. Should we stop at the hotel first?"

"No, no, I can go later. Aren't you scared to drive back?"

"A little. Listen, she upgraded you to a Holiday Inn."

"What got into her?"

"Royalty called her cheap."

"Why'd he care where we were staying?"

"Nobody can figure it out. We think Ellen must be slipping him Valium. The kids are really growing up. Audrey's in that awkward stage. She's got the braces and she looks funny, but I think she's gonna be gorgeous. Don't you think she's gonna be gorgeous?"

"If the King doesn't turn her into an anorexic first."

"Oh, her stomach's been fine since she's been here. You know, she loves your mother. And I think Danny is damn clever. Don't you think he's clever?"

"Very clever. What about the Ramona situation?"

"I just keep my mouth shut. I'm afraid to say a word. You know how your brother is when he has a concubine, I mean wife. Should I be saying *wife* yet? They're off by themselves most of the time. They're probably shtupping behind a dune. Your mother's so terrified the kids are gonna find them she can't see straight."

•

Our condo was located in one of two severe beige high-rises. Between them was an impenetrable labyrinth of three-foot-tall beige stone walls. After beige, the primary color in the compound was blue: the candy blue of the twin pools, the blustery blue of the sky, the faded gray-to-green-to-turquoise blue of the ocean in the distance behind a locked gate. It was De Chirico surreal, especially in the off-season.

My mother was in the hallway when the elevator door opened. In her left hand she held the Dustbuster like a spear; with her right she thrust a sandwich at me. My father sneaked past her to his chair, where his newspaper and medical journals lay neatly stacked. In her Speedo, my mother resembled a stork. Her sizable breasts and bulging middle served as either a pivotal axis or a grounding device—I'm not quite sure which—for her long spindly legs and almost equally long spindly arms.

"Oh, honey, the layover, was it a hell on earth? Do you mind taking off your shoes, it's these damn white tiles, forgive me."

I started to open my mouth, but I wasn't quick enough.

"Honey, I was sick, just sick, thinking of the layover. Do you hate me? You must be exhausted. Are you starving? Honey, stuff this sandwich—no, don't even stop to stuff it down—bring it with you to the pool. Hurry. These are prime rays. Quick, change into your suit." She paused to listen to the special weather radio that was clipped onto her Speedo. "There are some clouds coming up from the Caribbean any minute now—cumulonimbus—that means trouble. I beg of you, get down there. They're all down at the pool. Audrey's been waiting for you all morning. She's beside herself."

"Mom, I can't believe you didn't tell me about the accident."

"I told that son of a bitch not to say anything. That pussy, was he complaining? He's fine, just fine. In fact I think it may have knocked some of those slipped discs back into place. The nerve—"

"Why don't you just fly back?"

"It was nothing. Did he happen to mention that not one bottle of wine was scratched? And only one cup broke."

"What about your ribs?"

"That snake in the grass. They're fine, a little tender, but fine. Get in your suit, goddamn it, I see a cumulonimbus approaching."

She bent down to pick up a crumb with a martyred grimace. There was no time to intervene—in order to help my mother with housework of any kind, you had to brutally shove her aside, which wouldn't help her ribs much. She was right behind me, picking up stray articles of clothing from the bedroom floor and the few beige crumbs only she could spy on the beige carpet. "Honey, are you glad you came? I wish you could stay longer. It seems like I haven't seen you in so long."

She tried to muffle a cough by bending to pick up nothing I was able to identify.

"Mom, don't keep bending over. I can't take it. I saw you a couple of months ago—remember, the show? So why won't you go and get the X ray? And how come you and Dad are coughing?"

"I don't know, it's so odd. First Daddy started, and I thought, it's the cardiac cough, but they changed his medication and now I've got it—who the hell knows? By the way, you won't recognize Royalty. You know, honey, I really think he's maturing."

"Mom, he's almost fifty!"

"Oh. Well. Still . . ."

"Why don't you come down to the pool with me?"

"Oh, I've got to make dinner, and . . . you don't know the half of it. Jesus, it's almost one o'clock, prime rays will be over. Get down there. And would you bring these sandwiches down for them? And be nice to Ramona."

•

They were gathered around the pool, each clutching some form of reading material. No family member was able to conduct a conversation without clutching some form of reading material, in case of emergency.

"Hey hey hey, look who's graced us with her presence—in what appears to be a very chic bathing suit." The King turned to my younger brother for assistance, but he didn't react. I guess he was trying to act mature in front of Ramona.

"They said you were on good behavior. What happened?"

"How was the layover?"

"I weathered it. By the way, this bathing suit was free."

"Oh, a perk? Isn't that cute?"

"Where's his Valium?"

Ramona jumped up to hug me. My younger brother nodded and looked sheepish. My brothers and I didn't hug. The only family member who hugged was my mother, who had to be sneaky to catch one of us off guard. My father delivered an old-fashioned kiss on the lips, usually at the beginning and sometimes at the end of each visit. Ellen, who came from a family of fervent huggers, was right behind Ramona. In the pool Audrey and Danny were hanging off my middle brother's body like appendages. I heard him say, "Hey, Audrey, I'll give you five bucks if you get Danny the hell off me," followed by the hysterical on-the-verge-of-a-breakdown giggle he'd adopted back when he lived in our basement and worshipped Charlie Manson.

"Hey, what about that fucking accident? We would have been dividing the goods right now. Dad's scared shitless to drive back with her." The King broke into a coughing spasm.

"What is it with the coughing?" I asked.

He shrugged.

"Can't you talk her into flying back? She might listen to you."

He shrugged again.

The King was one of those people who'd peaked in college: big football star, sixties radical, an intellectual who still had time to drop acid. But after a decade in the city, his career hadn't scaled the heights he'd anticipated and he'd realized that it might not— he didn't have it in him to be a New York asshole. So he changed his focus to his kids. In fact, he was trying to replicate our family group, only he didn't have as big a cast to work with. I was concerned that in his zest he might be in the process of creating two or three kids in one.

I lay down on a lounge chair between the giant blond females, my present and future sister-in-laws. They were my best bets. Not only did they speak in complete sentences, but chances were good that they'd even listen to your response. The kids disentangled themselves from my middle brother to tackle me. My middle brother remained floating in the pool, with a Jesus-like expression, staring out at nothing with his blue eyes. He was the most handsome of my brothers. The only thing marring the perfection was the missing front tooth that my mother always begged him to get fixed. (He always retorted that it was bourgeois to care about a missing tooth. "So I'm bourgeois, I admit it, who's pretending? Who said I was anything else? Please God, you're so handsome, I'll pay for the goddamn tooth," was her comeback.) He sidled up to me on his float, and I leaned down to listen. He muttered, "The key is not to speak unless spoken to. My advice to you is stay as far away as possible from the public domain." I nodded and watched the King try to rally the kids for a game of tennis. Danny wanted to play basketball because my middle brother had accused him of only playing white-boy sports.

"I don't want to go," Audrey said. She was on my upper torso while Danny rested on my legs. "How come you're not staying longer?"

"I've told you before. I'm your weird aunt. Weird aunts are always on the go."

Audrey giggled and settled in more comfortably on top of me. It was a perfect vantage point from which to spy on Ramona, with whom she was entranced. Ramona had her bikini straps pulled down for an even tan so Audrey pulled hers down until her entire eleven-year-old chest was exposed. Watching Audrey grow up was torture. Whenever I tried to act the older sister, to commiserate over her stomach troubles so that maybe she'd confide the real troubles, she'd run off or change the subject. It was too late—she was one of us.

"Kids, I brought some sodas." My mother arrived laden down with much more than sodas. "I can't stay long."

"Here, take a lounge chair." The King got up.

"Oh no, honey, I don't have to lie down. I'm happy sitting."

"Take my chair and lie down, for Christ's sake. We're leaving anyway to play hoops. All your sons together. And your grandson. Doesn't that make you happy?"

"Not particularly." She turned to my youngest brother: "Please God don't break your ankle like last time."

"Too bad the gray pretzel can't get out of his chair, or he could come along and watch," the King continued. "We could prop him up by a tree."

"Oh, honey, would you try to get him out of the chair? He needs some air. Would you mind just going up there?" She couldn't finish because she was wracked by a coughing spasm. "Ramona, what a nice bathing suit." My mother was trying not to peer too closely at Ramona's breasts, which had almost fought their way free of the bikini, European-style.

"Oh, it's so old, it's falling apart. I should really get a new one." Ramona hadn't said much, and I didn't blame her. I was eight or nine before I spoke in complete sentences, much less paragraphs, when the entire family was gathered.

"I have an idea," my mother said. "Let's buy you a new suit for your birthday. We'll go over to the mall. They're having a huge sale. I hate the goddamn mall, but you can get to this store through a side door."

"I think the sale's over," said Ellen. "I took Audrey over there yesterday."

"Aw, no, it couldn't be over. I was just there, wasn't it just yesterday? I could have sworn it was just yesterday." My mother looked perplexed. "They've got to be on sale still, I'm sure it said . . . wasn't it . . . maybe it was . . . well, there's got to be a sale somewhere. I know we'll find one if we go to that other mall."

"Let her get a full-price bathing suit." I couldn't help it. "Jesus, Mom, it's her birthday!"

"Listen to my daughter, the spoiled brat and now a fashion maven. Have I ever begrudged you kids a thing? Ramona, honey, forgive me. Ramona, we'll get you a goddamn full-priced suit."

"Grandma, you swore. Twice."

"Honey, I slipped. Is that a crime against the goddamn nation? Kids, admit it, isn't this heaven? Let's live it up, just us girls. Let's go over to the mall. We'll go in the side entrance. What the hell? Prime rays are over."

"Mom, you three go. I don't want to get back in the car. Ellen and I'll go check out the beach."

The clouds had arrived a little behind schedule, and we huddled on the windy beach under a dune obscured by some scraggly bushes.

"So what's the latest?" Ellen asked.

Ellen was family without the history or agenda or judgments, but still family enough to cast him as the ruthless villain and me as the helpless heroine. I delivered a brief update, and she surprised me.

"I don't know," she said matter-of-factly. "If you think about it, he has more to lose than you do."

I could only cough in reply. Either it was a sympathy cough or I was undone by the implication of her remark—that he might actually have a stake in this.

By dinnertime, everyone was wracked by the hacking coughing spasms. The newlyweds-to-be exchanged a lot of glances while my father and the King berated the latest philandering politician. The King ended the discussion: "She gave good head. But that's a dime a dozen in Washington. Everyone knows the service industry in Washington is like a mink farm. They just club them over the head and drag them away. He made a bad choice, that's all."

After the twelve-minute meal, I tried to help our own personal service industry clean up while she finished her vaudeville act for the kids. Then I sat on the stool watching her do everything I'd done all over again.

When I got back to the hotel I climbed gratefully into the king-sized bed in my pink-and-blue cocoon and turned on the eleven o'clock news. The newscaster reported a curious epidemic that had overtaken a particular five-mile radius of the coast. He called it the red-tide cough. That cleared up one mystery. I kept watching, hoping the newscaster would clear up all my other mysteries, but he didn't.

As I left for the airport late the next evening, my mother asked anxiously, "Honey, we did have a good time, didn't we? We did have some laughs, didn't we? Didn't it feel like a vacation?"

"Yes, yes, it was great," I assured her. "Yes, yes, it was like a vacation." It had resembled a vacation, I thought, but the kind of vacation I needed most—a vacation from myself—was eluding me. Not even my mother, the travel agent, was capable of arranging that kind of vacation.

CHAPTER

16

WHAT A DIFFERENCE A DAY DOES NOT MAKE—EVEN AN EXTRA-LONG
thirty-six-hour day in a beige-and-blue state.

"Try to remember you're having a bad day, not a bad life,"
Aaron advised when she called from the rehab hospital Kojak
was paying for. She'd been sequestered for little more than a
week, and already she was equipped with a stockpile of platitudes. She didn't miss the drinking yet, she said. "They keep you
so damn busy."

"Doing what?"

"Groups, lots of groups. In fact I can't talk long. I'm due at
abuse group in a few minutes because this asshole reported me for
being rude, or maybe she said I was a snob, I can't remember.
They keep you so busy I can hardly remember a thing. I don't
know, something's working—it must be because they scare the
fucking daylights out of you."

My neighbor was suspicious when I told him how well Aaron

was doing. "There has to be some kind of a religion thing going on—God's behind all those places."

"There was a New Age tone to her voice, but she didn't mention anything specific," I said.

"Believe me," he said. "There are some prayers going down somewhere." Or maybe that was my line. I can't remember, which is surprising because I remember most lines spoken to or by me that August. I remember distinctly that the month was taking forever to end, and I remember the silence that greeted me when I returned home from Florida.

You couldn't really call it summer anymore. We were in a holding pattern between seasons, so the balance was off in the city. The poor neighborhoods were too loud and the rich neighborhoods were too quiet. Joseph Pendleton hadn't responded to the message I'd left before I'd gone away and I was pretty sure he was back in town. I was positive she was back in town because the script had been approved. I left another message, not with the secretary this time but on his brand-new "voicemail," a surprising bow to technology, since he prided himself on keeping his office not up-to-date. On the message I stumbled through an abbreviated version of my side of the story for whatever had gone wrong that night, and then I waited for an appropriate amount of time— appropriate for what, I don't know. When I tried again, he answered.

"Oh, hello. Can I call you right back?" He did call me right back, but his tone made my spine go rigid. "I've been out at my Long Island place," he said.

"Oh, that's nice."

"No, it's not nice. Would you call the L.I.E. a nice highway? The commute is a nightmare. I've got so much to do in the city right now that I'm always coming or going at the wrong time, so there's nothing I can do to avoid the traffic."

"Well, maybe it would be easier to take the train? I kind of like the—"

"I wouldn't be caught dead on that filthy train. So what have you been doing?"

"Not much. I was away."

"Where?"

"It was only for a day or two."

"Can you hold on for a minute . . . you were saying?"

"I don't remember. Oh, what I've been doing. Not painting because I got an assignment. I have to write about a day in the life of a cosmetics clerk. No, sorry, they call them aestheticians. What have you been doing?"

"Whatever happened to the dead-shoe-designer article?"

"It came out."

"I'll have to look for it." I didn't tell him that the magazine was a weekly, that the issue was already off the stands.

"Well, can we see each other?" I said instead.

"Not in the near future."

"Near future?"

"I no longer have my evenings free. I'm at the club most evenings, and what with commuting . . . I'm gearing up for September at the club. Fall seems to start earlier every year, doesn't it?"

"No, I hadn't noticed. Well, it's good that you're busy." No evenings free. That had never presented a problem before. No, there had always been afternoons free.

"Not really. It's just a lot of bullshit to deal with. Tedious, really. It's pretty miserable."

"Okay, busy and miserable. Anything else to tell me?"

"What do you mean by that?"

"Well, let's be honest—oh, pardon the expression. You haven't called since . . . in a while. Are you mad about something?"

"No, I'm not mad. Why would I be mad?"

"You haven't called me back."

"I never got a message that you called."

"I left two messages."

"Oh, I haven't had a chance to listen to all my messages since I've been . . . since I've been, ah, around."

"I left one message with your secretary."

"Oh, I never got it. I apologize for any—"

"Inconvenience? Were you going to say *inconvenience*?"

"Oh, hold on, another call . . ." He eased up when he returned. "Your voice . . . you don't sound like yourself."

"I don't? Oh, I guess . . . well, are you trying to get rid of me?"

"What a terrible thing to say! Oh, damn, just a minute, I've got another call. I have to take this. Listen, we'll talk soon." His conscience made his voice brittle. "Ah . . . take care."

"We'll talk soon" was bad enough, and "I'll call you next week," an old standard, was a sure sign that he would not, but "take care" was downright deadly. It was irreversible, final, like something you'd say to your grandmother whom you weren't going to be seeing anytime soon. I didn't call again for a week, a week crammed with bad days, but at least Aaron called frequently to remind me that it wasn't necessarily a bad life.

Rachel wasn't around. She was with the groom-to-be in the place to be, the hub of the universe: glorious Paris. We talked regularly. Rather, she talked and when the overseas pauses grew too costly I prodded her in a dead voice. She told me that he had bowed out of the project.

"What was his excuse?" I asked. "Just out of curiosity."

"Apparently his collection is tied up. Some show just came up. He was very apologetic, you know, a real gentleman. He suggested some people to call and said I could use his name, and if that didn't work he said he would make some calls for me. I can't complain. He was perfectly lovely."

"I'm sure."

My neighbor avoided me. He hadn't been involved one-on-one for a long time, and maybe he'd just had it with being involved one-on-two with me. He'd probably forgotten how the rational part of the brain shrinks to infinitesimal size in these instances and how everything else goes into overdrive to compensate. Or maybe he deemed my behavior self-indulgent or delusional, a concept I had long since embraced. His fall was starting early, too, and he also may just have been too busy becoming famous as a hot deejay. Now he had the two-career problem, which I knew all too well was no small problem. Whatever the reason, he couldn't take my saga anymore. When we did speak, he was polite and I retaliated with reserve. Eventually I was so taut and high-pitched that he blew up, and he didn't blow easily.

"What the hell is going on?"

"Nothing."

I wasn't lying. It was that the whole experience had come full circle, as bleak and hauntingly as I'd anticipated. Medical bills had suddenly started to arrive at a brisk tempo, reminding me of how it had all begun, and it looked like my insurance wasn't going to cover how it had all begun. I flogged myself daily, if not hourly, over my weak will, my inability to cope with an ostensibly casual, short-lived affair, but my emotions were loose and floppy and no amount of flogging snapped them back into place. Joseph Pendleton and the ghost baby were bound inextricably together, triggering all the big-picture questions just as they had initially. Each day began at dawn, strong and proud. But by the time I lay prostrate on the couch for the apex of my day, my six o'clock show, I was spent, just spent.

In these circumstances you were supposed to be angry, but I wasn't. I would have welcomed anger. In fact I was counting on Aaron to give me explicit instructions on how to get in touch with my anger. When she finally called, she said that anger was the key to closure, and when I managed it, she assured me, I would "let go."

Closure? They were still pushing closure? To me the term, not to mention the concept, had always been suspect. Besides, didn't you need cooperation in order to reach the alleged closure? But I was willing to try. I called again, with a new tactic: upbeat and businesslike. After all, handling business and romance in the city weren't all that different. I was also determined to take him up on his long-ago offer "to pay half." I would bring it up once, only once; that was all the degradation I was willing to withstand. Then I'd swoop in like a stealth bomber to confront the real business at hand, and if all went according to plan, I'd trap some truth.

"There were just a few things I wanted to ask you," I said. There was still some sleeping potion in my bloodstream, so I sounded relatively calm and casual. "Do you have a few minutes?" Not giving him a chance to protest, I continued in my calm and casual voice. "Um, that cosmetics-clerk assignment, well, it's evolved into an article about what makeup women should wear at what age, I know it's ridiculous, but anyhow . . . should they or shouldn't they, you know . . . wear makeup, lipstick, mascara, all that kind of thing . . . how much, how little. Anyway, I have to ask men their opinions."

"You're barking up the wrong tree. I wouldn't know anything about that, I hardly have the time to look at women."

"Of course you don't, but I need one more man, so let me just ask you the questions. There are only a few. And also, um, it looks like my insurance isn't going to cover. I got some bills, and it looks like it's not going to cover the whole thing, the . . . you know—"

"How much do you need?"

"Um, I guess around two hundred."

Rachel had said right from the start that I should insist he pay the entire amount and not even mention insurance. I was entitled, she'd said. So what if I made money on the deal?

"Fine, I'll give it to you next week."

"No hurry. Anyway, do you think women should wear makeup?"

"It depends. Unattractive women should probably wear some. Really unattractive women shouldn't wear any—it just accentuates their flaws. Attractive women shouldn't wear any, either."

"I have a feeling that quote is not going to go over well. Let's try again. How about lipstick?"

"Maybe a little. Never bright colors, especially not that awful orangy red."

"You may not be aware of this, but bright orangy red is in."

"No, I have noticed. It's really awful, especially when they gob it on. Even on younger women—"

"But I thought you didn't look at women. And I'm sure you don't look at younger women." We were teenagers again, playing hooky in a paneled basement, and I egged him on. "What about women as they get older?"

"The less makeup the better. No lipstick or nail polish in funny shades."

"Even older women who look young shouldn't wear a little makeup. You know, the kind with no wrinkles, perfect bodies?"

"No such thing exists. They're kidding themselves if they think—"

I swooped in then. "So anyway, what's going on? And don't act like nothing's wrong."

"All right. I was mad. And guilty."

"Mad about what? Guilty about who? Me or your . . . your family?" The term *wife* still would not leave my mouth. You cannot play hooky forever, especially on your genes.

"My family. My son, he was up one night when I got home . . . from you. Adolescents, they're perceptive, they know. I mean, this is only going to get worse for both of us. There's just going to be another calamity. It's going to be disastrous." He left out "when it ends," like he always did. Like I always did, too. Why would we start putting it in at this stage? It was what always made our separate but equally pointed silences all the more ominous. It was the unuttered phrase at the end of every sentence either of us had ever uttered, the filler for every pause, the answer to every question we'd ever asked, or never asked.

"Why didn't you just say you were mad when I asked you before?"

"Because I didn't feel as strongly then, and you've been so persistent."

"You call this persistent?"

"I'm telling you, it's going to be a disaster. I don't know how you're going to react. Human nature is such that you never know . . . it's such a . . ."

"You still don't trust me?"

"I do trust you, I do. It's just . . . I don't know how you really feel, what you want." I would have liked to help him out, but I couldn't. "And then a friend of mine said he'd heard some talk about me . . . and some Soho artist. That pissed me off. Perhaps your friends aren't as reliable as you might imagine."

"Who said that?"

"I'm not going to play that game. It's not important who said what. That kind of information just keeps the game going."

"Okay, fine, but no one I know would refer to me as a Soho artist."

"Well, maybe I am being a little paranoid."

"Maybe? Maybe? You are the most paranoid person I've ever met."

"Well, maybe I've lived a lot longer than you have, just maybe long enough to understand what—"

"Forget it. But Joseph, the other night, that night, after that night, I mean, we do have to talk about . . . Oh, damn it, now *I* have a call. Hold on . . . the goddamn phone company. What was I saying?"

"You were saying I was the most paranoid person you'd ever come across."

"No, that wasn't it, let's see . . . Where was I? Well, I don't know, I don't know."

This time he said "Take care" so tenderly, so wistfully, that it was clear he hadn't quite made up his mind yet and I'd made a calm and casual dent. I was willing to wait for a decision, but I wasn't a good waiter. He'd said the near future was out. But he had also said he would give me the money next week. How would one define "near future"?

•

The near future, which I had decided to define as next week, was a long time in coming. It was not next week. Nor was it the week after next. I continued to pass the time. I spent a morning with Victor, who was heading toward the poorhouse via the waiting-for-a-corporate-check process. Now he had in his possession a bona fide corporate check. Unfortunately, he no longer had a checking account. He also no longer had a picture ID, and apparently without a picture ID, you can't cash a check or open a checking account. Victor was matter-of-fact about the situation, but I saw the defeat and humiliation in his eyes, and besides, my feeling about Victor was that any one of us could be Victor if we were so bold as to be what we were, if we just plain lost the skills to be what we weren't in order to play the game.

We celebrated our check-cashing victory in the concrete park. Victor liked the concrete park, too. I'd often see him sitting upright on his bench among the assorted bums with his cane standing guard, like a distinguished English gentleman, reading one of his enormous books. We sat close together on the bench, and I felt better than I had in a long time.

"We really pulled it off," I said smugly. "It was so easy. I wonder why it didn't work before. It had to be a racist thing, don't you think?"

"I wasn't going to bring it up," he said. "I think one of the bank tellers before was even black, right, but it didn't make a difference. It probably made things worse. Yeah, it's insane. We're sitting here congratulating ourselves like we pulled off some scam, a fucking criminal act, and all we were doing was cashing a check. A corporate check, for God's sake. Right? I was nervous with that last teller, the Indian guy. When he started giving us that officious Indian attitude—"

"Oh, are Indians officious?"

"Is the sky blue?"

The next day I had to undergo a makeover for the makeup article. It was a disheartening experience. When it was over, I conducted a hasty interview and took off. I was distracted when I sat down to write the article because, while I still hadn't gotten in touch with my anger, I was wildly in touch with my despair. I reminded myself that closure was imminent, that I'd see him soon. After all, he owed me money and he wouldn't renege on that, not Joseph Pendleton with his precious sense of propriety.

I spent a horrible evening with Hank, so horrible it may very well have been our last, a swan song to forced romance. I took him to an art opening where orangy-red lipstick predominated and the women wore summer clothes so tight that even flat New York bellies protruded and the men wore heavy black boots—in the summer. I had worn the pink shoes in an act of irrational rebellion, and it was a mistake. After the opening we had to undergo the food-and-dating challenge—the hunt for the perfect restaurant—which involved covering many cement miles. The blisters returned full force, and I was sweaty and cranky in the quaint French bistro. When Hank began pronouncing ludicrous romanticisms about what it meant to be an artist, my frustration almost caused a public to bubble up. When I segued obliquely into my current predicament, Hank was brusque and the public bubbled over, and though I apologized, he was even colder.

I told Rachel about the evening when she checked in from Paris, and she gave me hell.

What finally broke me was the party the downstairs musicians gave on Sunday night. It was a lost August weekend—even my neighbor was away. I knew better than to stick around for the party, since communal living was the price you paid for life in a so-called glamorous loft—that is, one with cardboard ceilings and walls. I stayed at my neighbor's apartment, which was the only tenement left in the neighborhood, at the very edge of the neighborhood, and what a barren, lonely edge it was. It was like the edge of a neighborhood you'd imagine on Mars. The water and the sky met there, and New Jersey hovered menacingly, and a single spanking-new skyscraper stood in a brand-new concrete park. I scurried over at dusk and huddled in my neighbor's musty brown living room, and then I huddled in his dark-purple bedroom. In the morning I woke with my face wet from bad dreams. When I got home I called him. It was like taking too many drugs or smoking—you know you're going to die eventually anyway.

The call was brief, considering. Even he was undone by the brevity.

"Okay? Okay? Is that all you have to say?" It was the first time I'd heard Joseph Pendleton come close to a stutter. "Okay? Is that it?"

My "uh-huh" was weak, but he recovered. Smoothly, he suggested we have lunch when he returned from Long Island, but his delivery was a little sheepish. "Don't forget, I owe you money," he added with a feeble half chuckle intended to be wry. "I'll call you when I get back."

Overall, the call had not been smooth. I had trapped him, once again, with the bomber technique, minus the stealth.

"Joseph, look, if you want to get out of this, just do it." No hello, and my voice was flat, an unfamiliar voice that provoked an uncharacteristic response.

"I don't know." His voice was also unfamiliar, unrehearsed, in fact, frighteningly real. When he repeated "I don't know," I wasn't sure if it was his voice or an echo inside me. "Things are . . . well, I'm not all there, and it's starting to show." He was practically whispering. My heart opened wide, and I tried to shut it.

"I know," I whispered back, and I did know.

"And the guilt . . ."

"I know, I know. But why now and not before?"

"My family . . . that's what's most important to me. I can't do this."

"But why couldn't you tell me before? I never had any illusions, but why didn't you just tell me? It was cruel not to."

"I wasn't sure. I didn't know. We don't know each other that well, and I . . . and I couldn't . . . look, it's not like it wasn't complicated from the beginning. And I haven't had my evenings free."

"Christ. We could have had fucking lunch."

He didn't answer.

"It was cruel."

"All right, all right, maybe it was, but it was only going to get worse. Look, this isn't good for either of us. You told me you wanted a baby."

"I know. I know. You're right. I just, I just . . ."

The rest of his words were vague and far away. I pretended to listen, but my answers were rote. Not that expecting the worst wasn't second nature, but I was losing my innate ability to gauge the worst. I hadn't gauged well this time at all. Afterward, I sat and stared, and out of sheer desperation I called my neighbor. He suggested politely that we meet at the downstairs bar, and I didn't argue. I had a feeling, which was confirmed when I saw his eyes. They told me he'd run out of steam and empathy. He cut me off before I began.

"It's just like what happened with Jack."

I said it wasn't like Jack at all, that I'd taken a risk this time, and he looked at me with polite exasperation, and then we both stared at the sidewalk until he muttered, "Well, I have to go."

I was almost glad. I couldn't take any more politeness.

17

GETTING THROUGH LABOR DAY WAS JUST THAT: LABORIOUS. TO RISK holiday exile in the city was asking for trouble, so I marched in time with the celebrators and when I got home I was bone tired. September had always been exhilarating in the past, but with every year it grew less so. This year was no exception. During the next few weeks, clumps of people straggled back to the city reluctantly but refreshed and ready for action. I greeted them stale and in a fetal position.

He didn't call, there was no lunch, and I was silly enough to be surprised, silly enough to feel betrayed. When I dialed, he answered on the first ring and I confessed in a frill-free monotone that I wasn't okay, that I needed a better finale—in person. I just don't want to hate you, I said. Maybe that reached him. Maybe it was my sudden candor. Whatever it was, something swayed him. He suggested coffee and I said fine.

I ignored the fact that summer hadn't really ended yet and dressed for fall. He was waiting when I got there.

"I tried to be late."

He smiled wearily. "That's a nice coat. But it's hot as hell out. Why are you wearing—"

"It is nice, isn't it?" I busied myself taking it off and placing it carefully over the chair next to me.

"It is nice, isn't it?" He repeated it with an expression of mock horror. "You're supposed to say thank you when someone gives you a compliment. Who taught you your manners? So who designed it?" I didn't answer. For one thing, I didn't care to take the bait; for another, my mouth was too dry. I rummaged in my purse for a mint, and my headphones fell out.

"I have a great new tape," I said. "Want to hear this song?"

He listened for a minute.

"It's not bad. Your neighbor's all over the place; he's turned into a real hotshot deejay."

"Oh yeah, have you read about him?"

"I didn't actually read the . . . I couldn't . . . I mean . . . do you want coffee or what?"

At four o'clock the coffee shop was deserted. It was a run-down coffee shop west of Times Square, but it was still too bright and shiny. We had arranged ourselves carefully at a round table that could easily have accommodated six. Neither of us was particularly forthcoming; he was brisk and snappy, and I gave stunted responses. When we gradually fell into our easy rhythm—it was inevitable—we moved closer, unwittingly, and when our knees touched we moved apart and looked away, and then he curtailed the festivities.

"You said you had some questions."

"You know, I never realized that this, what happened to us, well, what a common soap opera plot it was. I must've seen at least five movies based on it since. I'd never even seen that one, you know the one—"

"Yeah, well . . ." He started to smile, thought better of it, and tried again. "You said you had some questions." It was too late. He'd charmed me. I was easy game and I stepped into every trap. To make matters worse, each answer he gave me triggered twenty more questions. I asked him if he thought I'd been in this for a lark or did he think I'd cared, and he chose the former gratefully, without hesitation. I said, no, I did care. He looked toward me but past me, like I was the school principal across a great big wooden desk, and said that he cared, too, he still cared. "This isn't a rejection," he added.

I replied, and I meant it, that I had never taken it as a rejection. Then I said, "How come you could stay so late?"

"There's always the club, but she knows I don't usually . . . They weren't home." A fine-mesh screen lowered across his face. The screen fell away abruptly, and then softly but ever so vindictively he murmured, "You were there that night."

I stared with my mouth open and my mouth closed. Of course I was there! What do you think, I'd have left you? I wanted to scream, I know they weren't home that night. Were they away every time? Why didn't you tell me? But instead I diligently asked him what had changed so suddenly—at least it had seemed sudden to me.

"I couldn't go home anymore after being with you," he said. "My kid—" he began.

I interrupted: "I respect you more for that," and again I meant it, but inside I was screaming, Why all of a sudden? Does your goddamn precious kid have ESP?

"You're a good egg," he said, leaning in.

"No, I'm not," I snapped. That was the closest I came to expressing anger. Not very close.

He asked the waitress for more coffee. My bones ached from being solemn and mature, and though he would have denied it I'm sure his bones did, too. When I retreated tight-lipped, he didn't badger me like he used to. He cajoled me gently, earnestly; he even used my name once, but my mind was racing with loose ties and even anger. I believe I was finally getting in touch with my anger, maybe not expressing it, but I was absolutely in touch with it. The old questions were fading, the new questions were looming, and they canceled each other out.

Getting in touch with my anger now was probably not such good timing. He began to fidget, although he was too seasoned to glance at his watch. When my face began to fold, he looked away and said he had to go back to the club to take care of a few things. I said maybe I had the flu, change of seasons and all. I had been feeling fluish for the past few days, but I'd chalked it up to the change in Joseph Pendleton, not the change in seasons. He nodded, looked off to the side, and said, "Yeah, it's going around." He added, "I have to leave in fifteen minutes," and I told him I'd better go to the bathroom first.

When I returned, he'd paid the check. His lips were pressed together and his eyes lifeless. We walked together for a block, and he gave his all to the cause: the cause of cordiality, the cause of no hard feelings. Choked responses to his questions were all I could muster because, boy, did that anger make me dizzy.

"So is the coat new?" he tried.

"No, old."

"It doesn't look old."

"It is." I plodded, head down.

"You don't feel very well," he said softly. The voice hijacked me. I glanced up and realized he'd stopped. I turned to face him.

"So," he said. "Did I answer all your questions?"

"Uh-huh."

"And we're friends?"

"Uh-huh."

He was muddy-eyed but not in the old way; it was pure shame. When he hugged me, it was fake and awful.

"Be strong," he mumbled when we came loose, and that was worse, that was pitiful. I stepped back.

"I am strong."

"Oh, okay then, forget it. Hey, there's a cab. You take it."

"No, I don't need a cab. I want to walk."

"Okay, then I'll—"

"Oh, I don't know. Maybe I will take a cab. Maybe I should, I guess I should."

"All right then, we lost that one but there's another one."

"No, you go first. I can get one myself."

"If that's what you want. Listen, I've got to run . . . if you don't mind, I'm going to take this one."

It was all very mature, unrelentingly mature. I had never realized how exhausting maturity could be. I guess I wasn't as strong as I'd claimed to be, because when I got home and tried to resume sitting and staring, I couldn't. I had to lie down. I was more confused than I'd been when I set off. The solemn session at the coffee shop had been a farce. What was it about that night that made him run? Because it was clearly something about that night. My questions were the real farce. I was so concerned that he be able to emerge from the coffee shop guilt-free that I didn't leave room for the only question I needed answered: Was the whole thing a farce?

Seven-thirty and it was already dark, a blessing, proof that fall was making a valiant attempt to arrive, that summer was going to end after all. I curled up tighter on the couch and turned on the TV, but the fall programming season hadn't really blossomed yet. TV was in a state as graceless as my own.

In the morning nothing was fine, although there was good news: A cold front was rumored to be approaching from Canada around midnight. Midnight seemed as far away as Canada, as far away as that damn closure. I'd never get to the closure if I didn't act fast.

His hello was cocky, breezy. By now he'd had more than enough time to congratulate himself on the clean and honorable getaway I'd engineered, and he was probably feeling pretty good, pretty damn sanctimonious about the whole affair. He deflated instantly when he recognized my voice.

"Joseph, I hate to say it but I still don't get it. I just feel worse; everything you said just made me feel worse. There's something missing still." I sounded like a record at the wrong speed.

"Excuse me?" He was stalling for time. Or maybe he really hadn't understood—it was plausible. Either way his voice was harsh and poisonous, and I had to take a deep breath to continue.

"Listen, I promise it'll only take—"

"I asked you . . . I asked you yesterday if I'd answered your questions. You told me yes." He was furious.

"I really wasn't feeling well yesterday. And you charmed me. I couldn't think straight." The silence was thunderous, but I pressed onward. "Were they away every night?"

"No. Christ no, it was just that one night."

"What happened that night? Just tell me. It was that night. What happened to make you run? That night."

"I've told you, my family, I—"

"But before we were just going along and . . . why, all of a sudden?"

"You're not listening to me!"

"I am too!"

"I've explained over and over. I've told you, it's my kid, it's the way—"

"But it didn't matter before; it wasn't like that before."

"It's not before anymore! Listen to me! I'm telling you the truth. I swear. Oh God, I hate this, I hate going over things. It's not going to—"

"Why did you invite me to Paris? It made it more, it made it seem like something more . . ."

"I, I . . . you charmed me. All right? You charmed me. That's all. That's it. Simple. Case closed." His words sliced like paper cuts, deep ones, the kind that linger.

"It was that night, I know it was something that night. What was it?"

"Can't you stop with that? Look, this was doomed from the start. It was a mistake. Everyone makes mistakes. You don't need this in your life."

"I just thought it would go on . . . it was just so abrupt, I just wasn't ready and you never said anything. It was so cold."

"Christ, you're acting like a victim."

"I am not acting like a victim. Don't be ridiculous. I could have taken the victim route long ago if I'd wanted to. You said things that made me think . . ."

"Name one thing I promised."

"I don't know, I don't know, just things."

"I never said I'd leave home." His voice, bitter and malevolent, wasn't only directed at me.

"Leave home?" He said it, not me, the significance of which did not occur to me until later, much later. "Come on, Joseph, we never even got close to talking about . . . I'm not attacking you, I'm just trying to find out . . . I just . . ."

What had he promised? Nothing. I knew it almost as well as he did. Almost as well as he did, because though I'd fought hard not to, I'd heard silent promises—made wordlessly with his eyes, with his mouth, with his hands, and then there were the vague intimations. They were not silent. They were articulated, often quite eloquently, but they were never close to promises.

"Tell me. Tell me what I promised."

"Well, you said we'd have lunch and you would give me the money for . . ." It was all I could come up with. There was a pause.

"I forgot. Just tell me how much it is and I'll put it in the mail this afternoon."

"Did you ever care?"

There was another pause.

"I cared about you . . . as a friend," he said stiffly, and then he softened. "Look . . . we had fun."

"Oh, was that abortion fun? Oops, I forgot—you missed that part of the fun."

"That wasn't my fault! You didn't let me—"

"Joseph, just tell me, what was it? What happened? What was it about that night?"

"Okay, okay, okay! You won't let up. I felt so split, I couldn't do what I had to do . . . that night, that night . . . it was too intense! It was all too intense! Everything was getting out of hand, too serious. It was too intense! And it was only going to get worse."

"All right, okay," I interrupted. "I . . . all right, it's . . . okay." That was all I needed. I didn't need much. But I needed something—I knew without hearing the rest. His animosity was scaring me, and I tried to inject some levity. "Now, are you going to atone for your sins?"

"Oh, sure." He barked a short laugh. "How do you suggest I atone for my sins? My so-called sins?"

I couldn't answer. The animosity was too overwhelming, so I whispered good-bye. His "take care" was tacked on begrudgingly, accusingly; still, he had given me what I needed, maybe not everything, but I had to be satisfied with what I'd gotten, for now. My anger was gone. It had only lasted a day. How could I be angry at him? He had never promised me the future, and he had given me a taste of the present. It was a generous gift because I was ravenous for the present. But he'd overdone the present and needed to study the past so that he could better steer the future. He gave me back the present, and I like to think I nudged him toward the future. We both needed to change time zones. Unfortunately, we couldn't do it with each other.

I continued to search for the anger, the surefire path to the much ballyhooed closure. I searched during the coming weeks, which became months, no longer truant autumn months but real autumn months, and then winter months, and—can you believe it—spring months. But anger is sly. It can sneak up on you when you're not looking, but it can also be elusive, maddeningly elusive. I never found it again. It was nowhere to be found in the jumble of the past. I must confess that I wasn't letting go as fast as they said you were supposed to, I wasn't moving forward as fast as they said you were supposed to. That damn closure evaded me. How could you close something that had never been opened?

18

I RAN INTO HIM A YEAR LATER. TO THE DAY. I REMEMBERED BECAUSE I FILE notable dates as scrupulously as I file seasons. It's a habit that contributes to my flashback problem, and I don't think I can blame it on the genes. After all our tormented collisions that summer, it must seem peculiar that it took a whole year for us to cross paths (a year in which I didn't not try to run into him), but it wasn't. It was predictable. It happened all the time. Quite often the city collaborated with fate in an elaborate scheme to protect you from yourself. Really, the city could be quite solicitous.

It was a genuine fall night, cold enough to make me shiver and windy enough to make the air dance with the unknown. My flashback problem had queered the summer, but the dancing air felt rejuvenating. Okay, it wasn't just the fall. There was someone else in the picture, no big deal, but a step up, in my opinion. Not in my neighbor's opinion. "You've merely gone from a shiftless Negro to a lazy Italian," he'd insisted. But at least he wasn't a musician or an artist. In fact he didn't have one creative bone in his body, and as my mother pointed out (repeatedly), "It's a goddamn blessing."

I don't remember where the lazy Italian was this particular evening. I was just minding my own business, standing on a sidewalk outside a small club in the creepiest part of the Village. The club was sixties-style crass, but my brother and his friends could get paying gigs there. Hank was playing with a big band—he and I had come to a comfortable truce—and they were between sets, so I'd stepped outside for some air. I wasn't quite sure if it was the mirage that sometimes shadowed me or if it was the real Joseph Pendleton. I stood still for a moment, uncertain, and I may have backed up a few steps. I was wearing the same coat that I'd worn our prior September encounter, and he might have been experiencing his own flashback. I filed away his smile as he came toward me because it was one of the rare monumental ones.

"Are we allowed to say hello?" I said, and then I backed up so far I was inches from the brick wall. He came closer.

"I got your note. That was so nice. I've been trying to call you."

"You can't have tried too hard. I'm usually home at least twenty hours out of twenty-four."

He shrugged, flashing the demonic grin. Two smiles of some magnitude; that caused another inadvertent step back. "Your note. I didn't expect . . . well, at first I thought it was a liquid bomb, but then . . . really it was so sweet."

His record company had come to be. It was doing well and it wasn't just soft-dick jazz, it was the real thing—even my brother had given it his begrudging seal of approval. I had written him a note a month or two ago, a short impersonal note of congratulations. Really, I had sent it because after all this time, his animosity was still plaguing me. It would wend its way downtown purposefully; the trail of animosity came after me, off and on, for a year. It was unsettling; I had to curtail it, and I thought a breezy note might be a start. The last thing I'd expected was a response. My expectations were another year's worth of experiences lower, which, in my case, was not necessarily a bad thing. Not at all.

"Well, you're doing something worthwhile. I just wanted to tell you." By now the bricks were scraping the backs of my legs. Impulsively, he pulled me forward and kissed me on both cheeks.

"I really was planning to call you."

"Why are you here?" I stammered. I half sidestepped, half slid along the wall, the only conceivable way out.

"I'm checking out the band. Did you see the first set? Are they any good?"

"Really good. A guy I know plays with them, so maybe I'm biased. And you may remember, I'm not too discriminating."

"I'll trust your judgment this time. Are you . . . do you . . . well, do you want to go next door, have coffee or something?"

The place next door was even sleazier than the club. Everything ostensibly wooden was plastic, and there was an enormous shiny oval bar in the middle of the room like a big corral, with TVs hanging down from every angle. We were physically tentative as we sat down; otherwise it was as if the year had lasted less than twenty-four hours. That was the way it had always been though. Once the wavelength kicked in, it didn't waver—unless the stakes were high, and tonight there were no stakes.

"I've followed your company. I've read all the press."

"You're keeping tabs on me?"

"I am not. But really, it seems like it's working. And the music, it's good. Even my brother . . . I mean, there's real integrity behind . . . oh, I forgot, that's not your thing."

"You have to be able to afford integrity. I found a fat-cat investor who doesn't have a life, so this company is providing him with a vicarious one."

"How about yours?"

"Mine? Oh, I don't know. It's better than just running the club,

I suppose, but it's the same old thing, too many people to placate, too many egos, doing the dance for investors. I'm thinking about . . . well, I'm thinking about Paris, moving back. Maybe playing."

"Playing?"

"Well, we were only . . . I was only going to give this a year and now it's been more than . . . what about you?"

I ignored the *we* even though it was not an inconsequential slip. I stored it, for old time's sake.

"I'm painting, not enough, writing more of that crap than I want to, I guess. But it's okay. I guess."

"You guess?"

"Don't you sometimes wish you could go really low, to breakdown low, and then you'd have no choice, you'd have to change, have a transformation?"

"You have had a transformation. I can see—"

"Yeah, right, a transformation. Not really."

"Yes, really."

"I don't know. Well . . ." I blushed. "Oh, I don't know."

"I don't know? I haven't heard one of those in a long time." He laughed at me and I took cover. "You don't have to be nervous."

"I'm not. Oh, I guess, well, maybe I am."

"Don't be. Well, how did the show in Paris go? What was that guy's name?"

"It went well, surprisingly well. I'm going to have another show with him in a few months. Yeah, he's been great so far. It's just here in New York. I'm probably the one who should move. Oh, by the way, you were right. He did hit on me."

"I'm always right. What'd you do?"

"No, you're not."

We retreated to safer ground instinctively, just as we always had. We continued to think out loud, but only safe thoughts. We moved in closer but not too close. It was strenuous to keep up the conversation without saying anything, but probably less strenuous than it would have been to say something. I kept my hands busy lest they stray.

"So what else is new?" I asked.

"Nothing."

I tried another tactic. "Hey." I spread my hands out in front of him. "Look." He was puzzled. "My fingernails—I stopped biting."

"I forgot about that." The fingernails got us through another few minutes, but fingernails are attached to fingers, fingers are attached to hands, hands are attached to arms, which are attached to the torso. Forget about the head, it's useless when it crowns a body afflicted by the human condition. Fighting the human condition—in its extreme form, that is, in the form of Joseph Pendleton—made my mind go blank and my limbs stiffen, so I tripped on a land mine in enemy territory.

"Oh, I know what else. I wrote another movie for another cosmetic company, equally as stupid, I . . . oops."

"It's okay. All right, I can see it's not okay. You were there, now I lost you. Damn."

"I'm sorry." My face got red, and the haunted year, the year he'd missed, crowded my eyes.

"Don't be sorry. Christ. You're upset, that's all. But you won't . . ." He looked equally pained. Oh, maybe I'm exaggerating, but pained enough that he couldn't look at me. "We were having a good time, before, and now it's ruined."

My mind had been in motion, overflowing for so long, and here was my opportunity, here was my receptacle sitting directly across the table. "It's just that, what happened with you, it triggered things, a lot of things. It's not your fault. You just happened to be there. It's just . . . the baby thing." And then I broke down, for the first time in his presence, not the grandiose fabrication in my mind, but his quite ordinary human presence. He'd never witnessed my tears, and I wouldn't be surprised if he'd had doubts as to their authenticity in the past. I wouldn't be surprised if he had never truly believed that he or the ghost baby were the cause of any anguish—melodrama maybe, but not anguish. I never left a whole lot of clues, so why would he have believed it—especially when it would be easier not to. But he did now.

"The baby thing." His voice was as empty as his face.

"It's okay, it's okay. Really, it's just . . . you were in the wrong place at the wrong time, that's all. Now tell me, what's next? Tell me something fun. What's your next record? Are you traveling much? Are you going away somewhere fun?"

"Fun? What's fun? Look, you don't have to change the subject. I can handle it. You don't have to do that for me." His voice softened into lullaby territory, and that, in tandem with the reproachful look, was insurmountable. I was in deep trouble. "A year . . . after all the . . . well, I never imagined we'd be friends. You know, it was brave, writing me that note."

"No, no, it wasn't, I just figured you don't get much credit, and I . . . I . . . well, I just didn't want you to hate me anymore."

"I never hated you. I had to . . . well, it doesn't matter. I don't hate you." He didn't look away but I had to. "It's later than I thought. I have to go. I'm supposed to have a drink at the club with this—"

"That's okay, I should go back in anyway. Oh, maybe I should just go home; it is late."

"Well, why don't I put you in a cab?"

"All right." It was more than all right. I wanted nothing more than to get up from the thick plastic-wood table. I stood up clumsily but fortunately landed on my feet. I think he came to me, but maybe I went to him. You see, it didn't feel like a year had passed, and we stood in a raunchy bar causing yet another scene. Even though it didn't feel like it, it had been another year, and I stood like a baby chick finally being fed, and he held me up for what seemed a long time but probably wasn't. I opened my eyes because I wanted to commit this one to memory, get this one right. This go-around I wanted to make sure I had all the details.

"It's different," he whispered. "It feels different."

I was wobbly and I have to say he was, too. But by the time we got out the door he'd recuperated.

"So, are you going to tell your friends about this?"

"No! How humiliating!"

"They're probably so bored by it now anyway."

"Don't flatter yourself."

"Hey, let's get this cab."

"I don't really need a cab—it's not that far, I can just walk . . ."

It was true. It wasn't very far. I could've walked, and maybe I should've walked, but I didn't walk, and we surrendered to the human condition in the cab, and just before I got out he mumbled, "Maybe I'll call you later."

"Maybe?"

"Yeah, maybe." He got huffy. "Yeah maybe. That's the way it . . ."

"Yeah, yeah, yeah." But I was smiling as I got out, and he flashed one back from the cab.

•

When I consulted Aaron the next day, she had trouble coming up with an appropriate platitude. I had to prompt her. "What about closure?"

"Oh, screw that sorry old closure," she said. "There are some people you just don't get out of your system." But then she added that "you do move on," and then she assured me that I had moved on.

And when my eyes got moist later during my six o'clock show—it was the episode where the token nerd on the show killed himself by mistake with his father's gun—they weren't moist because he hadn't called. In fact I hadn't even waited for his call. Nor was I thinking, Hell, duped again. Foiled again. No, I knew, and knowing tears are nothing to be ashamed of. They were not the tears of a deceptor or the tears of a deceptee, they were tears of consequences, of circumstances, maybe even adult tears, and they would cease, because no matter what year it was, even if the years that passed felt more like days, he and I were always going to be in the wrong place at the wrong time.

ABOUT THE AUTHOR

BETSY BERNE is an artist who has written for *The New Yorker*, *Vogue*, and *The New York Times Magazine*. A graduate of the Rhode Island School of Design, she lives in Manhattan.